SOUTHSIDE HUSTLE

Lou Holly

First published by
The Book Folks, 2016.

Typeset in Garamond
Design by Steve French
Printed by CreateSpace

Available from Amazon.com and other retail outlets

THE BOOK FOLKS
106 Huxley Rd, London E10 5QY
thebookfolks.com

Dedicated to my wife, Liz

A special thanks to the Naperville Writers Group

TO
SHIRLEY
THANK YOU

ALL MY BEST
ALWAYS

Lou Holly

Prologue

"Hands in da air!" Benny called out in the dark, walking up with Sal. "Dis is a stick up."

Trick looked unfazed as he leaned against his 1979 Lincoln Continental under the hazy moon that hung in the bleak December sky.

"Look at this dapper bastard. Trick, ya dress more like a bank president than a drug dealer." Benny's laugh sounded forced. "Dis is my friend, Sal Bianccini."

Trick nodded to Sal as he walked toward them and looked around the deserted parking lot behind the Ace Hardware on Cicero Avenue. He turned his attention back to Benny and squinted as icy pellets stung his face. "This is an odd place to set up a buy."

"Dey closed at 9:00, not a soul around. Don't worry. If ya got the stuff with ya, dis is gonna be a quick exchange, di beep di boop di bop."

"Yeah, I got it right here in the car." Trick blew onto his cold hands and looked back at Sal who was standing to Benny's left. "You got the money? It's $45,000 for one kilo."

"Right here." Sal unzipped his jacket and pulled a small satchel from his waistband.

Trick hesitated when he saw the handle of an automatic handgun sticking out of Sal's inside coat pocket. He asked Benny, "You two know each other long?"

"Yeah, yeah, we grew up tagether in Bridgeport. We gonna do dis or what? I'm freezin' and I got a

New Year's party ta go ta."

Removing the car keys from his camel hair topcoat, Trick walked several feet back to his Lincoln and unlocked the door. He pulled a brown paper bag from under the driver's seat, then walked back to Benny and Sal and held the bag up. Looking at Sal and nodding his head toward Benny, Trick said, "Give the money to Ben." When Benny took the leather satchel, Trick said, "Look inside. Everything copacetic?"

Benny unzipped Sal's satchel, inspected it, shrugged his shoulders and tilted his head back. "Of course. Ya think I'd set ya up?"

Trick tossed the paper bag containing a kilo of cocaine to Sal, who responded, "I'd like to test it."

"C'mon, Sal," Benny urged. "I told ya Trick's stuff is always top shelf. It's too cold out here ta be fuckin' around. I give ya my personal guarantee ya won't be disappointed. If it's not da real deal, I'll give ya back your dough myself. That's how sure I am."

"OK, give me the money." Trick reached out his hand. "Let's get out of here."

Benny handed the satchel of cash to Trick and said, "Oh, wait a second. Got somethin' for ya in my car. Hold on."

Hustling back to his car that was parked close to the side drive next to the hardware store, Benny opened the driver's door and hopped behind the wheel. He looked at Trick with round eyes, started the car and sped away toward Cicero.

Sal shouted at Trick and grabbed the automatic pistol from his coat. "What's goin' on here?"

Trick stood holding the money with his mouth hanging open, then said, "Oh, no."

Oak Forest Police cars flew in from the north and south entrances to the rear parking lot. Trick ran for cover behind his Lincoln and looked at the satchel in his hand. Sal followed him behind the Lincoln, crouched down next to Trick and said, "I'll kill that shitbag. I swear to God."

Looking behind them to the east, toward the backyards of the houses on Waverly Avenue about fifty yards away, Trick considered his options. There weren't many. Try to run or give up.

The police officers, dressed in dark blue uniforms and heavy zipper jackets, jumped out of their vehicles with guns drawn, shielding themselves behind their idling cars. A voice from a loudspeaker echoed in the night, "This is Detective Frank Murray. Throw your weapons to the ground in front of the vehicle and come out with your hands over your head."

"Do it," Trick commanded, looking at Sal. "What choice've we got?"

"I just got out of the joint. I'm not goin' back." Sal looked at his pistol. "I'd rather be dead."

"Well, I wouldn't. I got a little boy at home."

"You give yourself up, that boy'll be callin' someone else daddy by the time you get out."

The frigid fresh air stung Trick's nostrils as he breathed heavily. "It'd be better than never seeing him again."

Detective Murray's voice boomed across the large parking area, "Come out now! Throw down your weapons."

"You got a gun on you?" Sal said, without looking at Trick. "Got one in the car?"

"No. Look, I'm liable to get one in the back if I run. I'd rather be locked up than end up dead or crippled."

"You're along for the ride whether you like it or not." Sal stood with his knees bent, just enough to see over the trunk of Trick's burgundy Lincoln. He aimed his gun and shot once at the police.

The officers immediately returned fire as Sal quickly ducked back down.

"Oh, shit." Trick's voice wavered. "Are you out of your fucking mind?"

"Top of the world, ma!" Sal stood up and started blasting away at the police. "Aghhh, son-of-a-bitch!" Sal involuntarily dropped the pistol as bullets riddled his shoulder and arm, shattering bone and shredding nerves. He fell to his side moaning, "My fuckin' arm. Pick up the gun. Either start shootin' at them or put one in my head. I told you, I'm not goin' back to prison."

Trick reached around the front wheel of his car and put the satchel of cash on the axle, leaving a grease stain on the camel colored sleeve of his coat. "Give me the coke."

Sal groaned and handed the bag of drugs to Trick, who tossed it behind them as far as he could. He picked up the handgun and stared at Sal who writhed in agony, holding his injured arm.

"I can't take the pain. Do it. Put me out of my misery." The broken bone of Sal's upper right arm protruded through his cotton jacket, now soaked in blood. "You'd do it for a dog, wouldn't you?"

With the smell of hot steel and gunpowder in the air, Trick sat on the snow-dusted stones and leaned his back against the car with the automatic pistol in his shaking hand. "OK," Trick shouted. "We're giving up!"

"You lousy mudder fucker. I swear to God, if I live, I'll hunt you down and kill you." Before passing out, Sal whimpered, "You lousy prick."

Trick threw the weapon over the car in a high arc; it hit the ground with a metallic thud. "You see it?

That's the only one. I don't have a gun."

"Stand up with your hands clasped over your head," Murray's voice called out again, "where we can see them."

Trick knelt facing his car and put his hands over the hood. "I'm getting up," he called out. "Don't shoot me." He stood to see several police vehicles and one unmarked car and started walking slowly toward them.

"Lay on the ground, face down." Trick recognized Murray's voice without the loudspeaker, then complied.

Several officers ran toward Trick with their guns drawn. One of them kicked him hard in his ribs and another landed heavily onto his back with one knee while the other officers approached the Lincoln with their weapons aimed in front of them.

"He's unarmed," Trick pleaded, as he lay in the icy snow and winced in pain while his hands were forced behind his back and cuffed.

"We know there's only one weapon," Detective Murray said, kneeling next to Trick and pulling his wallet from his back pocket. "Go on, help him to his feet," Murray instructed one of the officers. Flipping open the wallet and removing Trick's driver's license, he read out loud, "Patrick Neal Halloran, May 19, 1954 … 27 years old. What's a nice Irish boy like you doing in a mess like this?"

Trick glanced back to his car where several officers joked and argued about whose bullet hit Sal first. Wheezing from the pain in his ribs, he looked down at his silk tie, wet with snow. "I'd like to speak to my lawyer."

"Oh, listen to this," Murray's older partner, Detective Armbruster, said, getting in Trick's face. "Someone watches *Hill Street Blues*." Armbruster slammed a wide fist into Trick's solar plexus, causing him to double over and lose his breath. "You like shootin' at cops, huh?"

Trick gasped for breath and managed, "I didn't shoot at anyone."

"If your fingerprints are on that gun, you're goin' away for a long time. Attempted murder of a police officer, you mongrel."

"Of course my prints are on it," Trick said, between labored breaths. "I threw the gun out like you told me."

Armbruster grabbed a handful of Trick's dark blond wavy hair and shook his head around. "You think a judge is gonna buy that?"

Trick smelled coffee on Armbruster's breath when he leaned in close and threatened, "How'd ya like it if I bit your nose off, pretty boy?"

One of the officers returned with the bag that contained the cocaine and told Murray, "We found the drugs but can't find the money. Does he have it on him?"

Murray answered, "See the soot on his sleeve? What does that tell you?"

"I … I'm not sure. He got it dirty?"

"You'll never make detective that way. Use your noodle." Murray pointed back to Trick's Lincoln, "Look up under the car … try the wheel wells."

An ambulance flew in with siren blaring and was waved back behind Trick's car. Two EMTs loaded Sal into the ambulance on a stretcher and roared away again.

Armbruster sniggered and said to Murray, "Looks like 1982 is gonna be a good one for us. C'mon, let's wrap up our paperwork and head over to Kicks on 66. We'll ring in the New Year together."

"I don't think so." Murray rubbed his graying

brown whiskers with his palm. "I'm bushed."

Back behind Trick's Lincoln, the officer held up the satchel of money and shouted, "I got it!"

"This is one asshole who's not gonna be celebratin' tonight." Armbruster smacked Trick across the face with an open hand spinning his head to the side. "Are ya, Mr. Fancy Pants?"

"All right, you've had your fun. That's enough." Murray squinted as his face changed to one of disapproval. "Let's get him in the car and bring him in."

Armbruster raised his voice and his ruddy face became redder. "Even if he didn't shoot at us, he was party to it." He grabbed Murray by the arm and pulled him aside. "What's a matter with you tonight? You usually like to twist the knife a little once we got it in. What? 'Cause he's Irish?"

"No. I don't know." Murray studied Trick shivering in the cold, looking down at the ground. "Something about that kid."

Chapter 1

The fragrance of the red maple leaves swirling lightly around Trick in the Indian summer breeze overwhelmed him and triggered something in his 31-year-old mind. Youthful nostalgia and lost innocence competed with the sadness that became his unwelcomed everyday companion. It was great to be a free man again but he still had serious problems to deal with.

Walking up the sidewalk to his ex-wife's apartment, Trick wondered how his five-and-a-half-year-old son would react to seeing him again. November 3, 1982, a date he hated remembering. The look on little Pat's face when Trick told his son he wouldn't be seeing him for a long time haunted him every day he was away. Once a week, Ginger allowed him a two-minute collect call with Pat while he was locked up. It had been two years, eleven months and four days since they last saw one another. He thought he had it all back then, a pretty wife, a beautiful little boy and a legitimate business. Attempting to phase out of drug dealing and into the straight world. Straight downhill is what it was. Why was it he always did so well breaking the law but fell flat on his face in the legit world?

After getting buzzed in, Trick bound up the steps to the second-story apartment. The heavy wooden door opened slowly. "Well, look at this. The absentee father's returned," Ginger said as he walked in. "I want Patrick home by 8:00. That gives you less than three hours."

"After all this time, that's what you want to say to me?"

With little Pat standing behind his mother, clinging to her leg, Ginger rolled her eyes. "Don't get on my case."

Trick self-consciously ran his fingers through his hair. "Well, how do I look?"

"You fishing for compliments? OK, you look good ... lost that boyish look. Prison agrees with you."

"Ixnay on the isonpray," Trick said, shooting Ginger a stern look.

"Oh, that's right. You were in college," Ginger fired back in a sarcastic tone.

Pat peeked around to look at his father, then retreated from view. Trick got down on one knee and said, "Hi, Pat. Let me get a good look at you."

"Go on. Say hi to your father," Ginger coaxed flatly.

"Hi, Daddy." Little Pat looked at the floor, rocking from one foot to another as he held his cloth Spiderman doll tight to his chest.

"Want to go to Bengtson's Farm and pick out a pumpkin for Mommy?"

Pat looked to his mother with questioning eyes, then hesitantly asked Trick, "Can I bring Spidey?"

"Yeah, you can bring Spiderman. He can help us find a good one." Trick reached out and pulled his blond, blue-eyed boy into his arms and felt the child's body stiffen. "I missed you so much, Pat. I thought about you every day."

"Well?" With one hand on her hip, Ginger cocked her head with an impatient look on her pretty but overly made up face. "Money? That $5,000 you gave me before you went away didn't last that long, you know."

Trick looked Pat in the eye and said, "Why don't you go wash your hands … or something. We'll get going in a minute." As Pat scampered off, Trick stood and turned his attention back to Ginger. "I hope you know that five grand was the last of my cash." Trick reached in his pocket. "Look, I've only got $125 on me right now but Reggie owes me and he's good for it. I'll have more in a couple days." He studied Ginger's face in the late afternoon sun that filtered through the swaying branches from the picture window. "You look tired."

"Well, thanks to you, I'm back at the Tinley Teacup. Never thought I'd still be waitressing at 29. You can pick Pat up there Thursday if you have my money."

Trick glanced around the living room trying to locate the aroma that kept pulling him back in time a few years, then spotted the bowl of potpourri on Ginger's coffee table. "I've got something big in the works. If my ship comes in, you can get off your feet again. Maybe set you up in your own place … a little coffee shop or something."

"Oh God, here we go again." Ginger shook her head. Bleach blonde hair danced on her shoulders as she smirked. "You and your big plans. Now that you're out, why don't you just get a job like everyone else and quit hustling?"

"Yeah, doing what? I don't have any practical experience. I'm used to being my own boss and not everyone wants to hire an ex-con."

Ginger sighed as she turned to look out the living room window at the fading leaves on the trees.

"If I get back on my feet, I'd like to take you out to dinner," Trick continued. "Circumstances could change overnight."

"I don't think Petros would like me going to dinner with my ex-husband," Ginger said, walking to the living room closet to get Pat's jacket.

"You kidding me? Pickle Nose? You can't be serious."

"At least he has a successful business ... a legal one."

"He also has two ex-wives." Trick stepped closer and tilted his head to catch her gaze. "I'd like to talk about getting back together. I never wanted a divorce and I sure don't want to be a weekend father. If I wasn't locked up at the time ..."

Pat eased back into the living room like a cat creeping along the back of a sofa. Ginger waved Pat closer and helped him on with his cowboy jacket, "Getting back together just so you can see your son more often is not on my agenda. Your three hours with Patrick is now two hours and forty-three minutes. I suggest you get going."

Trick surprised his son when he scooped him up in his arms. He started for the door, hesitated and turned to Ginger. "You lost a lot of weight. What are you on, the Karen Carpenter diet?"

"I'm fine ... just working too much. I need a good long rest. Just get going, please."

As Trick drove the twelve miles to the pumpkin farm with Pat, an uneasy feeling hung in the car like a heavy fog stalled over Lake Michigan. Trick turned off the radio when he heard Paul Young singing, *I'm Gonna Tear Your Playhouse Down*. "How are you, Pat?"

Pat sat silent for a moment, then held his Spiderman doll out in front of him and seemed to speak to it. "I don't remember you."

"Pat, we talked on the phone every week."

"I looked at your pictures in Mommy's album. But I don't remember you being my daddy."

"We'll change that." Trick slowed down when he noticed a young doe standing by the side of the road. "We're going to get to know each other all over again."

"My friend Will has a daddy. He reads him a story every night."

Trick put his window up as the warmth of October seventh cooled into early evening. "I might not be able to read you bedtime stories but you're going to see a lot of me from now on."

Pat finally turned to look at his father and shrugged. "How do I know you're not going to leave me again?"

Trick reached over, took Pat's hand and was taken aback by the softness of his skin, the delicacy in his care. He thought of when he was Pat's age, how he grew up being bounced from one foster home to another, not receiving much that could pass for love and caring. "That little shit will eat you out of house and home," he recalled one of his foster fathers telling his wife. He remembered the way the older biological sons of another family tormented him mercilessly behind their parents' back.

Trick gently rubbed Pat's hand and said, "I promise I'll never leave you again. You can trust me, Pat. I love you more than anything in the whole world ... anything." He pulled a folded white handkerchief from his back pocket and handed it to Pat. "Here, dry your eyes. We're going to have fun tonight. No more tears. OK?"

"OK, Daddy." Pat broke into an unexpected giggle and more tears streamed down his face.

***

While walking through the pumpkin patch and going on a hayride with Pat, Trick struggled to make conversation. His son, whom he treasured more than anything else in life, was solemn and quiet the whole evening. On the way back home, Trick realized it would take more time than he thought to re-establish a close relationship with his son. He dropped Pat off at Ginger's living room door with the large pumpkin they picked out together along with a small one just for him.

Getting back in his car with that final clang of steel gates still echoing in his mind from earlier that day, he had the urge to hit a bar, have a drink and talk to a pretty lady on his first night of freedom. But knew he had better get going to his destination before it got too late.

Chapter 2

Trick pulled into the parking lot of Reggie's condo. He nosed into a spot under an ancient cottonwood tree, got out and looked up to see a crow fly across the moon.

"Trick," a gravelly, nasal voice called out making him flinch. "You duckin' me?"

He turned to see Eddie Starnes walking up with a bottle of Jack Daniel's in his hand, his muscle, Moogie, right beside him.

"No, of course not," Trick replied, backing up against his driver's side door to keep Moogie from circling behind. "I had every intention of coming to see you. Just got out today ... wanted to get my ducks in a row first."

Starnes walked up nearly toe to toe with Trick. "Well, you got my $60,000?"

"I'm working on it," Trick said, feeling a cold breeze sting the back of his neck. "I've got a couple of irons in the fire. Just need a little time."

"Time? I been waitin' for three years. You're lucky I'm not chargin' interest."

"Hey, come on," Trick said, pulling his face back from Starnes' whiskey breath. "I was locked up. What the hell do you expect?"

"I expect you to come up with my money. I don't care how you do it. Go rob a fuckin' bank. But you will cough up some coin. Otherwise you'll find your son's head on the front porch with the mornin' paper."

Trick grabbed Starnes by the lapels of his motorcycle jacket. "You mother fucker, don't ever threaten my son's life again." His voice raspy from dryness, Trick managed, "If anything ever happens to him I'll kill you with my bare hands."

Trick heard Moogie's .45 caliber revolver click next to his head. "Just come up with the dough." Starnes shoved a fist into Trick's chest. "I could hurt you in ways you couldn't imagine. Never see it comin', boy."

With the exception of Moogie's asthmatic breathing, they stood in silence, glaring at one another. After a few moments, Moogie tailed Starnes back to his pickup truck and they drove away. Leaning against his 1979 Lincoln Continental, Trick took a few deep breaths in an effort to compose himself. It was one of those times when an unfiltered Old Gold would taste great again.

He walked to the entrance he remembered so well and pushed the lighted button next to the name LeChat. A hand pulled a curtain aside and a familiar ebony face peered at him. The annoying sound of the buzzer unlocked the door, giving Trick entrance to days gone by.

"Look atcha, man. Put on some size while you were in da house. Been hittin' dat iron, boy. Face looks different too … became a man while you were gone."

"Hey, Junebug, it's been a while. Yeah, I'm not the same person." Trick shook Reggie's hand and glanced around the first floor condo. "I appreciate you letting me bum here."

"S'ok, man." Reggie's tone changed as he dropped the street dialect. "It'll be good havin' someone here keepin' an eye on things while I'm gone."

"Yeah," Trick said, changing the subject. "I just

had a run in with Starnes and that neanderthal, Moogie, out in your parking lot. Got any idea how he knew I'd be here?"

"Who me? No. How would I know? Must have heard you were out, I guess. Maybe tailin' you."

Trick tried to lock eyes with Reggie, who looked away with a wave of his arms and said, "Well, what do you think?"

"Place looks good ... new couch, bigger TV." Trick breathed in a combination of incense and lemon-scented Pledge. "A fishing boat, huh?"

"Yep, north to Alaska. Ten Gs for three months. Can't spend any of it either. You're on a boat the whole time. Work your ass off. Come back with some of that mean green. You know what they say, money talks."

With deadpan delivery, Trick answered back, "Well, all it ever said to me was goodbye."

Reggie chuckled and shook his head. "Why doncha sign up for the fishin' boat? They're always lookin' for guys."

"I've been away from my son way too long. I need to make up for lost time." Trick looked at his gold Omega watch, wondering what it would bring at a pawnshop. "Ten grand wouldn't solve my problems anyway."

"Gotcha. Sit down, make yourself at home." Reggie spread his palms out. "It will be for the next few months. Wanna beer?"

"Hell yeah, I haven't had a drop of alcohol in almost three years. Well, except for some homemade hooch over in Cook County on Thanksgiving a couple years ago."

Reggie walked into the kitchen and returned with two open bottles of beer. He handed one to Trick, and said, "Gentlemen, start your livers," before settling into a velour recliner.

Trick took a big gulp of cold Michelob, wiped his sandy-brown moustache with his thumb and said, "Damn that tastes good." He let out a long sigh. "I'm going to give my parole officer your address as my residence."

"Why not? S'ok with me."

"So, you're out of the business?" Trick picked up a copy of *Penthouse* from the coffee table and thumbed through a layout with nude photos of Madonna.

"Yeah. After you got popped, then Mossimo, then Herbie. I knew what time it was."

"Don't blame you," Trick said, settling back on the couch. "It's not the same out there. Guys rolling over on each other left and right. No honor left."

"What was it like? I was only in jail once, for a few hours in Chicago lockup. I can't imagine. What did you do, like, three years?"

"Just about," Trick said, pulling at a loose edge of the gold Michelob label. "Prison is not what you think. Not like the movies, TV shows. Hollywood writers need to make their stories interesting so there's all this shit about guys getting shanked or raped every day. It's not like that. What it is … is boring. Every day's like the last. Once in a while there's a fight. No big deal."

"Anybody ever try anything funny with you? You know."

"No, man. No. You got to understand." Trick paused, running his fingertips over the rough synthetic sofa fabric. "Men don't suddenly turn queer because they have a set of bars in front of them. If a guy's got a proclivity toward men on the outside, he'll have it on the inside. The ones that do get reamed are usually just the punks, guys who want it.

They get passed around. I don't care if I was locked up for the rest of my life; I'm not going down that road."

Reggie shook his head. "Hope I never have to find out."

"You'd do OK." Trick held his beer bottle up to the light, watching bubbles race to the top as he chose his words. "I didn't have much trouble. A couple of little scrapes. Most of those thugs didn't want to mess with me. They saw me jogging the yard in ninety-degree weather, hitting the weights every day, doing handstand pushups against the wall … Enough about prison, talking about it is almost as boring as being there. I'm out and I'm not going back. I'm through dealing too."

"Gonna get a straight job? Won't be easy for you. Gettin' by from week to week. You were up there. How much were you makin'?"

"For a while there, for over a year, I was pulling in at least ten a week."

Reggie's eyes popped open, "G's?"

"Yeah. It was a lot of fun. Taking Ginger to all the five-star restaurants downtown, shopping on the Magnificent Mile. I dropped over ten grand on clothes one week."

"Yeah, but, where's all that scratch now?"

"The money's gone, all of it. What the cops didn't confiscate I spent on lawyers and appeals. I'd have been better off just copping a plea. Would have got out sooner and saved a lot of dough."

"Speakin' of money. You got the run of my condo the next three months and we forget about the $2,500 I owe you. Right?"

"That's a little steep. Let's say we knock $1,800 off the balance for rent. I'm going to need a little operating capital. Ginger's already leaning on me for child support."

"I got a thousand. How 'bout I give you half?" Reggie stood and opened his wallet. He flipped through a stack of bills, counted and held some out toward Trick. "I'm gonna need a little foldin' money for the trip to Alaska in the mornin'."

"Yeah, that's cool … for now." Trick took a swig of cold brew and asked, "What's going on with Richie?"

"Rich Quigley?"

"No, man. You know, Richie C."

"Oh, I haven't seen that guy around in a couple years."

Trick leaned forward, setting his empty beer bottle on a Year of the Ox coaster. "Ask around about him, will you? Me and Richie were doing a few things together before they revoked my bond. Gave him the last of my dough for a kilo. Expected that jamoke to get a hold of me. I'm not only broke, I'm deep in debt."

"You just said you were through dealin'. What's with that?"

"I am. But if I can get my hands on that one kilo and sell it, I can pay off Starnes and have enough cash to get back on my feet."

"Let me make a couple calls." Reggie stood and grabbed Trick's empty bottle, "Want another beer?"

Trick nodded, then looked at the television that had the volume turned down. A big handsome lug with a full moustache grinned at the camera then pulled away in a red Ferrari. He listened as Reggie made calls from the kitchen telephone.

A few minutes later, Reggie walked back into the living room with another beer for Trick. "He's in Concord."

"Concord? On 95th? Son-of-a-bitch."

Chapter 3

Trick felt a chill as he walked into the Tinley Teacup restaurant at 159th and Harlem to pick up his son. He spotted little Pat sitting in a booth, drawing on the back of a paper placemat with an orange crayon.

"Mommy's mad at you again. She said you were supposed to be here a half hour ago."

Ginger shot Trick a perturbed look as she stood next to a table taking a late lunch order. He took a seat across from Pat and asked, "What're you drawing, buddy?"

"This is Rambo. He's beating up the bully at my school who makes fun of me. His daddy said you're a bad egg." Pat looked up. "Are you?"

"I'm trying, I'm trying. Don't pay any attention to guys like that. Inside they're not happy, so they want to make you unhappy too. Pat …"

Petros, the owner of the family style restaurant, strutted up and interrupted Trick's train of thought when he blurted out, "So, how does it feel to be a free man again?"

"What does he mean, Daddy?" Pat stopped drawing and tilted his head. "Free?"

Trick looked up at Petros and shot back, "I'd appreciate a little discretion there, *malaka*."

"You should leave Ginger alone. She don't love you no more. You're a good looking guy. Go find another girl."

Trick fished a quarter out of his pocket and handed it to Pat. "Why don't you go get yourself a prize?"

Pat took the coin, gave Trick a funny look, and walked to the hostess station where three vending machines stood; one with salted peanuts, one with gumballs, and one with little toys in clear plastic egg-like containers.

With Pat out of earshot, Trick turned his attention back to Petros, "Not that it's any of your business, but I'd do anything for my son. Even remarry Ginger and put up with her immature, selfish bullshit. As long as I'm with my boy … that's all that matters to me."

Stroking his thick black moustache with his thumb, Petros rebuked, "Look, my friend. After I marry Ginger, we let you see him a couple days, on weekends, so I can take Ginger to Greektown and show her off. Give her the things a lady like her deserves. I'm going to be raising Pat. I'll see he gets everything he needs. Don't worry, if you go back to prison, I'll be there for him."

"You know what I don't like about you guys? You get set up in a restaurant by the Greek Syndicate and think the waitresses are your playthings. You think American girls are a bunch of whores you can impress with your little restaurants." Trick laughed. "Big shots in a tiny little corner of the world."

"You American men are so jealous of our success." Petros smiled smugly. "Get used to it. Me and Ginger are going to have lots of kids, give Pat some brothers and sisters."

"Yeah, well, let's hope they don't end up with your schnozzola."

Ginger finished setting plates of Reuben, French Dip and Monte Cristo sandwiches in front of customers, then stomped up to Trick and Petros. She put her hands on her hips and demanded, "What's going on over here?"

Standing and taking four hundred dollars from an inside pocket of his calfskin jacket, Trick tossed the folded bills on the table. "Here, this is for child support."

"Where'd you get this?" With customers looking at each other, trying to hide their amusement, Ginger picked up the money and waved it in the air. "What're you up to now? Huh?"

"Don't worry about it. Damn … you complain if I don't have it and complain if I do."

Pat crept up unnoticed and asked, "How come everyone's yelling?"

"We're not yelling, Pat," Trick said, taking his hand. "This is what's known as a spirited discussion."

Walking toward the entrance with Pat in tow and bumping shoulders with a Tinley Park Police officer entering the restaurant, Trick looked back at Petros. "You want her, you got her. She's your problem now."

Petros grabbed the officer by the arm as they both watched Trick storm out. "He's a drug dealer. You should keep an eye on this one, my friend."

Chapter 4

Trick had a bad feeling walking into Concord Nursing Home. Was Richie really here? It didn't seem right.

"Can I help you?" asked the chubby young lady, seated behind the open sliding glass window.

"Yeah, Richard Caponigro. He here?"

"Let's see." Her long purple fingernails flipped through a large notebook. "Room 218 West."

The expansive day room, trimmed in log cabin motif, was sparsely filled with bouquets of silver hair scattered here and there. A young man, dressed in a barbershop quartet outfit, jubilantly played the piano in a corner, singing *Oklahoma!* to the few that noticed. One octogenarian gentleman with a pencil thin moustache and a white, well-worn navy hat tapped his foot in time. As Trick turned the corner and proceeded to the west wing, he felt nauseous from the smell of urine and feces while patients cried mournfully for help. Through open doors he viewed the living dead, on their backs, waiting to go on to their husbands and wives who already left the material world. Some not even aware of where they were or who they were, with open mouths and thin skin barely covering ancient bones that looked as though they were trying to make a break for it. Others sat in wheelchairs in the hallway nodding and saying hello, studying, as though they knew you somehow.

"You said you were going to take me out for steak

and a glass of whiskey." A frail black female patient with wiry white hair chastised him. "Come back here, Joe," she called after Trick, who just smiled and winked.

Locating the even numbers to his left, Trick counted them off in his head, "212 … 214 … 216 …" The wide wooden door to 218 was partially closed so he slowly swung it open. On the first of the two small beds lay an obese man who seemed to be staring past the ceiling to a land above. The second bed was empty but in a wheelchair looking out the window sat another elderly looking man. As Trick moved closer, he could make out the profile of someone from his near past. Was this Richie's father, Angie?

"Richie?"

The unshaven, thick-skinned man turned from the light of late afternoon sun and looked Trick in the eye. "Hey, man. I know you."

The voice was raspy like Richie's dad, a low level Outfit guy whose specialty was break and entry jobs, but it was unmistakably Richie.

"How you doing? I thought it was your father sitting there for a minute."

"Trick, man. These fuckheads round here don't know their ass from apple shit. You remember I was on the moon?"

"The moon?"

"Yeah, that orderly, Tyrone, just left here. Tellin' me I'm crazy. He's fuckin' crazy."

"What's this about the moon?"

"Yeah, they sent me up there in a rocket. You don't know nothin' 'bout that?"

Trick just looked at Richie incredulously while he continued, "You know the moon doesn't spin around. You should see the Earth from up there …

beautiful … clouds and shit."

Trick sat on the edge of Richie's bed and spun the wheelchair around so they were face to face. "Who sent you to the moon?"

"The Marines."

"You were never in the service. What year did they send you to the moon?"

Richie's eyes glassed over.

Trick leaned forward on the bed. "What happened to my money? I gave you thirty grand for a kilo, then they revoked my bond. You got the kilo or the cash stashed somewhere?"

"When they sent me to the moon it was top secret shit. That's why it isn't in the record books."

"Richie … my dough. You owe me thirty Gs. What did you do with it?"

"Oh wow, man. That's right, you're undercover … FBI. I don't know nuthin' 'bout that shit. Remember I was heavyweight champ? Only one I couldn't beat was Ali. He broke my nose so bad the doctors said I couldn't fight anymore. Might kill me."

"You goofy goombah, I only remember you getting in one fight in your life. We were in eighth grade and Pete Ryan kicked your ass. Yeah, bang zoom, to the moon. Maybe that's what you're thinking."

"I boxed under a different name. Look it up in the library."

"Richie, look at me. You never did any of those things. You dropped out of high school in our sophomore year, the oldest one in our class. First time you got locked up was 1974. You've been a car thief and drug dealer all your miserable life. In and out of the hospital and rehab."

"I beat George Foreman. His arms were so big he couldn't hold 'em up the last few rounds."

"Look in the damn mirror." Trick stood over Richie, raising his voice, "You're five-foot-seven, never weighed more than one-sixty in your life." Trick grabbed Richie by the lapels of his robe and shook him. "Tell me where my stuff is!"

"Let go of me." Richie looked away and whimpered, "I want some ice cream."

As Trick walked out of the room, Richie yelled after him, "I walked on the moon! I brought back rocks! They sent me up there when I was a detective with the Chicago Police!"

Trick walked to the nurse's station and asked a doctor of Asian descent who didn't look up when he asked, "What's the matter with Richard Caponigro? He faking it?"

She didn't say anything for a moment, then looked up from her paperwork. "Mr. Caponigro has been diagnosed with the early onset of dementia. Usually doesn't know what year it is or even how old he is. He struggles to remember his brothers' names, although he usually recognizes people when he sees them."

"He was talking goofy, about being on the moon and stuff."

"It's not unusual for patients with dementia to have false memories, to imagine their lives more interesting than the ones they've lived."

"He's only 33 ... what happened to him?"

"It could be one thing or many things, drugs and alcohol ... particularly cocaine ... staying up for days on end without sleep. Chronic dehydration can do irreparable harm to the brain. There is so much we don't know about the human mind. He might have been genetically predisposed to it."

"Do any of these people with dementia ever get better, remember their real lives ... important things?"

"They rarely, if ever, get better. It's a downhill slide. Once in a while there might be a small flash of cognizance."

"You never know when though?"

"Exactly."

"Thanks for your help," Trick said as he turned to leave. Under his breath remarking, "Time to get a job."

Chapter 5

"Patrick," General Manager Nick Notara called out, motioning with his hand. "Have a seat." He looked up from Trick's application. "So, you know Jay. He told me you'd be by."

"Yeah, we go back a long way." Trick folded and unfolded his hands. "Said you could use a salesman."

"You sell cars before?"

Trick shifted on the hard, molded-plastic chair, searching for a comfortable position. "No, I haven't."

"Good, I don't like unteaching bad sales habits. Ever done sales at all?"

"Well ... I sold stuff but basically it sold itself." Trick shifted again. "Just a matter of supply and demand."

"Jay filled me in." Nick peered at Trick over black, half-frame glasses. "When did you get out?"

"Two days ago." Trick felt pained answering personal questions and realized it was the first time he applied for a job in close to eight years.

"I don't need guys walking around here high. You have to be sharp, on your toes to do this kind of work."

"Jay didn't tell you? I never used drugs, just sold them." Trick waved his hand to the side. "I'm through with all that. I lost three years of my life, even more when you consider the hell you go through fighting a case. Knowing that you're probably going away, having that hanging over your head. It's rough. I'm not going back to selling drugs or prison. Just want to work and get back on my feet."

Nick leaned back in his chair, folded dark hairy knuckles over his ample belly and studied Trick. "Where do you see yourself five years from now?"

Trick looked away, studied one of the older salesmen sitting at a desk with his head resting on his hands, dozing. "Five years. I … I don't know. I'm just worried about right now, making money, paying the bills. The things I need to accomplish have to happen sooner than five years. The only thing I really care about is my son Pat. I just want a normal life with him. I want to see him every day, watch him grow up. I heard that some guys make over a hundred grand a year selling cars."

"Let's hope you're one of them." Nick let out a long belch and patted his belly. "Got to cut down on those onion rings. Patrick, a lot of guys and gals come and go in this business. Not as easy as it appears. Maybe one in twenty make the big bucks."

"I'll be one of the money guys. I've got to." Trick let out a nervous sigh and looked up at the ceiling. "Not sure where else to turn."

"OK, Patrick, I'll give you a chance. You'll start out getting a draw against commissions. Come in tomorrow at 8:30. We go on the floor at 9:00 but we have a sales meeting every morning. Be on time. If you're running late, don't bother to come in at all."

"Gotcha," Trick said, jumping up from the chair and extending his hand.

"You don't need to tell anyone you were incarcerated." Nick looked at Trick's hand and paused before shaking it. "Don't need to offer any information that might reflect badly on William Buick."

Trick walked out into the cool evening air and looked west to see the sun setting next to the Oak Lawn Water Tower. He got in his car and headed east on 95th Street, turning up the radio to drown out his stomach calling to be fed. He made his way through the multitude of traffic lights to Palermo's restaurant. Finding a spot in the rear parking lot, Trick's mouth watered from the aroma of freshly baking pizzas as he walked around to the front entrance. There were only a couple people at the bar so he took a stool and leaned back into the tufted leather, happy to see a familiar face.

"Trick. Oh my God. It's good to see you." Dotti, the bartender, reached across the bar grabbing his hand.

"Good to see you too." Trick stared into Dotti's eyes and smiled. "Still beautiful as ever."

"Thank you, Sweetie. When did you get out?"

"Just a couple days ago." Trick sighed and looked around. "You know, I came here the night before my sentencing. Got loaded on Bailey and Stoli. Knew it would be a long time before I had another drink."

"I bet the first thing you did was go see your son. How is little Pat?"

"He's great, but it's awkward. When I left, he was two years old. I doubt that he can remember much, if anything, from that age. I'm this guy who called him on the phone once a week."

"It'll work out, give it time. Can I get you anything?"

"Johnnie Walker Black, on the rocks. Make it a double."

Dotti set Trick's Scotch on a cocktail napkin but couldn't ignore the harsh stares she was getting from her manager, Tony. "I'm sorry," she said. "I'll be right back." Trick turned to see Tony talking animatedly with his hands but couldn't make out what was being said. She returned flustered. "Tony wants to know what you're doing here."

"I came to get dinner." Trick put his palms out and shook his head. "Why don't you put in an order of spaghetti and meatballs. I'm starving."

Savoring his Scotch, Trick remarked, "You know, Cesar Romero sat in this very seat. He was performing down the street at Drury Lane. I was having lunch here about ten years ago and he was sitting right in this spot."

After a little small talk, a waitress put a hand on Trick's back and pressed her breasts into his arm as she set a steaming plate of spaghetti in front of him.

"That was quick. Thank you," Trick said, as he slipped a five-dollar-bill into the waitress' hand.

Trick was twirling his first forkful of spaghetti when Tony walked up next to him brandishing a butcher knife. "My nephew died from that poison you sell."

"I don't sell drugs anymore." Trick put his fork down and turned in his seat to face Tony. "I did my time, paid my debt."

Tony waved the knife toward Trick's face. "You pushers should get life for bringing drugs into our neighborhoods."

"I'm sorry," Dotti said, as Tony stormed off red-faced.

Unable to eat, Trick pushed his plate away. "How much do I owe you?"

"This is on Tony. He told me to tell you not to come back. He doesn't want your business."

Chapter 6

Trick glanced at the dashboard clock, 8:29 AM. He fumbled with his tie, got out of his Lincoln and looked down. He tied it too short but there was no time to adjust it so he buttoned the top button of his old Armani sport coat and hustled to the back door of the dealership in the fog and cool morning drizzle. He cut through the service department, stepping over oil patches.

Nick Notara shot a stern look toward Trick, who walked in trying to look inconspicuous and blend in with the other salesmen seated at desks and standing around. He continued talking to the sales team, "One thing I do not tolerate is tardiness. If I say to be here at 8:30, I expect you to be here at 8:15, get your coffee and be ready to learn something," Nick continued, glancing at Trick. "Anyone here think they know everything there is about selling cars? Anyone think they know more than me?"

Trick kept his mouth shut as he stood in the back, nowhere to sit, and watched the other salesmen glancing at each other uncomfortably. While Nick continued berating the group of sixteen men who ranged from their early 20s to their late 50s, Trick leaned against a 1986 Park Avenue, surrounded by the smell of new cars, fresh tires and cheap carpeting. He tried his best to absorb the non-stop diatribe of the general manager but his mind kept wandering back to the early 1980s, when he had "fuck you" money. When he was married and would come home to a hot meal and play with baby Pat. The spell was broken after the sales meeting when a pudgy, fair skinned, rosy cheeked guy about his age appeared in front of him. "Hi my name's Steve Zajaczkowski. Most people can't pronounce it." He extended his hand and gave Trick an enthusiastic salesman handshake. "Just call me Stevie Z."

"Name's Patrick Halloran. People call me Trick. Round here, probably better if we stick with Pat."

"Follow me, Pat." Steve walked ahead and motioned with his hand. "Looks like we'll be sharing a desk. I'll squeeze the rest of my stuff into these two drawers and you can have these two. OK?"

Trick watched as Steve knelt down and began moving an extensive filing system from one drawer to another. "You're gonna need copies of all this stuff for your own system. You don't want to go around looking for paperwork when you got a customer hot to sign. Don't want to give them a chance to think about what they're doing. Might change their mind, just like that." Steve snapped his fingers for emphasis. "Car sales have a lot more to do with impulse and emotions than logic."

"I'll remember that." Trick sat on the edge of the desk. "How long you been here?"

"Just started last week. I've made the rounds. This is my seventh dealership in the last few years." Steve's expression changed from his polished salesman smile to one of dread. "Oh shit, here comes Wickerstock. He's our sales manager. Seems I'm his whipping boy around here."

Todd Wickerstock walked up and looked down on Steve with an expression that was a cross between amusement and disgust. "Z, get up off your knees. What are you doing down there?"

"I ... I'm making room for Patrick. You said we

had to share this desk."

"You look like you want to blow someone. Stand up like a man and put these flyers under the windshields of all the new Buicks out there."

"Well ... yeah but, if I'm out doing that I'll be missing ups. I can't sell anything if I'm fiddling with those things."

"Oh, you're too good for this? Everyone's got to pitch in around here. You want to handle the flyers or pack your shit up and hit the road?"

"Well, I mean, if everyone has to do it ... I guess I don't mind."

Wickerstock held out a stack of pink flyers with black lettering and said, "Right now would be good."

"Guess I'll finish organizing later." Steve's pale face turned red with embarrassment as Wickerstock walked out of earshot. "Wish I had the balls to flatten that asshole." Steve looked at the floor and shook his head. "Who am I kidding? He'd whip my ass. Heard he played left guard at Purdue."

***

Trick hesitantly knocked on the aluminum screen door a second time. A petite Filipino woman with straight, black hair, opened the faded, wood-paneled door.

"What you wanted?" Her facial expression looked as though she had just sucked a lemon.

"I'm looking for Charles Brummerstedt. Does he still live here?"

"Yes." She spoke as though Trick might be half-deaf. "Mr. Charlie listen to radio program."

"Could you tell him Patrick Halloran is here to see him?"

"OK, wait on porch, you," she said, then slammed the door.

Trick turned to look at the towering, cottonwood tree in the front yard. The rope he tied to a high branch his first summer there when he was thirteen was weather-worn but still hanging there. The same rope he would climb up and down over his teen years, hand over hand, attempting to develop his physique.

The door opened again and the round faced woman said, "You no stand on porch now, you walk in door."

She led Trick to the family room at the rear of the house where he was surprised to find his former foster father in a wheelchair, shocked at how Charles had aged since he last saw him. "Hi, Pop." Trick breathed in stale air that seemed to have aged with the house.

After adjusting false teeth that were too big for his shrinking gums, Charles replied. "Well, look what the cat dragged in."

The Filipino woman pointed a finger at her chest and said, "No. Me no drag cat."

Charles gave her that look, the one Trick used to hate being on the receiving end of. "Why don't you go clean something and give me time to talk to this prodigal son-of-a-gun."

Trick smiled. "See you haven't lost your charm."

"You come here to be a wise acre?" Charles aimed a crooked finger from a hand that shook with palsy. "I don't need none of that sass talk."

"No. Just kidding, really." Trick sat on a doily covered arm of a vintage Herculon sofa. "Just wanted to see how you're doing."

"Well, how does it look like I'm doing? I'm 79 years old and stuck in this wheelchair."

"How is Martha?" Trick's words caught in his throat. "Is she …?"

"Martha died a year-and-a-half ago, while you were in the hoosegow."

Trick's face dropped. "I'm sorry. I didn't know."

"You should be sorry. She washed your clothes, cooked your meals, treated you like her own flesh and blood. Only to have you take off once you turned 18, with hardly a word."

"I appreciated everything she did for me. I just couldn't stay here any longer." Trick noticed the cocky, smirking photo of himself when he was 15 on the mantel over the fireplace, still sitting in the same spot. It seemed to mock him, reminding him that he thought he knew it all back then. Maybe he didn't know as much as he thought he did now at 31. "This is your house. Always felt like I was living in your house, eating your food, breathing your air."

Charles wrung his veiny hands. "Being a foster parent wasn't what I thought it would be."

"Why did you take me in?" Trick stood, stuffed his hands in his pockets, and walked a small circle on a worn area rug. "Never could figure it out."

Charles looked out the rear bay window at a gnarled tree with a few stubborn leaves that clung to the branches. He seemed to drop his hands on soup-stained, gray work pants in defeat. "Martha couldn't have any more children after Joanne was born. And then she grows up and goes off to that fancy college where they filled her head with a bunch of communist notions. That's when we brought you into our home. I always wanted a son. But you were so damn bullheaded. Mister Independent, didn't trust no one. Always hated authority."

"I give you and Martha credit for your efforts, but I never asked for much. I was always working."

"Yeah, and always getting fired. Wouldn't listen to no one. Always knew better, so you thought."

Charles shook his head. "Even got kicked out of the Marines."

"Well, I'm working again ... wanted to wait until I had a good job before I came to see you."

"That won't last long," Charles said. "Probably get mad and punch your boss on the nose."

"No. I'm trying real hard, for my son."

"Did you ever think maybe me and Martha would have liked to see your boy? No. You were too busy running round with that waitress you married. Too busy to come by and see us old people. Maybe thought you got too good for us. Big shot with a lot of blood money."

"I'm sorry. I didn't know ... didn't think."

"See you still got that gold watch I gave you on your eighteenth birthday, right before you disappeared. That's not plated you know, it's the real thing. Railroad gave it to me after 44 years of dedicated service. Never did like wearing no watch no how."

Trick looked at the wristwatch. It always amazed him that Charles gave him something so nice. He never bought Trick new clothes, only passable ones from the second hand store. The bicycle he gave Trick on his fourteenth birthday was an old one that someone in the neighborhood left out on the curb for the garbage truck to pick up. He thought of the inscription Charles added on the back plate of the watch. *To Patrick, May you always obey the Golden Rule, Pop.*

"What can I bring you next time I come? You still like those butter pecan coffee cakes?"

"You don't have to bring me nothing. It would be better if you didn't come back at all. You know how embarrassing it is to have all the neighbors know you're a jailbird? All looking at me. I know what they're thinking ... I didn't do a good enough job raising you. No, boy. Just stay away. Let this old man shrivel up and die. Can't come soon enough for me. Just want to go be with my Martha again." Charles looked away.

"OK, Pop. I won't bother you again. Just want to say thank you ... for everything." Trick walked closer and extended his hand but Charles didn't seem to notice. A tear slowly made its way down one of the deep lines in Charles' gaunt face. Trick pulled his hand back, then walked slowly through the old house one more time, drinking in as much as possible.

Chapter 7

Within earshot of the desk he shared with Steve, Trick rested against a brand new LeSabre that reflected the high overhead lighting on the red enamel. He could tell by the body language of Todd Wickerstock walking toward Steve Z that something was up.

"Z," Wickerstock blurted out, looking down on Steve, who was sitting at his desk working on his follow-up list. "William Buick has decided that it would be best served if we had a parting of the ways. Pack up your things and be out of here as quick as you can."

"You've got to be kidding. I'm a good salesman," Steve pleaded. "I've got deals in the works. Customers are coming back to see me."

"Oh, that's no problem." Wickerstock smirked in his annoying smug way. "We'll take care of your people."

After Wickerstock was back in his office, Trick approached Steve. "Hey, man. That's a bum deal. You're so knowledgeable about car sales. You don't deserve this."

"That chicken fucking egg sucker just doesn't like me. I have no idea why."

"If they'd treat *you* like this," Trick ran his fingers through his full wavy hair and sighed, "what's in store for me?"

Steve fumbled with his paperwork, his already rosy cheeks now red as wild strawberries. "This is the way a lot of dealerships work it. You haven't been here long enough to notice but they bring in two new guys every week and fire two guys every week. The managers browbeat the salesmen, treat them like shit. They give the good deals to their top earners like Coleman to keep them happy. Then they purposely make it hard for you to sell so you get desperate. That's when they lean on you to bring in friends and family members. After they've exhausted all your connections, they boot your ass out the door."

Wickerstock walked back to the desk as Steve was putting his car sales paperwork in his brief case. "What are you still doing here? I told you to get the fuck out. What do I have to do, throw you out of here bodily?"

"I'm going," Steve said as he stood with briefcase in hand.

"And you better have left all your William Buick deals in your drawer." Wickerstock poked Steve directly on his polyester tie, just below his slight double chin. "Otherwise, I'll call every dealership on the south side and have you blackballed."

Steve sidestepped Wickerstock, turned to Trick and shook his hand. "Good luck, Pat. Watch your back."

"It was brief, but it's been good knowing you." Trick watched Steve walk out the door appearing to muster as much dignity as possible.

With Steve gone, Wickerstock turned his full attention to Trick. "Halloran, don't just stand around waiting for someone to pull up. Get on the phone and call all those ups you let leave without buying."

***

"OK, go ahead and write it up," Wickerstock said, tossing the sales proposal sheet back across the desk.

"You got lucky today. This is a laydown, an easy one. Don't go thinking that'll happen every day."

Trick spent the next four hours running back and forth, doing paperwork, getting his customer through the finance department, having the new Buick Century prepped by one of the porters and attending to all the other various duties that go along with selling a new car.

Waving goodbye to his customer as she drove off in her shiny new car, Trick excitedly asked the more experienced salesman, Ralphie, "How much do you think I'll make on this one?"

"Let me see your deal." Ralphie grabbed Trick's paperwork from his hand. "Looks like they weren't able to rape her in financing, credit's too good. You didn't sell her any extras, not good. No spiffs or spins. After taxes, maybe twenty-seven bucks."

"That's all? I've been hiking back and forth, working up a sweat for less than seven bucks an hour?"

"You gotta tip the kid who prepped the car too. You know that, right?"

"Tip him?" Trick became annoyed when he heard a few salesmen laugh. "How much?"

"Couple bucks," Ralphie replied, rubbing his thumb and forefinger together.

"Damn," Trick said, walking away with his paperwork.

"You wanna make any money, you gotta sell a few used ones every week along with the new ones," Ralphie called after Trick. "Only way you'll be able to eat."

***

Ginger opened her door as Trick knocked a third time. "What are you doing here? How'd you get in?"

"Someone left the door open downstairs." Trick loosened his silk tie, a leftover from his clothes shopping days when the cash was rolling in. "Today's an early day. I was hoping to spend some time with Pat."

"You making any money over there?"

"Well, not really. But I will. Things are starting to come together for me. I'm learning the ropes." Trick rubbed his light brown stubble. "Do I smell cherry popovers?"

Holding a pot holder in one hand and the other on her hip, she snapped back, "Never mind what you smell. Pat needs a new winter coat and a Halloween costume."

"Sure, no problem. Don't worry. I'll have some cash next time." Trick smiled at his son, who sat cross-legged on outdated shag carpet, playing Frogger on his Atari. "Has Pat eaten yet? Thought I'd take him to McDonalds."

Pat dropped his joystick and jumped on the couch, bouncing up and down, chanting, "McDonalds, McDonalds, McDonalds!"

"Well, now that you've opened your big mouth, what else can I say?" Ginger's eyes rolled to the ceiling. "Go ahead."

"Thanks. I'll have him back in a couple hours." Looking around for signs of Starnes and Moogie lurking around, Trick led Pat down to his car. He buckled him in the front passenger seat, then headed east on the Midlothian Turnpike. "Pat," Trick said to his boy, who was looking out the open window of his Lincoln, watching the world go by. "What are you thinking about? I want you to know you can ask me anything."

"I was thinking about outer space." Pat pointed in the air. "How far does it go?"

"That's what you're thinking about? Infinity? Well ... gee ... let's see. Umm, that's a tough one. When I said you could ask me anything, I didn't think ..."

"How does God remember everyone's names?"

"Oh, boy. Well, Pat, that's another ... hey, that's what goes on in your five-year-old head? When I was your age I was thinking about frogs and yo-yos." Trick let out a big sigh and continued. "Men have been pondering those questions for centuries. Outer space just keeps going, on and on. It doesn't stop, far as I know. And, only God knows how he does things. He's a lot smarter than us. He has infinite wisdom."

"What's infinite?" Pat shrugged his shoulders up and down.

"Uh, it means ... it means Mommy will look it up for you in the dictionary when I drop you off."

"Hmmm." Pat sounded disappointed and waved his hand up and down through the open window as though trying to catch the wind.

"Did you know I love you more than anything in the whole world?"

"I guess so." Pat folded his hands on his lap and hung his head.

"I do." Trick turned to study Pat's face. "I would do anything in the world for you."

Pat finally looked Trick in the eye. "Why did you go away?"

"I didn't want to go away." The smell of burning leaves from a nearby backyard swirled in the breeze, triggering autumn memories of years ago. "I had to."

Pat spread his upturned palms outward. "Where did you have to go?"

"I had to go to college. Needed to learn a few lessons."

"Was it more important than being with me?"

"No, it wasn't. I know that now," Trick said as he turned left onto Cicero Avenue. "I'll never do anything that will take me away from you again. See, I got smarter in college."

Trick drove north a few miles and pulled into the parking lot of McDonalds and unbuckled Pat's seatbelt.

The boy got on his knees and leaned forward, putting his nose to Trick's cardboard air freshener hanging from his rearview mirror. "How come this thing looks like a skunk but it smells good?"

"Things aren't always as they appear, remember that. Life is full of contradictions. You'll find that out as you get older."

Pat scrunched up his nose. "What's a contradiction?"

"Well … hmm … a contradiction. See, It's kind of like when something opposes something else. No wait, it's like a conflict or inconsistency … I think."

Pat just stared at him.

"Pat, I'm not too good at this. I don't have much experience talking to five-year-olds." Trick raised his eyebrows and shook his head. "They didn't teach me that in college."

"I'm hungry," Pat said, sighing. "Can we eat?"

"Yeah. Good idea."

Chapter 8

"You blew another one?" Wickerstock berated Trick, as spittle stretched between his lips while he spoke. "You need intense sales training, green pea. You'll be shadowing Ralphie. He's going to be on every deal with you and get half of your commissions."

"Half?" Trick's temper rose. He thought about the last guy who talked down to him in prison and how it ended in a fist fight. "For how long?"

"Until I say different."

"Oh, fuck." Trick realized he had just vocalized his thoughts when he saw an orange 1953 Chevy pickup pull between two fading yellow lines in the customer parking area. He walked away from Wickerstock and headed toward the front entrance as two formidable figures exited the restored, polished truck.

"Hey, I'm not through with you," Wickerstock barked.

Trick ignored Wickerstock, walked out the door and up to the two. "What are you guys doing here?"

"This is your plan? This is how you plan to pay me back? Sellin' cars?" Starnes bitched in his nasal tone. Moogie slouched behind him with the noon day sun shining off his freshly-shaved scalp.

Starnes grabbed Trick by the lapels of his navy blue William Buick sport coat. "Polyester? You're comin' down in the world, boy. Hey, I need you to start makin' heavy payments to me, like yesterday. Don't make me do bad things to you. I almost like you."

"I'm going to do good here. Sold my first new car yesterday. Be reasonable."

"Be reasonable?" Starnes let go of Trick's jacket and poked his finger at him. "I don't gotta be nothin'. You gotta be somethin'. You gotta be figurin' out a way to pay me my dough real quick."

Shadowing Starnes, Moogie stroked his chest-length copper-colored beard, grinning, showing off nubs of discolored teeth.

"Hey, Moogie," Trick asked, in mock sincerity, "you ever say anything, or just stand around looking pretty?"

Moogie's grin changed to an evil grimace in the blink of an eye as he put his hand on the box cutter he wore in an oxblood leather sheath on his belt.

Starnes slapped Trick lightly on his face, then gave an exaggerated, overly friendly wave to Wickerstock, who was standing on the other side of a showroom window surveying the interaction between the three. "Don't get cute just 'cause there's witnesses around."

Trick turned to see Wickerstock's scrutinizing face, then returned his attention to Starnes and Moogie. "You guys are going to screw things up for me here. Then I won't have any way of paying you."

"OK, Trickmeister. Better start sellin' a lot of cars real quick. I'll be in touch." As they got back in the pickup, Moogie gave Trick a mock pull of a trigger from a finger pistol.

Trick did his best to act nonchalant as they pulled away with a squeal, leaving two strips of noxious smelling rubber on the graying asphalt. He slowly walked back into the showroom knowing Wickerstock was watching his every move.

"What was that shit? You bringing drug dealers around here now?" Wickerstock stood with fists on his hips and a scowl on his broad square face. "Or did you muff another sale? Which is it?"

"Neither. It wasn't a customer. Just an old friend ... stopped by to say hi."

"Friend? Didn't look too friendly to me." The gooey bit of spittle still on Wickerstock's lips nauseated Trick. "I swear, if you're using William Buick to move drugs, I'll have you back in the slammer before you can take a crap."

***

"Don't argue with me, Halloran," Wickerstock scolded Trick. "Everyone here has to send letters to their family members, friends, people you went to school with, anyone and everyone you can think of. You want them all to know you're here and ready to give them a deal on a new or used car. Say whatever you have to. Just get them in the door. Understand?"

"Yeah. I got to tell you though; I don't like the idea of leaning on people I know to make a buck." Trick shifted from one foot to another. "Why can't I just work on walk-in customers?"

"You've been here three days and only sold one car." Wickerstock folded his arms across his chest.

"Yeah, but I have a few prospects," Trick said, raising a finger in the air. "One guy said he'd call me tomorrow."

"I've been doing this a long time. That guy was being polite. The minute he walked out the door he was heading to another dealership where a more experienced salesman sold him a car. You worked eight ups since you've been here that walked. That means you blew eight sales. It cost William Buick a lot of advertising dollars to get those customers in the door. So far, you're costing us a lot of money to train you with no guarantee you won't jump ship and go to another store."

"But if I send out sales letters to everyone I know," Trick squinted and continued, "I'm kind of stuck here."

"No shit. Go to your desk, formulate a sales letter and bring it back to me. Either that or take off your team jacket and hit the bricks right now."

Walking back to the desk he used to share with Stevie Z, Trick weighed his options and thought about what other work he might be qualified for. The only real experience he had was working in factories, mind-numbing work that he hated. The only success he had was selling drugs. His work record was spotty. Prospective employers always wanted to know why someone like him went so many years without holding a legitimate job. And then there was the prison thing. If they asked, he couldn't lie. If they found out that you lied about being a convict, they had call to fire you. The problem was, he needed a job that paid a lot of money in order to get out of the financial trouble he was in; otherwise, just about anything would do.

Trick sat with pen and William Buick letterhead and thought about the words that would get people in the door without humbling himself too badly. He jotted down notes while watching other salesmen greet enthusiastic looking customers. About fifteen minutes later, Trick finally felt he had just the right combination of words and sentiments that would have everyone he knew rushing up to see him with money in hand. He brought it back to Wickerstock as he heard one of the walk-in customers say, "OK, you got a deal," to Jimmy, who started the same day he did.

"Here, I'm done," Trick said, holding the piece of paper up.

Wickerstock snatched it out of Trick's hand and read it. He gave Trick a distasteful look and said, "Go back and work on this some more. You're on the right track but it could be better. Go on, get going."

Trick sat back down and looked his sales letter over. While he doodled on the large calendar desk mat, a cream colored Audi pulled onto the lot as three salesmen chased it down. Jamile, who had the longest legs of the trio, got to it first. A shapely young lady in a business suit emerged to find an outstretched hand ready to pump hers.

"What do you think of this one?" Trick asked, handing Wickerstock the same exact letter he had ten minutes earlier.

Wickerstock looked it over and answered back, "There, that's better. See? Go ahead and bring it to the office and have one of the girls make as many copies as you need. They'll give you envelopes. Address 'em, fold 'em and stuff 'em."

"Pompous ass," Trick muttered under his breath as he headed to the business office with his letter.

***

"Anita!" Trick was happy to see a familiar face. "Good to see you."

"I heard you were working here. I'm looking for a good used car. I know you won't cheat me."

"I'd never screw a friend. How's your family?"

"Everyone's doing good. Jodi just started high school."

"Damn. Little Jodi?" Trick felt the harsh stare of Wickerstock burning down his good mood. "What kind of car you looking for?"

Trick put a gentle hand on Anita's back and led her out the door to the used car lot and showed her around. After an hour of running back and forth, retrieving car keys, going on test drives and getting the trade-in appraised, Trick brought a signed deal into Wickerstock's office and said, "Sold."

"What've we got?" Ralphie walked in right after Trick and picked up the sales sheet. "Hey, good one, nice profit. Oh, trade-in too, fuckin' A." He smiled and dropped the sheet back on the desk.

Wickerstock looked it over, initialed it, handed it back to Ralphie and said, "Go ahead and deliver it."

"Hey, that's my sale. I worked that all by myself."

"What'd I tell you? You're in intensive training. You split all deals with Ralphie."

"This lady's a friend of mine." Trick began wondering what was worse, prison or selling cars. "She wouldn't even be here if it wasn't for me."

"Put it on the board, Ralphie, your name over Halloran's. Pull it up next to her old car and have one of the porters switch the plates. Get it on the road."

"You got to be fucking kidding. This is bullshit!" Trick asserted, "that's it, I'm through."

"I didn't think you could take it. Nick told me you were a drug dealer. Too used to that easy money. Different when you have to work for it, isn't it?"

"What the hell makes you think you know what I can handle? I worked all my life, doing odd jobs as a kid, cutting grass, delivering papers before school. When I left high school I worked my ass off in a lot of hell-hole factories. You think you know what I can take? I'll tell you what you can't take, you spoiled mama's boy. You wouldn't last a day in some of the places I lived through, Cook County, Joliet, Statesville. They'd pass your sissy ass around like they owned you."

"I'll see that you never work for another

dealership in Illinois again!" Wickerstock screamed red faced, "you're blackballed, jailbird!"

"You think I give a rat's ass?" Trick's voice became raspy as he stepped closer to Wickerstock and looked him dead in the eye. "I'd never do this again in my life. I'd rather go back to selling drugs. There's more honor among drug dealers than you thieves. The only way you can make any money in this business is if you cheat people. I never cheated anyone in my life. Anyone who ever dealt with me got a square deal, got what they paid for. I don't know how you people can feel good about yourself, how you sleep at night, you fucking crooks."

Trick stepped back, took his William Buick jacket off, rolled it in a ball and threw it in Wickerstock's face. Wickerstock grabbed the jacket, tossed it to the floor and hunched forward. Trick stood his ground and said, "Go ahead, I dare you to talk to me in that tone again." Wickerstock stood with his fists clenched, snorting like a bull but didn't say a word. Trick stood with his eyes locked on Wickerstock's for a few moments, then added, "Yeah, I didn't think so." Trick turned, walked out the door and remembered all those sales letters that went out with that day's mail.

***

As Trick walked into Ginger's apartment, she put a finger to her heart shaped lips and whispered, "Shhh, Pat's sleeping. He conked out about an hour ago. He ought to be up soon. C'mon, back here."

Trick followed her back to the kitchen in the wake of her Dior's Poison perfume, watching her ass as she walked, throbbing memories haunting him with every step. She suddenly stopped, pivoted and folded her arms across her chest. "OK, why the

61

hangdog look? Wait, don't tell me. You got fired."

"I quit." Trick recognized that look. "OK, here comes the *I told you sos*."

"Big man with big ideas." Ginger smirked and shook her head. "Couldn't hack it, huh?"

"No real man would have put up with that bullshit."

Ginger toyed with the emerald pendant that hung from an 18 karat rope chain he bought for her birthday four years earlier. It was just another reminder of how much he had then and how little he had now. The precious stone, that was easily affordable to him then, picked up the green in her hazel eyes. Those eyes that had a way of looking down at him, even though she was five-foot-five and he was six inches taller. "I thought a real man can put up with things weaker men can't."

"You weren't there. You don't know." Trick looked away and studied the crude finger-painting of a man, woman and little boy holding hands that was secured to the refrigerator with black and white Scottie dog magnets. "I'll find another way."

"You're thinking about it," Ginger said, arching her left eyebrow. "Aren't you?"

"No. I mean, of course it crossed my mind. That doesn't mean I'm seriously considering it. There's a difference."

"You're going to fold," Ginger taunted, waving a finger at him, "go back to it."

"You're wrong. I wouldn't do anything that would take me away from Pat again."

Ginger tapped a Virginia Slim out of a tight pack and put it between her full, red painted lips. "Well, if not drug dealing, what are you going to do? I need that child support coming in every month."

"Don't worry." Trick ran his fingertips over the

lumpy texture of little Pat's finger paint. The humming vibration of the refrigerator seemed to breathe life into the idealized, two dimensional family. "I'll figure something out."

"Don't give me that false bravado, Mr. Pessimism. Where are you going to find a good job? You hardly have any experience." Ginger took a stick match from an open box and ran it up the zipper of her jeans. She lit her cigarette with the tiny bluish flame and blew smoke out the side of her mouth. "It's not like you're going to get an executive job somewhere."

"I'll tell you something I've learned. Sometimes you don't know if a situation is good or bad until some time has passed."

"Oh, boy." Ginger rolled her eyes in an exaggerated manner. "I feel one of your speeches coming on."

"Give you an example. Before I met you, I was coming back from Baltimore. Just wrapped up some business out there and needed to get back quick to make another buy before my connect left town. I was driving to the airport and missed my turn on the highway. It was a while before I realized I had gone out of my way. So, I'm racing to get to the airport but when I got to the terminal it was too late, saw my plane pulling away from the gate." Trick's serious expression changed to a whimsical one. "Well, turned out that Southwest Airlines had another flight going to Midway an hour later. So, no big deal after all. Went to the bar, relaxed and had a drink." Trick motioned with both hands. "Here's the thing, the flight that I missed had mechanical problems and got diverted to Milwaukee. Turns out I got in a lot earlier than I would have if I made the first flight. Taught me something."

Ginger tapped a gray ash into the kitchen sink and

asked, "So, what do airplanes have to do with you getting a job?"

"Nothing. What I'm trying to say is, you don't always know about things. Time tells the story."

"So, you're trying to put a positive spin on getting shit-canned?"

"Forget it. I'm casting pearls ..."

"Pearls? What do pearls have to do with anything?" Ginger took a deep drag, blew smoke out of her nostrils and extended her palms out upward like she was checking for rain. "I'm not giving you back those pearls you got me."

"Oh, my God. Are you really that ..." Trick hesitated and turned to see little Pat stumbling toward them rubbing his eyes.

Pat stopped and looked up at his father. "Are you fighting?"

Trick knelt down and patted his son's shoulders. "No, no. Me and Mommy were just having an intelligent conversation." Lowering his voice, he added, "Kind of."

Chapter 9

Pulling away from Ginger's apartment, Trick didn't know where to turn and started driving aimlessly. He knew he had to do something to get out of the mess he was in.

He traveled all the way to the Village of Willowbrook before getting on Interstate 55 and starting back. Heading east and passing a sign that read *Historic Route 66*, he looked in his rearview mirror to catch the last remnants of the sun disappearing behind massive purple clouds that reminded him of the Rocky Mountains. He contemplated Ginger's weight loss as he drove along in the middle lane listening to the radio. Putting his headlights on, he took another look in his mirror to see the clouds already changing colors, losing their brilliance when something else caught his eye. A blood-red Dodge Charger was flying up from behind, darting in and out of lanes dangerously close to the other vehicles. Trick turned to see a white Chevy Blazer in the right-hand lane quickly move onto the shoulder to avoid getting clipped. After making its way past a number of vehicles driving in a pack, the Charger had room to run and flew past the First Avenue exit.

Trick then spotted a black unmarked police vehicle, with alternate flashing headlights, speeding up from behind on the right shoulder. The police car swerved, with screeching brakes, stopping just short of slamming into the Blazer, still on the side of the road. He looked ahead in the distance to see someone in the front passenger seat of the Charger throw a large dark bag out the window. The bag landed somewhere among the high weeds and cattails of the sloping ditch next to the expressway. After the bag was thrown, the unmarked car maneuvered around the Blazer and continued pursuit of the Charger.

Trick thought, "Did people in the other vehicles not realize what just happened?" He was in the business long enough to know what this might mean. Changing lanes, he quickly decelerated and pulled onto the shoulder. The two speeding cars were now out of sight and he carefully exited his Lincoln. He walked back about thirty yards and began looking through the tall growth and dry cracked mud that was at the bottom of the ditch. The sound of vehicles going past came in loud waves as he continued searching. Then he saw it, a fully stuffed black leather bag lying between an empty bottle of Gordon's gin and a faded McDonald's wrapper. Trick grabbed the zipper bag by both handles, climbed the incline and hurried back to his car with surges of wind from semi-trailer trucks nearly rocking him off his feet. He threw the bag onto the passenger seat as he hopped in behind the wheel.

Trick made his way into the right-hand lane and drove cautiously, breathing heavily with excitement. He looked over at the bag and pulled it closer, running his hand over the cracked leather. Toying with the zipper, he was unable to pull it open with one hand. He passed a sign indicating one mile to the Harlem exit. Steering with his knees, he made a quick move using both hands and finally got the zipper open a few inches. His heart started pounding when he caught a glimpse of cash.

Turning onto the southbound Harlem Avenue exit, Trick steered into a Shell station a short distance ahead on the street's west side. He pulled up on the far right in the parking lot and slammed it into park. After looking around, he opened the bag all the way. Paper-banded stacks of 100s, 50s and 20s practically jumped from the open bag.

"Son of a fuckin' whore," Trick said out loud and turned the radio off. Removing wads of bills, he saw something at the bottom of the bag. Pushing the remaining money aside, he pulled out what appeared to be a kilo of cocaine. He'd seen enough of them to know what they looked like and counted a total of three identically packaged kilos. Taking a pocket knife from his glove compartment, he cut into the taped surface of the solid rectangular package. He pulled out a small amount onto the flat surface of the blade and examined it, taking the small iridescent, flaky rock between his fingertips, breaking down the luminous layers and feeling the texture. Bringing it to his nose, he smelled the combination of bubblegum and cat piss fragrance that told him it was the real deal.

He looked into his rearview mirror to see a car slowly pulling up behind him. He could see the look on the man's large square face. It wasn't a friendly one. Trick jumped when the man blew his horn and his heart pounded faster still when the man yelled though his open window.

"Hey, *kolo*," the man called out in a Polish accent. "Can you pull up? I want to get some air in my tire."

Trick turned around, smiled and waved. He drove around to the rear of the service station and hastily put the contents back into the bag. Continuing south on Harlem, past the Candlelight Dinner Playhouse, he spotted a payphone in the parking lot of Prince

Castles Hamburgers. Getting out of his car, he fished some change out of his jacket pocket, stepped up to the payphone and dialed.

He heard Starnes' nasal voice mumble, "Yo, what's up?"

"Glad you're home. I got good news for you. It's Christmas, a white Christmas in October. Can I come by?"

"Get your tinhorn shanty-Irish ass over here."

"I told you, I'm not Irish. I'm not sure. I mean … I might be." But Trick realized the call was already disconnected.

Trick took the bag to the back of the car, opened the trunk and carefully looked around. He unloaded the cash, covered it with an old plaid blanket, then drove the rest of the way to Starnes' Palos Hills home cautiously, no more than five miles over the limit.

Ringing Starnes' doorbell, Trick waited a few seconds, then impatiently knocked. The red painted door flew open, followed by a gruff command, "Get in here, boy. We'll go down to my bar in the basement."

Starnes carried his beefy frame around to the back of the bar and said, "Grab a stool." He took two crystal rock glasses from a silver serving tray and set them on the bar. "What can I getcha? I'm havin' my usual, Jack and Coke."

"I'll have the same." Trick couldn't hold back a smile as he patted the black leather satchel sitting on his lap. "I suppose you're wondering what I got in the bag."

"I'm kinda hopin' for somethin' old, green and wrinkled," Starnes said, preparing two drinks. "That's a big bag; I hope you don't disappoint me." He ran his grease-stained fingernails through his prematurely graying curls and locked eyes on Trick. "I wouldn't like that very much."

"I got something better than cash," Trick said, setting the bag up on the bar. "I owe you sixty grand." He opened the bag, took out a kilo of cocaine and set it down between them. "I got three kis. If you want to take these instead of the dough."

Starnes jumped back a step and yelled, "What the hell's the matter with you!" Lowering his voice, he admonished, "I never bring drugs into my house. This is where I live with my wife and kids. You tryin' to get me busted?"

"You want me to leave or you want to listen to my proposal?"

"You crazy gutterslag ass-monkey." Starnes sat on a stool behind the bar. "Say what you gotta say and make it quick."

"This product is pure, you fucking butt slug," Trick replied, holding his ground. "Open it up and try it."

Starnes looked at Trick like he could kill him and pulled a knife from behind the bar. He paused, then made an L-shaped cut into the tape-wrap of the sealed kilo. He scooped out a generous portion, dumped it on the bar and started chopping the soft rocks and flakes with the knife. "Where'd this shit come from?"

"Columbia," Trick said evasively and shrugged. "What do you think?"

"No, funny guy." Starnes separated the cocaine into two generous lines. "I mean, where did *you* get it?"

"Look … that's my business." Trick put his hand on the kilo. "Either you want these three or you don't. I know damn well you could wholesale them just the way they are for at least twenty-five G apiece.

You'd be ahead like a bandit. I know you have those kind of connections."

"Yeah, but you owe me moolah not drugs. I still have the risk of sellin' this shit to get my money back." Starnes snorted a line up his right nostril and pinched the bottom of his nose. "Oh yeah, that's money."

"Come on, this is what you do. That tow and snowplow business is just for show, a way to pay some taxes so the feds don't get suspicious. You're a drug dealer. That's how you got rich."

Starnes snorted the other line up his left nostril. His head flew back and his eyes closed. Composing himself, he said, "Even if I say yes, you gotta get this stuff outta here right now."

"What do you mean, if? I know damn well you wouldn't pass up a deal like this. And, no, if I leave with this stuff, the deal's off. I'll break it down and sell it myself, give you back your sixty and walk away with a nice profit."

"This doesn't smell right. Why *don't* you sell it yourself? You tryin' to set me up?" Starnes raised his voice. "After you leave I get a knock on the door?"

"I quit the business, that's the only reason I'm offering you this deal. I did my time and I'm not going back. If I have to jump back in, I'm jumping in with both feet. I could make some real dough on this. Whack it in half and re-rock it, break it down into ounces and make buku bucks. Walk away with over three-hundred Gs. But I can't take the chance of being separated from my son again."

"None of this makes sense. Where did your broke-ass get the scratch to buy three kis? You steal this shit?"

"I was in the right place at the right time, just sort of fell in my lap. That's all I'm going to say." Trick gulped the rest of his drink, stood and put the kilo back in the bag. "You're not the only person I can sell this stuff to. I'm just giving you first crack at it because I owe you and I want to get this stuff off my hands quick. I'm leveling with you."

"Alright, take it easy. Sit down. You want another drink?"

"No, I'm going." Trick grabbed the handles of the bag. "With or without this stuff."

Starnes stood up and leaned forward on his knuckles like a gorilla. "If I get raided after you leave, I'll have someone throw a stick of dynamite through your ex-wife's front window while she's watchin' Johnny Carson."

Trick acted as though he didn't hear Starnes' last remark. "I want to hear you say this makes us even. That you're not going to come back later with some bullshit about interest or street tax or any other catches."

"Yeah, even-steven. Square business."

"Good. You and I don't have anything else to talk about." Trick pulled the three kilos from the black bag and set them on the bar. "That's the last threat I'm ever going to take from you. We're finished."

Without another word or looking back, Trick walked up the stairs and out the front door with the empty bag, felling a great weight lifting.

***

Driving to Reggie's condo that would be his home for the next few months, something nagged at Trick but he couldn't put his finger on it. It just seemed too damn easy. "Quit worrying," he tried convincing himself. "All your problems are solved."

In the parking lot of the condo, Trick got out of his car and looked around. He could hear the laughter and shouts from older children playing at nearby Walker Park. It was close to 9:00 pm, all would be quiet soon except for the occasional barking dog or roar of a motorcycle from Cicero Avenue. He watched an elderly couple walk past holding hands on Laramie Avenue, each with hair white as cotton. When they were far enough away, he opened his trunk, loaded the cash back into the black bag and entered the condo, feeling as though he were walking through a dream.

Trick turned the stereo on and tuned it to the Oldie station. After making sure the drapes were completely closed, he unzipped the leather satchel and dumped the cash on the living room carpet. The Bombay Sapphire that Reggie left in the freezer seemed to beckon him, so he mixed himself a strong Gin and Squirt on ice while a love song from The Skyliners carried into the kitchen. Gulping half of his drink down, he topped it off with more liquor. Trick walked back into the living room and stared at the pile of cash.

Money by Barrett Strong came on next. He cranked it up and called out, "Perfect." He gulped some more of his cocktail, set it on the coffee table and danced wildly around the pile of banded bills, laughing and singing.

When the song was over he did a backflip, landing on the cash, and rolled around in it for several moments. He lay there with his eyes closed and caught his breath before getting up and turning the music back down. "Down to business," he said, grabbing his drink and sitting on the floor in front of his newfound fortune. One by one, he slid a band off a stack of bills and carefully counted before replacing it back in the band. Once tallied, they were placed on the coffee table in sections of 100s, 50s and 20s.

After making another drink, he sat on the couch in front of the coffee table with pen and paper and counted his windfall over and over. "Two-hundred-and-eighty-five-thousand dollars," he said, dragging out his words. "Two-hundred-and-eighty-five."

Chapter 10

Trick had forgotten how it felt. He was happy. No, it was more like giddy. He turned up the radio as he drove to Ginger's apartment. "Ain't nothin gonna break my stride," he sang along, "nobody's gonna slow me down."

Trick shut the car door behind his back and felt a spring in his step as he crossed the parking lot. Multi-colored leaves from ornamental pear trees lining the parking lot rained down as he tried to contain his excitement. After getting buzzed in, he climbed the stairs two at a time and pounded on her door.

"All right, all right." Trick detected annoyance in Ginger's voice as the chain unlatched. When they came face to face, she demanded, "What's so important? You know Pat's in kindergarten."

"I came to see you." Trick rocked back and forth from his heels to his toes. "Good news. Money's not going to be a problem for us anymore."

"Here we go again." Ginger motioned with her hands in an exaggerated manner as though performing in a high school play. "What's it this time? You borrowed money and invested in another oil field?"

"This isn't some pipe dream. It's already happened. No more risks. I'm done." Trick pulled a Ziploc neatly stuffed with cash from the inside pocket of his brown leather bomber and held it out toward Ginger. "Here, get yourself a new car. Trade in that piece of shit you're driving."

Ginger took the money and asked, "How much is in here?"

"Fifteen-thou. If you want, I'll come with you and negotiate the deal. I know how those thieves operate."

"What did you do? You do something stupid?" Ginger tossed the money on a knick-knack shelf like it was burning her fingers. "You finally did it, didn't you? Robbed a bank. You always talked about it."

"The less I tell you the better. It's unmarked, that's all you need to know." Trick pulled a folded wad of cash from the back pocket of his Jordache jeans and added, "This is for child support, for the next year."

"Petros already told me he'd get me a new car when we get married. I really don't need you to buy me one," Ginger said, putting the loose cash in the pocket of her yellow terrycloth robe.

"Forget that Greek Mafia wannabe. He's all talk, not who you think he is. Believe me."

"You've been away. What do you know?"

"I know people. You don't go through what I have without getting an education in people. Don't trust this guy."

"You're just jealous."

"Of what? I can buy and sell that restaurant right out from under him now if I wanted." Trick became annoyed with Ginger's mocking expression. "Yeah, that's right. Look at me like I'm crazy. I'm telling you, every dog has his day, Honey, and I'm barking."

"You're serious."

"Damn right, I'm serious."

"I trusted you before and look where it got me." Ginger picked up the Ziploc of cash and held it out toward Trick.

"No. You keep it. Get yourself a dependable car

to drive Pat in. No strings attached." Trick started for the door but hesitated and turned. "Have you been to the doctor lately?"

"No. Why?"

"Have you looked in a mirror lately? You're getting too skinny."

"I just haven't had much of an appetite," she said, tightening the belt of her robe.

"You look sick. Go see a doctor, will you? I'll pay for it."

Ginger looked at Trick's concerned expression, biting her lip. He thought he saw tears welling up as she turned and walked into the bathroom.

***

Making way for a cocktail waitress zipping past with a tray full of drinks, Trick took a step back, turned and bumped into a very attractive young lady walking with a Manhattan cocktail. A cherry flew from her drink and landed in his beer glass. Trick took a second to compose himself, took the cherry from his glass by the stem and held it out to the young beauty, "Did you lose your cherry?"

She flipped a long lock of shiny black hair behind her shoulder with a flick of her wrist. "Do you ask all the girls you bump into if they lost their cherry?"

"Only the ones I want to marry."

"Whoa, slow down, buddy. You might get a speeding ticket," she said, taking the dripping cherry and holding it away from her as though she might be holding a dead mouse by its tail. "Besides, I never marry guys unless they tell me their name first."

"Sorry I bumped into you. My name's Patrick. People call me Trick."

Her clear alto voice seemed to cut through the loud music and clutter. "My name's Collette. My friends call me Collette."

"Can I buy you another cherry with a fresh drink around it?"

She giggled and dropped the beer soaked cherry into an ashtray on a nearby table. "No, thanks. It's all right. I've been meaning to cut down on cherries anyway."

Noticing two stylishly-dressed young ladies watching them intently, Trick motioned toward them with his thumb. "Friends of yours?"

"Oh, those are my girlfriends," she said, waving to them. "They watch me like a hawk. Always think somebody's going to try and pick me up."

"Well in this case they might be right. Why don't we grab a table ... over here," Trick said, taking her gently by the elbow. They sat at a tall, wooden table and set their drinks down. "You live around here?"

"Yeah, right here in Orland." She opened her clutch bag, took out a cigarette and placed it between plump lips. "Did you say your name's Trick?"

"Short for Patrick." He pulled a cigarette lighter from the side pocket of his tight-fitting Perry Ellis sport coat and lit her cigarette. "Patrick Halloran."

Collette slowly blew smoke from parted lips and held her cigarette up like a 1940s Hollywood star. "So, you're Irish."

"Think so?" He leaned in closer to hear better over the DJ's blaring speakers.

"Well, sure. With a name like Patrick Halloran."

Trick caught Collette's girlfriends scrutinizing his advances from the corner of his eye. "I mean, do you think I look Irish?"

"I guess so." She sipped her drink, studying his face. "Am I missing something?"

"No, forget it." A young guy strutted by in a patterned polyester shirt, half unbuttoned, showing off gold chains. He bumped into Trick's elbow as he was bringing his glass of beer to his mouth. Trick's demeanor changed in a split second as he quickly shot up and glared at the guy. The young man pivoted, put his hands up in apology and kept moving away. Noticing Collette's shocked expression, Trick sat back down and said, "Sorry, forgot where I was."

"You looked like you wanted to kill that guy."

Trick let out a long breath and dabbed beer from the front of his cashmere sweater with a cocktail napkin. "It's OK, forget about it. Where were we?"

"You remind me of someone … that actor. What's his name? Tough guy, did a lot of cowboy stuff in the 60s, cops in the 70s?"

"Yeah, I get that once in a while. I was born with a lucky face." Trick did his best to lighten the mood and said, "You look like my second wife."

"You've been married twice?"

"No, just once."

"Oh … oh." Collette giggled again and crossed her legs.

"I'd like to take you out. How about dinner tomorrow night? We'll go somewhere nice."

"Tomorrow? You're assuming I don't have plans?"

"No. I'm not assuming anything." Trick examined Collette's body language and studied her crossed leg swinging in short quick movements. "Do you have plans?"

"Maybe." Collette put a hand to her cheek. "I just met you. Never had a guy ask me for a date … so quick."

"I really like you. Why wait?"

Collette tilted her head to the side. "I don't know. It's just …"

"Look, it's not that complicated. It's a yes or no question," Trick said with a smile. "I won't be offended if you say no."

"How about I give you my number and you call tomorrow afternoon?"

"Perfect." Trick clasped his hands together as a sign of sealing the deal.

Collette's girlfriends approached the table as she was handing Trick her phone number that she jotted down on the inside of a matchbook cover. "C'mon, Collette. We're leaving."

Trick stood and extended his hand to the closest girlfriend. "Hi, my name's Patrick."

She looked at Trick's hand as though it might be a viper. "Hello and goodbye."

Collette shook Trick's hand as it hung there. "G'night, Trick. It was nice meeting you."

The heavier-set girlfriend pulled Collette by the arm. "God. We leave you alone for a minute and you're giving your number to some hooligan."

Trick stood and waited as the three walked toward the exit. He watched Collette closely and got what he was hoping for when she looked back and smiled.

As Trick sat alone in a bar full of people, his sense of wellbeing began to ebb. He had every reason to feel great, but something kept gnawing at him. It was like that feeling he got when he left the house knowing he had forgotten something, but couldn't remember what it was.

Chapter 11

Trick stretched, his bare toes brushing against the cool smoothness of fine cotton sheets. His eyes shot open, realizing he was no longer in prison. How long would it take, he wondered. Weeks, months? Maybe years until he got used to waking up not surrounded by several other inmates, snoring, coughing, belching and farting. He got up, looked at the bag of cash on the floor next to the bed and walked to the bathroom. His own bathroom, he marveled. No waiting for a toilet. No watching eyes.

After taking his time shaving and showering, he walked back to the bedroom, sat on the bed and pulled the bag up next to him. He opened it and ran his hand over the pile of cash. He loved the texture, the way it looked and smelled. He loved everything about it.

Trick decided to head downtown to the Magnificent Mile. He needed some new clothes that fit the extra muscle he had gained lifting weights in prison.

***

After purchasing a couple of new sport coats, silk shirts, slacks and other items at Bigsby & Kruthers in Water Tower Place, Trick treated himself to lunch next door at the Ritz Carlton Café. As he sipped his Perrier with a lemon wedge, he smiled, taking in the animated conversation from the next table. Actor, singer and game show host, Bert Convy sat at a white linen covered table with several women who gushed over his thick curly hair and long eyelashes. He wondered who the ladies were, members of a fan club, hosts of a charity event? One table away was a different world.

Trick gathered his bags and left a fifty-dollar bill to cover his meal plus a healthy tip for the comely young lady who waited on him. Walking past the huge fountain in the center of the expansive lobby, he spotted a few pay phones near the elevators. He walked over, set his bags down and took out the matchbook containing Collette's home phone number.

"Hello, Johnston residence. How can I help you?" Trick recognized Collette's sweet, sexy voice.

"You can help me by saying yes."

"Is this Trick?"

"Is that a trick question?" Trick examined his fingernails, considering a manicure. "What time should I pick you up for dinner?"

"You're pretty sure of yourself, aren't you?" Collette didn't bother to hide the sarcasm in her voice.

Trick glanced at his watch and waited several seconds before responding. "I'm waiting. Going once, going twice."

"You're a real character, aren't you? I should say no." Collette manufactured her own uncomfortable pause. "OK, Mr. Halloran, you're on. Come by and pick me up at 7:00." She gave Trick her address and closed by saying, "And you better be on your best behavior. You're not the only guy asking me out."

***

Trick retrieved the bag of cash from the bedroom closet and sat in the living room staring at it. He knew he had to find a place to stash the money very soon. When he was shopping earlier that day, he kept worrying about who else might have access to the condo. Maybe Reggie's old girlfriend, Tamla, still had a key. Safe deposit boxes, he thought, five of them. Probably get a false identity too.

As he freshened up and brushed his teeth, his concerns grew. He put on a new sport coat and grabbed the bag, deciding the money would be safer in the trunk of his Lincoln while he was out with Collette.

***

"Dinner was great," Collette said, taking Trick's arm as they exited Toby's restaurant. Feeling the texture of his sport coat, she remarked, "You really dress nice. What are you wearing?"

"Armani. Thanks." Walking across the damp red maple leaves that littered the parking lot, still wet from the night's earlier rain, Trick was moved by the earthy aromas that filled the autumn evening air. He wanted to breathe in all the things he missed when he was locked up.

"What did you say to the hostess?" Collette leaned her body against Trick in a way that made him want to stop, put his arms around her and kiss her. "You got us such a great table and she took us right back while all those other people were standing around waiting."

"Oh, I just told her that if she took care of us I'd let her sleep with you. I slipped her your number. Said she'd call you tomorrow around noon." Trick turned and looked at Collette with a serious expression. "Use a sultry voice when you answer."

"What?" Collette's mouth hung open as they stopped next to his car, but then burst out laughing when Trick could no longer keep a straight face. "You are such a bad boy."

"I slipped her a ten-spot." Trick unlocked the passenger door and held it open. "Told her my name was Doctor Halloran and I was on call. Works every time."

Collette surprised Trick with a soft kiss, then placed a hand on the front of her short skirt as she got in, preserving the mystery of her femininity. He closed the door and walked around the back of the car thinking the kiss seemed promising. He got in and asked, "Would you like to come over to my place for a drink?"

At first he thought Collette must not have heard him because she took a compact out of her purse and opened it, using the reflection to apply a fresh coat of lipstick. After pausing, she turned and said, "Something about you. I don't know, maybe it's not a good idea."

"Come on, I'll take you back home the minute you say so." Trick held three fingers up in a mock Boy Scout salute.

"OK, just one drink. But you have to promise to be good. I've never been alone with a man before."

Trick squinted, furrowing his brow. "You mean ...?"

"No, I'm not a virgin and I'm not gay if that's what you're thinking. I've never been with a real man, just guys my age."

Trick was at a loss for words so he just nodded and turned on the radio. While Sade's sultry voice moaned, "Smooth Operator," Collette lit a cigarette and put the passenger window down a few inches. She studied Trick's profile and said, "You know, you're not a bad looking guy, a little rough but kind of nice too."

"Thanks. I've been taking handsome lessons."

Collette giggled. "What?"

"Yeah. Correspondence course, nine easy lessons to look more like Cary Grant."

"Oh, really? How's that going?"

"Lesson number one ... have good looking parents. High cheekbones are a plus."

"What about lesson two?" she asked, playing along.

"Stand tall, shoulders back. Think handsome and you'll be handsome. Doesn't matter if you have blue eyes or brown eyes, but if you have a nose like Jimmy Durante you're liable to flunk the course."

"What about three?" Collette laughed.

"That's as far as I got. So, after seven more lessons, watch out. You might not be able to control yourself."

"Oh, boy, I can't wait."

***

Trick opened a kitchen cabinet that contained several liquor bottles. "How about a twenty-four-year-old Scotch?"

"Jumping bunnies," Collette exclaimed in a way that made him feel a little uneasy. "That's three years older than me."

Settling on the living room sofa, Collette inquired, "There's still something I don't get. Your name's Patrick Halloran, but you don't know if you're Irish?"

"It's a long story." Trick swirled the ice in his Chivas Regal and took a sip. "I started out as Baby Patrick in the orphanage, no last name. From what I've been able to find out, I was adopted by a couple named Halloran. The records were sealed but I paid someone under the table for information. I was told the Hallorans adopted me in a last ditch effort to save their marriage. It didn't work out so they ditched me. The first thing I can remember as a kid, think I was about four, was being brought back to the orphanage. I didn't understand. There was a lot of crying. I had this lump in my throat that didn't go away for a long time."

"I'm surprised you can remember back that far," Collette remarked.

Trick could see sadness in Collette's eyes. Compassion he could take but pity was something he couldn't stand. He learned to differentiate between the two long ago. "Something like that you don't forget. I felt like I wasn't good enough. That stayed with me all through my childhood. Can't remember all the details but there were other foster homes. I was bounced around like a paddle ball, so were my feelings. Every time I went to live with a new family, I prayed they would keep me, even the ones who treated me like shit."

"Sorry I touched a sore spot," Collette said, looking uncomfortable. "Did you ever try to locate either of the Hallorans?"

"No. Why would I? They didn't want me then. Don't think either of them would want to see me now. Besides, there's a lot of Hallorans out there. Phonebook's full of them." Trick held an imaginary telephone to his ear. "Can you picture me? 'Hello, Mr. Halloran, are you the guy that broke my heart?'" Trick shook his head. "No, I don't see that in my future."

Collette leaned closer and gently rubbed the back of Trick's neck. He set his glass down and turned to kiss her as her mouth opened in response. He slid his hand under Collette's cropped sweater and felt her softness through the thin laciness of her bra.

"C'mon, be good. You promised," Collette moaned. She pulled away and adjusted her clothing. "We just met. It's our first date. I'm not like that."

"I understand. It's just that I'm very attracted to you and … I haven't had sex in three years."

"A good looking guy like you?" she asked, wrinkling her forehead. "Come on."

"No really, I'm not kidding. It might be better if I told you a little more about myself." Trick looked down and rubbed his forehead, hiding his eyes. "I just got out of prison. Did a few years on a cocaine beef."

"Oh, no." Collette pulled the hem of her skirt further down over her tanned thighs. "That must have been horrible."

"The worst part was being taken away from my son." Trick straightened up and continued, "It's understandable that if you break the law there's got to be some consequences. But it doesn't seem right that a guy's family has to struggle while they're in there playing cards, lifting weights, killing time. I think it would be better if we were forced to work at full wages, doing anything, construction, manual labor, whatever. As long as the money was sent to your wife and kids, you know, people on the outside who depend on you."

"I can't get over you being in prison. I never went out with a bad boy before, not a real one." Trick thought he detected a hint of glee in her voice. "If my dad found out … oh boy."

"What does your dad do?"

"He's a police officer, detective with Orland Park."

"Oh, great. Say … what did you say your last name was?"

"Johnston."

"I better take you home now."

***

Trick shut his headlights off just before turning into Collette's driveway. "Collette … I was thinking. I'd love to see you again, but your father could be a problem."

"Really, you think so?"

The vague sarcasm in her voice gave Trick a twinge of anger, reminding him of his ex-wife. "Maybe if he got to know me, found out I was legit, not dealing anymore. He might give me a chance."

"I don't know." Collette watched the living room window of her house. "Maybe. They say anything's possible."

"What does a guy have to do? I lost everything when I got busted, everything. I did my time, paid my debt to society." Trick turned the radio off. "Tell you what. If your dad asks about me, tell him my last name's O'Connor. OK?"

"I don't like lying to Daddy. I love him but sometimes he scares the snot out of me. How long do you think that would work anyway?"

"I don't know. But I'd love to take you out again. I really like you. You got class."

Trick leaned over to kiss Collette but she quickly turned her cheek to meet his lips. "I better get in before Daddy gets up and looks out the window. I'll let myself out. Bye."

"I'll call you," Trick's voice trailed off as Collette shut the car door behind her.

Chapter 12

"What the fuck?" Trick kept glancing in his rearview mirror on the way home after dropping off Collette. He slowed down to five miles under the speed limit on 143rd Street and hoped they would turn off. "Undercover cops? What the hell do they want?" He first noticed the glow from the yellow fog lights on the vehicle behind him as far back as LaGrange Road. When the driver blew the red light at Harlem Avenue and kept up with him, Trick knew this wasn't going to be a good night. He drove cautiously the rest of the way to the condo complex, pulled into the parking lot and turned the engine off. A coffee brown Oldsmobile 98 pulled directly behind his Lincoln, blocking him in. Trick turned in his seat to see four men exit the vehicle. "These guys aren't cops," he said under his breath.

The four dark figures broke into pairs and approached both sides of his car. Two of them, who looked like brothers, went to the front passenger window, while the shorter of the two men by the driver's side tapped on his window with a tire iron. He made a circular motion with his left hand as he said, "Roll it down."

Trick lowered his window, and calmly as he could manage, said, "What did I do, cut you off or something? Sorry."

"We want to talk to you, *whetto*," said the short, stocky young man with wide-set eyes and slicked-back hair.

"I've got a gun," Trick said, putting his right hand inside his sport coat, trying to bluff.

"I don't think so, parolee." The short guy, who seemed to be in charge, opened his long topcoat revealing an automatic pistol in a shoulder holster. "But we do," he said, fingering the gun. "You have something that belongs to us. The black leather bag, where's it at?"

Trick didn't have time to think. The first thing out of his mouth was, "I don't know what you're talking about."

With the tire iron resting on the open window a couple inches from Trick's face, the leader said, "C'mon, outta there, on your feet."

"You must have the wrong guy," Trick said, getting out of his car.

The tallest of the group, wearing a Chicago Bulls jacket, shoved Trick out of the way and pressed the trunk release button, popping it open. He went to the back of Trick's Lincoln, found the black leather bag under a blanket and held it up. "Why you lying to us? You think we're *stupido*? Now you make me feel like hurting you."

"Let's go, Homes." The short stocky guy pushed Trick from behind with the tire iron in his spine. "Get in my car. We're going for a ride, have a little *conversación*." He motioned toward the front seat as the guy in the Bulls jacket opened the passenger door. The leader got behind the wheel, pinning Trick between him and the big guy. The two brothers, who had not said a word yet, got in the back.

As they pulled out of the parking lot, Trick asked, "Where we going?"

"Not far." The leader looked straight ahead. "Somewhere we can have a little privacy."

Trick felt his filet mignon coming up into his

throat. He swallowed hard and said, "Why don't we just stay here and discuss this?"

"Shut the fuck up, thief. We'll tell you when to talk," one of the brothers said in a heavy Mexican accent, pushing a pistol hard into Trick's ear.

They drove to woodsy 147th Street and pulled onto a service road just east of the Missionary Sisters of Saint Benedict. "Get out of the car, bean bandit," the short guy said, as the others began exiting onto the uncut grass behind a cove of trees. "I don't want any blood in my 98."

A pistol, from behind, tapped Trick on the side of his head. He felt dizzy as his heart beat even faster getting out. Feeling wobbly on his feet, Trick pleaded, "Look, I'm open to any kind of negotiations. Just tell me what can I do to make things right."

Still holding the bag, the tall one in the Bulls jacket rummaged through it. "How much *dinero* is missing?"

Trick felt cold metal at the back of his neck. "Uh, let me think. Give me a minute." Trick breathed heavily. "Twenty thousand, that's all. Just twenty."

"The coke's not here," the big guy said, raising his voice. "You're going to give it all back, just the way it was, the twenty that's missing and the three kilos. Or we'll have to do very bad things to you and your family."

"Oh, fuck," Trick mumbled as his teeth began chattering uncontrollably.

"Where's the drugs?" the leader asked. "In your crib?"

"No. Look, the drugs are … gone." Trick had the odd sense that he had been struck by lightning when he felt a bolt of pain run through his skull. Everything went dark and he collapsed to the ground. Seconds later, his vision returned and he looked up to see the short young man standing over him with the tire iron. The pain became more excruciating and centrally located as he realized he had been struck on the nose.

"Don't ever tell me what I don't want to hear. Understood, *puto*? Just tell me things that make me happy." The leader smoothed his slick hair back. "We know you won't go to the *policia*. Drugs ... drug money; you'd be right back in *prisión*."

Trick got to his knees and put his hand on his nose. When he looked at his hand it was full of blood.

The leader spit on the ground next to Trick. "Not so *guapo* now, eh, *maricón*? You're going to return the missing money, and the *yayo* just the way we left it. If you don't come up with the kilos, you owe us another $300,000. You got one week. *Comprendo*?"

"Yeah, got it." Trick waved his hands in surrender knowing this was no time to attempt a negotiation. "*Comprende*."

"In the meantime, we'll be watching your ass." The leader stood over Trick with the tire iron resting back on his shoulder. "Remember something, *bandito*. I'm a Mexi-can, not a Mexi-can't. I always take care of business." The four calmly walked back to their car and drove away, leaving Trick on his knees bleeding.

The moon behind the hazy clouds took on an eerie glow. Trick wondered if it was from the tears that welled up from the stinging pain he felt. Smelling his own blood, he made it to his feet and stumbled, looking around to get his bearings. He took a clean handkerchief from his back pocket, held it to his nose and thought – a couple miles, maybe less, to the condo. The sooner he started moving his feet, the sooner he would get home. Cutting through the darkened Midlothian Country Club around midnight, a lone rabbit stopped in his tracks and watched Trick cautiously. He thought the cottontail had a look of concern, then it hopped away without glancing back. Tasting the blood that dripped into his throat, he kept spitting, trying not to swallow too much. The high wind brushed the treetops with early warnings of a cold November while he kept putting one foot in front of the other, walking, stumbling, until after a span that didn't seem to be measured in regular time brought him to the doorway of his temporary digs.

Trick unlocked the door, thankful that none of his neighbors saw him in his current condition. The last thing he wanted was to answer questions. He staggered in, half expecting the condo to be ransacked but nothing looked out of place. He went straight to the bathroom, threw the blood-soaked handkerchief in the wastebasket and inspected the damage. It was broken, just as he thought. Along with the swelling and sick looking color his face was taking on, his nose had a pronounced curve to it. So he tried his best to shove it back in place with his fingers and thumb. Screaming in pain as his knees buckled, he crumpled to the floor. Trick gasped for breath as the blood flowed freely again. He grabbed the sink, pulled himself to his feet and spit a big clot of blood from the back of his throat into the toilet, then flushed the blob away. His nose was noticeably straighter but still swelling.

He went to the kitchen, got a popsicle from the freezer and ran it under hot water until only the stick remained. Locating a serrated knife, he held half of the popsicle stick over the edge of the kitchen counter and began sawing, with blood dripping over everything from his nose. He went back to the bathroom, found a roll of white surgical tape in the medicine cabinet and tightly taped up his nose with half of the popsicle stick on either side of it.

By now he was starting to resemble a raccoon, as blood collected beneath the skin under his eyes. He went back to the kitchen and made a cold compress with ice in a dishtowel. Trick grabbed a cold beer and sat in the living room with the icepack on his nose, wondering how he was going to get out of this mess. It was one thing owing money to that sadistic bastard Starnes. He knew where the son-of-a-bitch lived and could retaliate if things got too ugly. These Latino guys were a different matter. He had no idea who they were or where they came from. The bigger questions running through his mind were, how the hell did they know who he was and how could they have known he was holding the bag?

Chapter 13

After a night of sporadic dozing on the living room recliner, Trick got up and read 10:30 am through the blood splatters on his watch. He took off his new Armani jacket and ice-blue silk shirt, checked the pockets, and tossed them in the waste basket. Worried that Ginger might have already bought a new car with the $15,000 he gave her, he called her but there was no answer. So he took a shower, letting cold water run over his face, washing the dried blood away. Staring down at the red water swirling around his feet, Trick pounded his fists on the shower tiles, cracking one of them. His breathing became labored thinking about the wasted years he spent locked up and separated from his son. Now he had all this to deal with too.

Trick looked in the mirror and removed his homemade splint. He had two black eyes and his nose looked as though he was going to have a bump on the lower bridge, even after it healed. Trick redressed his nose with another homemade splint, then tried calling Ginger again. There still was no answer so he decided to go over there right away.

His heart pounded while he talked to himself on the short drive to her apartment: "Please. Say you didn't do it." But there it was; a brand new white 1986 Chrysler convertible where Ginger's old Chevy was usually parked. "Damn it!" He slammed his car door behind him and took big strides up to Ginger's apartment building.

"Who is it?" His ex-wife's dim, metallic-sounding voice crackled from the speaker.

"Oh, good God," Trick said into the intercom. "Are you looking out the window? Who else do you know that drives a burgundy 1979 Continental?"

"Well, you can't be too careful." Trick didn't appreciate her sarcastic tone, especially at this moment. The buzzer unlatched the front door of the apartment building and he climbed the steps feeling woozy. Ginger's door was open with no one in sight. He walked through the living room and down the hall to find Ginger standing in front of the medicine cabinet mirror touching up her eyeliner, a lit cigarette dangling from her lipstick coated lips.

"Don't you love my new LeBaron?" Ginger didn't take her eyes off her reflection. "I think it's sexy."

"I was praying you didn't pull the trigger. When did you buy it?"

"I just got back a few minutes ago." The tip of her cigarette bobbed up and down with every syllable. "Why?"

"I kept calling you." Trick squinted and waved smoke away from his face. "I was hoping to stop you."

Ginger finally looked at Trick and exclaimed, "Holy bejesus. What happened? Did Starnes and Moogie do that to you?"

"No. Never mind my face. I need you to take the Chrysler back. I need that money."

"What?" Ginger threw her cigarette into the toilet making a hissing sound like a snake lying in wait. "No one is taking my convertible away. I finally get a new car and you want me to take it right back? Are you bananas?"

"Tell them you changed your mind. Tell them anything. Say the IRS came by demanding money."

"No!" Ginger threw her head back and stomped her foot which always reminded Trick of a spoiled little girl.

"Is any of the money left?"

"No. It cost more than $15,000. Petros kicked in the rest."

"He went with you?"

"Yeah. Why? What's wrong with that? He knows people. Got me a good deal."

Trick slumped against the wall. He rubbed his forehead with his fingertips and moaned, "Never mind … never mind. Forget it."

"Does getting beat up have anything to do with you wanting the money back?"

Without saying another word, Trick turned and walked away. He knew what he had to do. The last thing in the world he wanted.

Chapter 14

Officer Perkins knocked on Detective Homer Johnston's open office door at the Orland Park Police Station. "Hey, Boss. Got something I think you wanna hear."

Johnston looked up from the file in his big paws and barked, "Get in here."

"I been keeping an eye out for your daughter like you told me. I happened to be at Fat Sam's the night before last and saw Collette with some guy. Looked older, rougher than the boys she usually runs around with."

"What do you mean, runs around with? What're you implying?"

"No ... no, I mean ... y-you know."

"Quit stammering, Perkins," Johnston growled with an unlit, half-smoked cigar situated in the side of his mouth. "What about this guy?"

"He looked familiar so I tailed him to his car and got his plate number."

Johnston dropped the paperwork onto his desk. "Well, whadaya got for me?"

Perkins stepped closer to Johnston's desk, handed him a sheet of paper and backed away saying, "I ran the plate. It belongs to Patrick Halloran. You know ... Trick Halloran, the drug dealer. The guy in the big shootout in Oak Forest a few years back."

Johnston held the paper up to read it. By the time he set it down, his face had turned red. Perkins slowly inched backward toward the door.

"Goddamn it!" Johnston picked up his glass ashtray and threw it in the general direction of Perkins where it sailed dangerously close over his head, smashing in countless pieces against the wall.

"Whoa, Boss!" Perkins pleaded as he flew out the door. "Don't kill the messenger."

Johnston mulled the situation over and took his pulse. He removed a pill bottle from the inside pocket of his polyester suit coat, shook out a couple tablets and swallowed them dry. Opening the leather bound address book on his desk, Johnston dialed his phone.

"Hello, this is Detective Frank Murray," the voice over the phone answered.

"Murray, this is Detective Homer Johnston over at Orland Park. Heard you're part of the new drug taskforce they put together. How many suburbs that take in?"

"Eight of them here in the southwest suburbs. Something I can do for you?"

"Remember a guy you put away a few years ago," Johnston asked, removing a blood pressure kit from a drawer, placing it on his desk and slipping his arm in the cuff, "a Trick Halloran?"

"Oh yeah, of course. What's up?"

"Well, I have reason to believe this Halloran is dealing again. You might want to keep an eye on him."

"You got something tangible?"

"It's from my informant," Johnston lied sincerely, "that's all I can say."

"OK, thanks for the heads up."

"It's my pleasure, trust me." Johnston hung up the phone and smiled his crooked smile.

***

"Collette, get your little ass down here!"

Bouncing down the stairs, Collette became embarrassingly aware that her braless breasts were wiggling like two bowls of Jell-O and put her arm across her chest. "What's the matter, Daddy?"

"Who you been going out with?"

"What? Who?"

"Don't play stupider than you already are. You know goddamn well who."

"You mean Patrick?"

"What's Patrick's last name?"

"Uh ... O'Connor. Why, what's wrong?"

"Is that what he told you his name is, or is that what he told you to tell me?"

Collette stood with her mouth open and stared wide-eyed. "W-well ... he said his name was Pat O'Connor."

"I can always tell when you or your mother are trying to pull some shit. Don't lie to me!"

"I'm not, Daddy. He said his name was O'Connor. Why?"

"Never mind why. Next time he calls, give him the air. No debates. Don't ever see him again."

Chapter 15

Trick dialed the payphone and heard the last voice he wanted to hear. "Starnes Towing. What can I do you for?"

"Hey, it's me. I want to see you." Trick thought how that statement didn't really convey his true feelings. He didn't want to see Starnes at all. He needed to see him.

"Oh, now you want to see me, huh?" Trick hated Starnes' nasal, condescending tone. It was like nails on a chalkboard to him. "What happened to, 'you and I don't have anything else to talk about'?"

"Yeah, OK, I know what I said … can I meet you somewhere? It's important."

***

As Trick walked over to the 1953 Chevy pickup, Starnes cackled out of the driver's window. "So, Trick, you come crawlin' back. Hey, what happened to your beak? You owe someone else money too?"

"Forget about my nose, that's not important. Can I get those kilos back?"

"Are you fuckin' crazy? Two of them are practically sold and the third one's been cut, broken down and put on the street."

"I need to get as much of it back as I can; just the way I gave it to you, right away."

"I smell a rat here." Starnes studied Trick's face. "You win the lotto? Got the cash to buy three kilos all of a sudden?"

"What I'm proposing is, you let me sell them and pay you back with the profits."

"For argument's sake, let's say I still got the stuff just the way you gave it to me. Why would I take the chance of handin' it back to you? You could get busted, then I'm out the dough. You're back in the pokey and I'm waitin' another three years or more to get paid again. This is the stupidest conversation I've ever had. No way in hell."

"Well ..." Trick looked sideways at Starnes. "Could you front me *one* ki?"

"Front you? You made a big deal about how you were out of the business; didn't want to take a chance of gettin' busted, goin' back to the joint again. There's somethin' else goin' on here. I didn't get to be where I'm at by playin' the patsy."

"Circumstances have changed. Can't say much more than that. I need to come up with a lot of dough, quick."

"Tell you what." Starnes rubbed his prematurely graying stubbles and smirked. "Let's say I took a chance and fronted you one. I'd have to charge you $40,000."

"Oh, come on. What the fuck? I just gave you those kis at $20,000 apiece three days ago. Give me a break here."

"You know the only breaks I give are arms and legs. No. The price is $40,000. Take it or leave it. I don't give a rat's ass. I can sell that shit to anyone. I don't need you."

"All right, I'll take it."

"You realize that ki is spoken for, all but sold. That means I gotta disappoint someone I do business with, a valued customer. If you fuck up, I don't think I have to tell you, we're gonna be like a snake and a crab in a bucket and I'm the one with the pinchers."

"Yeah, I know … I know." Trick waved him off. "When can I get it?"

"Meet Moogie in the Willowbrook Ballroom parkin' lot on Archer at midnight."

***

Arriving a little early, Trick waited in the ballroom parking lot with his window down smoking a Cohiba. Listening to the hoot of an owl hidden somewhere in the treetops, he waited for Moogie to bring him one of the three kilos of cocaine that was in his possession just a few days earlier. Blending in with the other cars, he sat facing the entrance, scanning each vehicle that pulled in. A few minutes after midnight, a black Ford F-350, sitting high off the ground, turned in off Archer Avenue. Trick flashed his lights and the pickup truck slowed to a stop in front of him. Getting a better look, he recognized Moogie behind the wheel from the silhouette of his shaved head and long full beard. When Moogie revved his engine and continued on to the dimly-lit rear area of the huge parking lot, Trick pitched his cigar, started his car and followed him.

Trick pulled up next to Moogie's truck, got out and walked to the passenger side. He tried to open the door but it was locked. He stood holding the handle, looking into Moogie's scowling face. The lock finally popped up and Trick climbed in. He squinted at Moogie, who just glared back at him.

Putting some bass in his voice, Trick asked, "Well, you got it with you?"

Trick sat waiting for an answer and after a few moments of silence, Moogie, with a revolver in his left hand, said, "I never did like your monkey-time ass. Was up to me, I'd put a bullet in your head right now and leave you in a ditch somewhere."

"Don't try to sell me any wolf tickets. I faced guys badder than you every day I was in the can," Trick said, looking Moogie straight in the eye. He knew the worst thing he could do was show the fear he felt. Guys like Moogie sniffed it out like a dog. "Just give me the kilo."

"Ya walk around thinkin' you're better'n people. Fuckin' pretty boy," Moogie wheezed, then took a long pull from his asthma inhaler. "What'd ya do, get a nose job to look cuter?"

Looking at the third eye in a triangle tattooed on Moogie's low forehead, red beard with strands of gray covering the chest of his bibbed overalls and teeth the color of moldy bread, Trick thought that almost anyone sitting next to Moogie would look good. "I don't have all night." Trick grabbed the door handle. "If you got it, give it to me or I'm walking. Tell your boss man to make his own deliveries next time."

Moogie reached under his seat and tossed Trick a brown paper bag. "Here, ya fuckin' pussy. Go home and pull your prick while ya stare at yourself in the mirror, probably your favorite pastime."

Trick hopped to the ground, but before he slammed the door, said, "Go ahead, get a good look. I know you'll be thinking about me when you turn off the lights tonight."

Moogie slammed it into low gear and the big Ford fishtailed, laying two patches of rubber as Trick jumped out of the way to avoid being knocked over. The smell of burning tires overtook the aroma of damp leaves as Trick felt a chill from the northerly wind. Opening his car door, Trick stopped when he spotted a red fox hobble through the trees with the lower portion of one of its rear legs missing. With his head hung low, the fox moved silently through the shadows and disappeared into the brush surrounding the I&M Canal just to the west. He wondered if the fox lost its leg in a trap.

Chapter 16

Trick spent the next afternoon with his son and assured him that he had just bumped his nose and it would be all better the next time he saw him. He went on to explain to little Pat that the movie they were about to see was just that, a movie, a make-believe where no one really gets hurt. They watched *Commando*, an Arnold Schwarzenegger film, where the hero has to rescue his kidnapped daughter. Then later, after an hour of climbing on the monkey bars and swinging on the tall swing set at Walker Park, a pizza and RC Colas hit the spot at Vito & Nick's Pizzeria. But his mind was distracted, thinking about what he had to do after dropping Pat off.

A hug from his little boy sent Trick on his way to the evils that lay ahead of him. After running around from store to store and buying enough baby laxative powder to cut the cocaine, Trick got to the Ace Hardware on Cicero just before closing. He pulled into the rear parking lot and got out of his car. It was his first time back there since his arrest. A cold wind blew across his face as the memories of New Year's Eve 1981 came flooding back; icy rain assaulting his face, gunshots echoing in the night, the odor of his damp camel hair topcoat, and Detective Frank Murray's voice booming from a loudspeaker.

"Here we go again," Trick muttered, as he walked into the hardware store. Purchasing everything else he needed for the night, he headed straight to the condo. Once inside with the door locked and dead bolted, the drapes fully closed, Trick put on a dust mask and latex gloves. He proceeded to break the kilo up, pushing the soft rocks through a large flour sifter with a tablespoon, turning it into powder. Measuring out a little more than a kilo of the baby laxative, he added it to the nearly pure cocaine in an extra-large Ziploc bag. He turned the bag over and over for ten minutes to get the two powders completely mixed.

Trick then emptied the contents into eight white handkerchiefs folded into envelope-like containers. He set the envelopes into a big pot and drenched them with acetone. Next step was putting the cloth envelopes between two small, raw blocks of wood and squeezing the excess acetone out with the help of a vice he attached to Reggie's kitchen counter. A pan on the floor collected the acetone drippings. When all eight were prepared, he placed them on a cookie sheet and baked them in the oven at a low temperature for twenty minutes. Once they cooled off, Trick broke the cocaine patties into stone size rocks.

With a little extra cut thrown in, the 35.3 ounces of coke were now 72 ounces, and still a much higher quality than almost anything else on the street. Trick got out a small calculator and figured an average of $1,650 an ounce times 72 ounces equaled $118,800. He knew he could sell some of the ounces for at least $1,800 but to move them faster, he would have to turn some of them through a middle man who would take multiple ounces. For those people, he would have to come down on that price some. Now if he could move that much stuff in the next five days with all the cash in hand, he felt he might be able to make a deal with the Mexicans and at least buy more time.

Move it all in time and not get busted again. It seemed an almost impossible task but he couldn't think of another solution. He headed out the door with samples to get things going. Trick knew he didn't have an hour to waste.

***

Trick spent that night and the next day contacting old customers. Some were out of the business, some were in prison, and one was dead, shot in the head from an impatient supplier. The handful left were a huge disappointment. He knew what he had to do. It was his last resort.

"Bob's Bondage, all of our operators are tied up," came the high-pitched, scratchy voice over the phone.

Trick groaned. "Still pulling those tired gags."

"Trick? Is that you?"

"Back from Hell."

"Whenja get out?"

"Ten days ago. I want to get together and talk. When are you free?"

"Right now. Where do you wanna meet?"

"The old spot, last place you saw me. Half hour?" Trick touched his homemade splint. "One thing, do not ask me what happened to my nose. I've been answering that question night and day."

***

Walking into Fast Break Billiards on 147th Street in Midlothian, Trick savored the aroma of grilling onions from the White Castle hamburger restaurant across the street. A breeze of unusually warm eighty-two-degree weather accompanied him into the pool hall as he looked around adjusting his eyes to the light. Spotting Bob in a back corner at a pool table, he made his way through the other tables and players and extended his hand.

"Wow, man. How long's it been?" Bob looked at Trick over round, rose-colored shades and shook his hand. "Two ... three years?"

"Almost three. Time is different on the inside, moves much slower. When you're in there you know exactly how much time you got left. You start getting short; you count the hours."

"Long time. Your pooper must be sore there, Trick." Bob giggled and started placing the balls in the wooden rack.

"Real funny. No one takes my manhood from me."

Bob's round belly jiggled under a tight tie-dyed t-shirt as he racked the balls and retorted back, "OK, tough guy." He pulled a quarter from his vintage pin-striped vest and flipped it off his thumb. "Call it."

Before the coin landed on the green felt, Trick said, "Tails."

"Tails it is. Speakin' of tail, you get any in there?" Bob held out his cue stick and looked down the end toward the tip checking for straightness with Trick's eyes in his line of vision.

"I told you, I don't play those kind of games," Trick shot back, already annoyed with Bob, who kept staring at his splint-covered nose and black eyes.

Bob pushed back his sweat-stained pork pie hat revealing the thinning, cropped hair in the front area of his black, stringy mullet. "Break 'em, free bird."

Trick slammed the cue ball into the triangle of balls with a loud crack and watched the striped 13 ball roll into a corner pocket.

"I'd have thought you had enough stripes for a while."

"You don't wear stripes in prison anymore. That

went out with black and white James Cagney movies." Trick looked around and lowered his voice. "You still in business?"

"Does Hugh Hefner like big tits?" Bob smirked at Trick. "Whadda you think?"

Glancing around the room at the other pool players and the owner to make sure no one was watching, Trick knelt down, pulled a sealed envelope from his sock and handed it to Bob before standing back up. "I could use your help moving this stuff. Most of my old customers are out of the biz. I need to sell a lot of shit in a short time."

"How much we talkin'?" Bob asked without looking up from his shot, sending the yellow 1 ball on a slow roll into the side pocket.

"Tell you what … I can front you ounces at $1,600. This stuff's fifty percent pure. You can whack the shit out of it and still sell ounces for $2,000 … grams for eighty-five, ninety. You know the rundown."

"You didn't waste any time. Hit the bricks runnin'." Bob shook his head and smirked. "Make that $1,500 and we deal. If it's as good as you say, I'll start with twenty O-Zs."

"OK, but keep this quiet. Cops'd love to put me away again. I copped a six-ball first time; it was a Class X felony. You do a little less than half if it's state time. Second time, for the same offense, they give you at least twelve. Means I wouldn't get out in less than five-and-a-half. That's with good behavior. So don't mention my name to anyone." Trick stopped lining up his next shot and turned to face Bob. "Got it?"

"You know me," Bob answered in a stage whisper.

"One more thing. Don't front it out. Cash only

with your people. I can't be fucking around."

Bob shrugged, looked at Trick with mock sincerity and said, "Yeah, yeah. No problem. But look, I gotta ask. What did happen to your snout, she shut her legs too quick?"

Chapter 17

Pulling away from Fast Break, Trick looked at the dashboard clock. It wasn't quite 4:00 so he started heading toward Collette's house, figuring her father was probably still at work. Steering into the tree-lined parking lot of Jack Gibbons' restaurant along the way, he examined his face. Trick carefully peeled the white tape away from his cheeks and removed the splint from his nose. It had been three days since his nose was broken and most of the swelling had subsided. But his black eyes were in full bloom with deep shades of purple, tinged with yellow.

Running a conversation with Collette in his head, Trick drove the rest of the way to the older, modest home section of Orland Park. Seeing Collette's car in the driveway, he pulled to the curb, debating whether or not he should go to the door. He took another look at his face and remembered he still had an old pair of black Wayfarer Ray-Bans in his glove compartment. He didn't have the luxury of time so he put the sunglasses on, walked up and rang Collette's doorbell.

He waited several moments, realizing that coming there without calling was a bad idea. As he turned to walk away, the door opened. When he pivoted and faced Collette, she said, "Oh my God, Trick. What happened to your face?"

"That's … nothing. Just bumped my nose." Trick leaned closer, taken in with Collette's perfume. "It'll be fine in a few days."

"Did the police do that to you?"

"No, of course not. It's nothing, really, just ran into an open door in the middle of the night." Trick's eyes ran up and down Collette's smooth, tanned legs, as she stood with her bare feet apart in her tight, baby-blue jogging shorts. "Are you going to invite me in?"

"No, I better not," Collette said, looking everywhere except Trick's eyes. "Not a good idea."

"OK, what is it? Something's wrong."

"I've been dreading this the last couple days." Collette looked down and ran her toe back and forth across the door sill. "We can't see each other anymore."

"Why?" Trick watched a handful of leaves in the front yard get swept up in a swirl of wind like a mini tornado. "Is it something I said or did?"

"I don't know how my dad found out about you but he knows your name's not O'Connor. He must have run a check on you. When he found out I was seeing a guy who's been in prison, he flipped."

"You want me to walk away, just like that, without a fight?" Trick gazed at Collette's cleavage pouring out the top of her tube top as she folded her arms across her chest. "I haven't had these kind of feelings for someone in a long time."

"You don't understand. He'd kill you if he caught us together. If he came home right now ... you don't know. I've heard stories. He blew a guy's heart right out of his back with his police revolver in a barroom brawl when he was off duty. The cops showed up and protected him. He wasn't even charged. They called it self-defense."

"Damn." Trick shook his head. "Let's forget about daddy law for a minute. I want to know how you feel."

"I never met anyone like you ... the way you carry yourself. You know people watch you when you go by?" Collette flashed an uneasy smile. "I had so much fun when we went out. You made me laugh."

"Yeah." Trick's face dropped. "A lot of laughs."

"I'm sorry, Trick. You better go now."

Trick looked over at a white Trans Am pulling into Collette's driveway. "Who's this?"

"He's ... a friend."

"We need to talk. Meet me at Petey's on 159th."

"I ... I really can't. It's better we, you know, just say goodbye."

"Can I call you?"

"No! Daddy would find out. Please go, don't make this so hard."

"Will you at least give me a call?" Trick said as he backed away from the front door. "Call me. OK?"

"Goodbye, Trick."

Trick slowly walked past the Trans Am locking eyes with the young man behind the wheel. The pretty faced, college-age kid with a thick blond mullet and handful of pimples on his cheeks gave Trick a nervous smile and nodded to him. Trick got in his car, slammed the door and watched the kid strut up to the front door still held open by Collette. The guy stood on the porch, turned at the hip and motioned with his hand toward Trick. Collette's expression changed when she saw Trick getting out of his car again. She pulled at the kid's white Members Only jacket while he looked back defiantly. As Trick walked toward them, the young man allowed Collette to pull him in the door that she quickly shut behind them. Trick thought about the cocaine in his trunk, got back in his car and drove away.

Chapter 18

Trick sat in the dimly-lit condo massaging his black eyes with a mixture of warm water and vinegar to speed up the healing. He felt sick to his stomach, thinking about his financial problems. He was going to have to put off paying Starnes or stiff him altogether in order to come up with as much money as possible to appease the Mexicans. But if he didn't pay Starnes for the kilo that was fronted him, he would have to find another source to get two more kilos in order to square up with the Mexicans, and hopefully Starnes too, at the end.

Trick remembered a jailhouse proverb: when your back is up against the wall, come out swinging and don't stop. The ounces of coke weren't moving fast enough. He hated to get down to the street level of drug dealing, it meant more exposure but he felt he didn't have a choice and turned the lights on. He took an ounce of coke, added 14 grams of cut to it and turned 28 grams into 42 grams which he knew he could easily wholesale for $60 each and retail for $85 and up. After carefully weighing out the grams on Reggie's Ohaus triple beam scale and packaging them, he headed out the door to make the rounds.

***

Trick walked into the haze of cigarette smoke at Fat Sam's bar on LaGrange Road and recognized a couple faces from the early 80s through the dark tint of his Ray-Bans. He spotted a huge, beefy biker with a short mohawk, shaved on the sides, revealing FTW tattooed on the left side of his head. Joker, just the guy he was hoping to bump into. Trick walked up next to Joker as he was taking a big swig off a bottle of Miller High Life. Trick called out to the bartender, "Two more of these," motioning with his thumb toward Joker's bottle then setting his sunglasses on the bar.

"Trick! Tricky Trick … long time, dude." Joker's deep, hoarse voice broadcasted over *Smuggler's Blues* by Glenn Frey blasting from the DJ's speakers. "How'd ya get the black eyes? Someone ya want me to take care of?"

"Nah, that's a situation I have to deal with personally. But hey, I appreciate it."

"Change your mind, let me know. I haven't fucked anyone up in a while and I'm getting twitchy." Joker took an Erik cigar from behind his ear and lit it with a Zippo he pulled from his leather motorcycle jacket. "When did ya get out?"

"Week-and-a-half ago." Trick looked up at Joker and smiled. "Same old Joker. How's things?"

"Wrecked my knucklehead a couple years ago. Busted my right leg up real good. Got a rod holdin' it all together. That Softail parked right out front's my new ride." Joker threw his head back and laughed loudly over the blaring music. "I can't complain. Makin' money, gettin' laid, got kids all over the state. Life's good, man. How 'bout you?"

Trick leaned closer to Joker and under the music said, "I'm back in business." Trick motioned with his eyes down to his hand. Joker looked down as Trick opened his hand then quickly closed it again. "The real deal. Top shelf."

"Hey now. You always had the best shit."

"You in the market?"

Joker watched two young ladies walk past in tight designer jeans and low cut tops. He wiggled his tongue at them, making guttural sounds. "Yeah, man, I'm always in the market for quality shit."

"Circus clowns," Trick said, shaking his head as he watched three guys in their early twenties on the dance floor breakdancing, surrounded by a circle of girls cheering them on. "How many you want?"

"How many ya got?"

"With me? These two and twenty more in the car."

Joker slapped his leather chaps, howled like a wolf and growled, "I'll take 'em."

Looking around, worried that Joker was attracting too much attention, Trick quietly responded, "All of them?"

Joker guzzled half a bottle of beer, slammed it on the bar and burped loudly. "Absofuckinlutely."

"I'm going to need cash, sixty each."

"Trick, who you talkin' to? First of all, make that fifty. Second, this is me, man. You know I'm good for it. I ever screw you?"

"No, but I need all the money soon, real soon."

Chapter 19

Arthur Patoremos looked up from the papers in his hand when Trick knocked on his open office door. "Come in, Halloran," he said loudly, over the rattling window-unit air conditioner. "You're three minutes late." He motioned to the chair across the desk. "Take a seat."

Trick navigated the narrow path through stacks of files piled on the floor in the tiny office. Easing onto the cold, steel chair and rubbing his goose-pimpled arms, he looked at the name plate that sat precariously close to the edge of the desk, competing for space. "What do I call you? Arthur, Art, Artie …?"

The heavyset, big-boned man behind the desk tilted his head back and scrunched up his nose that balanced the thickest glasses Trick had ever seen. The lenses made his eyes appear like goldfish swimming next to the edge of their small bowls. "You call me Mr. Patoremos. What are you, a wise guy? Is that how you got the black eyes?"

Trick kept detecting the smell of garlic and realized it was coming from a shriveled, half-eaten dill pickle sitting in an ashtray along with crumpled cigarette butts smoked down close to the filters. "No … to both questions, Mr. Patoremos," Trick replied, dragging out Arthur's surname. "Just trying to be friendly."

"I'm your parole officer, not your buddy. Give me half an excuse and I'll bounce your ass back to the joint. If there's one thing I hate, it's you drug dealers. So sit there, shut the fuck up and answer when I ask questions." He handed Trick a few sheets of stapled paper, an unsharpened pencil and instructed Trick, "Go sit in the hall, fill these out and bring 'em back. And don't take all goddamned day. I haven't had my lunch yet."

Trick went back into the hallway and remembered there weren't any chairs. He sat on the floor, leaned his back against the wall and filled out the questionnaire. Where are you currently living? When did you last use alcohol? When did you last use illegal drugs? Have you associated with known felons since your release from prison? Are you currently working? Several minutes later, he reentered the overly-chilled office and attempted to hand the paperwork to Patoremos.

"Put it down." Patoremos looked at Trick challengingly. "Drop it."

Looking around for a spot big enough to set them down, Trick settled on a short stack of files closest to his parole officer.

Patoremos snatched the paperwork off the pile and quickly scanned the information. "You're not workin'? Gotta have a job if you don't wanna go back to the joint."

"I had a job ... for three days but it didn't work out."

"Shit-canned you. Zat it?" Patoremos' nostrils flared as his stomach growled noticeably.

"No, I quit. No man should have to put up with that kind of crap. I'm looking for a better job."

"I want you back here in two weeks, November 1st ... employed. I don't care if you're diggin' ditches, shovelin' shit or flippin' burgers at Mickey D."

"Two weeks?" Trick felt his face getting hot and did his best to contain his rage. There was no way he could hold a regular job and still be able to move the cocaine in time. "I thought I was supposed to come in once a month."

Patoremos stood, knocking his chair backward and appeared much shorter than Trick would have guessed. "Don't question me." He raised his voice and pointed. "Look at the calendar. It's Friday the 18th. If you're not back with a paystub in your hand two weeks from today, I'm gonna recommend you go back. We're through. Get the fuck out."

***

Driving with his window down in the sixty-eight degree, mid-October weather, Trick could smell it from 87th Street, that wonderful aroma like no other. The red, white and green neon sign flashed in the late afternoon sun, *Ronaldi's Pizza*. His old business acquaintance and restaurant owner, Ronnie Diamond, with his straight, blond hair and pale complexion, didn't have a drop of Italian blood.

As Trick walked in, Ronnie, from behind the counter, waved his hands in the air and called out in a mock Italian accent, "Patrizio!" Ronnie wiped white powder onto his gravy stained apron, walked around the counter and stuck out his hand. "Well, how does it feel to be a free man again, *paisan*?"

"Not as good as I thought it would," Trick said, shaking hands and removing his sunglasses.

"Whoa. What happened?" Ronnie asked. "They give you a blanket party before you left prison?"

Trick put his sunglasses back on. "Hell no. I was voted most likely to kick someone in the balls from my prison GED class," Trick joked. "Look, I need to ask you something, in private."

"Sure. C'mon back. There's only me and one girl here right now and she doesn't hear nothing," Ronnie replied, waving his hand under his chin. "Wanna meatball sandwich?"

"No, I'm good." Trick patted his flat stomach and followed Ronnie back to the kitchen. "I heard you got three joints like this now."

"Yeah. Pizza business is booming."

Trick watched a short, bosomy teenage girl with headphones on, bobbing her head while spreading out pizza dough with a wooden rolling pin. "I'm proud of you, man," Trick said. "You got away from it and you got away with it. Seems like just about everyone we were doing business with a few years ago either has a bad coke habit with holes in their septums, or they're broke, in prison, or dead."

"Forget about it," Ronnie said, shrugging his shoulders and extending his fingers. "I still do a little tootskies once in a while but I quit selling the stuff altogether. If I got busted, they could confiscate everything … my pizza places, house, cars. I'm done with all that."

Pizza girl nodded her head in time with a tune only she could hear as she ladled out pizza sauce with a large spoon, then flipped the spoon over and distributed the sauce to the edges of the raw dough. "I need a favor, Ron."

"Done. Whatever it is. Done. I wouldn't be where I'm at without you. The money we made together, *ah Madone*." Ronnie waved his right hand like his fingertips were on fire. "Listen, if you need a job, I can put you on in one of my stores … making pizzas, deliveries. Hell, I could use a manager in my Evergreen Park location."

"Uh … no. Thanks for the offer." Trick paused and chose his words, watching the young lady toss handfuls of shredded mozzarella onto the sauce-covered dough. "I might take you up on that later but right now, I just need to show an income … pay stubs."

"Oh, that. I don't pay my people by check. Give 'em all cash, keeps things simple. That way I don't have to fool around with FICA, insurance or any of that mess. These kids come and go all the time."

"I'm sure you have a company checkbook. How about I give you $300 a week in cash and you write me out a check for the same amount. Add forty hours on the memo line."

"Oh, man. I don't know. Something like that … could get sticky."

"What happened to, 'done, whatever it is'?"

"All right … all right, but give me $350 in cash and I hand you back a check for three bills. I'm sticking my neck out … got expenses."

Trick shook his head and said, "OK, fuck it … I can live with that. I'll be by next Friday with the cash and pick up the first check." Trick grabbed an Italian sausage from a tray of a couple dozen and said, "Gotta run."

Trick drove away mumbling as he ate the hot, spicy sausage, "Cheap prick. Probably got the first two cents he made collecting pop bottles."

Chapter 20

After getting a message on his pager from Joker, Trick returned his call and drove to the Orland Square Mall parking lot and cruised around until he saw his 1968 El Camino parked along the outer edge near Marshall Fields. He pulled his Lincoln within a foot of Joker's driver-side door, lowered his window and got a lungful of unfiltered Pall Mall. "Hey, give me a break with that, will you?"

"Bitch, bitch, bitch. You sound like my old lady," Joker said, as he flipped his half smoked cigarette off his fingertip, sending it sailing over Trick's car. "Did you bring me those thirty grams?"

Trick coughed and waved his hand in front of his face, then tossed Joker a stuffed, sealed business envelope. "You got the cash for the last twenty-two?"

"I'll have everything wrapped up in a couple days. Square up with you then."

"Very important that you do." Trick tried reading Joker's eyes behind his aviator sunglasses. "I don't know about this other deal. You sure this guy's OK?"

"Yeah, he's good people."

Squinting into the setting sun, Trick asked, "How much does he want?"

"Half-pound."

"Whoa. That's a lot of product," Trick said, examining Joker's typical smirking face. "You sure he's not a cop?"

"Absolutely. What? I'm a jerkoff now?" Joker pointed a finger at himself. "I don't know what I'm doin'?"

"All right, don't get hot. What's this guy's name? Where you know him from?"

"Barker, we were in Nam together. I'd trust 'im with my life. In fact, I have."

"He's got to understand, cash only." Trick rubbed his thumb and first two fingertips together. "The price is $25,000."

"Not gonna be a problem."

"OK, go ahead and set it up for tonight." Trick put his car in drive with the brake on. "Get back to me with the details."

***

"Yeah, got it. I wrote it down," Trick said, holding the payphone just close enough to hear Joker but not so close that he had to smell the years of saliva buildup on the black plastic mouthpiece. "But I'd feel better if you were going to be there too."

"I can't, man. It's my daughter, Brandi's, birthday. Otherwise ..."

"What's he look like, this Barker?" Trick read the gang graffiti scratched into the clear acrylic panes of the phone booth.

"'Bout five-nine but he looks bigger. Heavy build, shaved head, fair. Kinda looks like a bulldog. Oh, and he's got the devil tattooed on the side of his neck."

"What the hell?" Trick got a bad feeling about the situation. "The devil?"

"He said meet him in the backyard of that address, on the patio, 11:00 tonight."

***

Trick drove to the Homestead Bar at Central Avenue and Southwest Highway looking for Bob. Seeing Bob's emerald green Eldorado in the parking lot, he went in and found him sitting on his usual stool.

"I want you to ride shotgun with me tonight," Trick said, taking a seat next to Bob.

"What're you talkin' about … shotgun?"

"I'll give you a grand for an hour's work. Easiest money you'll ever make."

Bob swallowed the last of his Sambuca, then spit a coffee bean back into his snifter. "What do I gotta do?"

"Just come along. Watch my back. Make sure nothing goes wrong," Trick said out of the side of his mouth as the bartender approached. "Bring your gun."

Chapter 21

"Look, let me ask you something." Bob fooled with Trick's power window button, raising and lowering it. "I got to know, what was it like in jail?"

"Prison. Jail and prison are two different things. Quit messing with my window." Trick turned his eyes from the road and gave Bob a stern squint. "It's a mind fuck. You don't want to go there."

"I always worried ... well, wondered," Bob said in his raspy, soprano voice, "how I'd do if, for some reason, I had to go to prison."

"If, for some reason, you have to do time, don't try to play the tough guy. Someone tougher will slap the shit out of you."

"I heard you should go up to the baddest looking guy and lay into him with everything you've got."

"Yeah, try that sometime, Bob." Trick laughed. "It would be worth it to go back just to see you pull that one. You better make sure you don't get busted for anything, that's all I got to say."

"What? You don't think I can handle myself? I'm not as macho as you, tough guy?"

"Wait, that's it, that's the address. Let's just drive by first."

"This one here?" Bob craned his neck as they slowly drove past. "What's with all the flags?"

"Must be a model house," Trick said, checking out the colorful plastic triangles strung across the front yard blowing in the wind. "This isn't what I expected. I thought someone lived here."

Trick continued along the street till it curved around, took two rights and headed back again. He turned off his lights and pulled over to the curb so he could see the house on the cross-street ahead. "There's no car in the driveway. Wonder if he's there." Trick glanced at his watch. "11:04. Wait here." He got out of the car, opened the trunk and took out the half-pound of cocaine that was inside a Kleenex box wrapped like a birthday present. He looked around; most of the lights in the surrounding houses were off so he didn't shut the trunk all the way, not wanting to make too much noise. He put the box into a plastic mailbox that looked like a tiny barn, then walked to the passenger side and motioned for Bob to lower his window. "Wait here, I'm going back there."

The wind whipped through Trick's dark blond hair as he walked up the driveway and into the backyard of the model house. He took note that there was vacant land for about a half mile behind the house, nothing but tall grass and weeds all the way to busy 159th Street to the north. Then he saw the orange ember of a cigarette bobbing in the dark.

A gruff voice called out, "You Trick?"

"Yeah." Trick saw moonlight shining off a shaved scalp. "You must be Barker."

"You got the shit with you?"

"You want to get right to it, don't you?"

"That's why we're here." Barker flipped his cigarette into the backyard.

"It's close by. You got the cash? $25,000."

Barker pulled a paper bag from his back pocket and waved it in the air with a leather gloved hand. "Got it all, right here. Where's the shit, in your car?"

"Yeah," Trick lied. "I'll be right back."

Trick walked back to the car and jumped in

behind the wheel. "I'm half tempted to just take off. Leave the stuff in the mailbox and come back for it later."

Bob fidgeted with a Rubik's Cube he had produced from his coat pocket. "Is he alone?"

"Yeah." Trick ran his fingers through his hair and let out a deep breath. "An old customer vouched for this guy but I got a funny feeling."

"Want me to come back there with ya?" Bob tried in vain to put some bass in his voice. "Earn my dough?"

"Tell you what. Wait a minute after I leave, then go up the sidewalk and come around the far side of the house. He'll have his back to you." Trick turned the car off and put the keys in his jacket pocket. "I don't have to tell you to bring the gun, do I?"

Time seemed to slow down as he retrieved the half-pound of cocaine from the mailbox and put it inside his half-zipped jacket. He breathed in the cool air that was laced with manure fertilizer from farmlands to the southwest and looked around at the houses. A few doors back a television set flickered in the living room window. The rest of the households looked as though everyone had gone to bed. "Working stiffs," Trick whispered as he walked up the sidewalk. A gust of wind blew through the small trees in the new housing development, drowning out the sounds of a barking dog and traffic from 159th Street.

Barker flipped another cigarette into the backyard when he saw Trick round the corner of the house and walk onto the concrete patio. "I thought you weren't coming back," he growled.

Trick didn't like the tone of Barker's voice. He walked up close enough to see the whites of Barker's eyes, or the lack of. His eyes were more red than white.

Barker, about four feet away, stood with his feet set far apart and his shoulders hunched forward. "Well, what the fuck? You got my stuff?"

"Yeah, right here." Trick pulled the box containing the cocaine out of his jacket and held it up.

"Joker said your stuff's top flight. But how about I take a look?"

Trick tossed the package to Barker and answered back, "Let's see the color of your green."

"Cute. Happy fuckin' birthday to me." Barker tore off the wrapping, ripped the box open, pulled out the drugs and threw the packaging to the ground. He set the Ziploc filled with cocaine on a wrought iron patio table and opened the bag. He took a deep whiff, zipped the bag closed and stood looking at Trick.

"Well?" Trick stared at Barker, looking for a reaction.

"Here." Barker pulled the paper bag out of his back pocket and tossed it to Trick.

Trick opened the bag and pulled out a stack of index cards held together with a rubber band. "What the fuck …?" He looked up at Barker, who was now holding the Ziploc full of cocaine in his right hand and an automatic pistol in his left.

"Shakedown, breakdown, mutha fucka," Barker laughed.

Trick looked behind Barker at the corner of the house. Bob was nowhere in sight. Realizing he should have been there by now, Trick sized up the situation. Not knowing what Barker was capable of, he knew he had to decide that second whether he was going to chance getting shot. He slipped the rubber band off the index cards and flipped them in

Barker's face. Trick dove for the gun, which went off as he grabbed it. With the sound of gunshot ringing in his ears, Trick was stung in the face by bits of concrete that flew up from the patio. Barker dropped the Ziploc when Trick dug his thumb into his wrist. Trick grabbed for the bag while holding onto the hot barrel of the gun but it slipped through his fingers. A powerful blow to the back of Trick's head dropped him to his knees. Everything went black and white. Barker yelled something that Trick couldn't make out. His voice was muffled and seemed to be playing at a lower speed.

In those short seconds Trick thought this was the end. This is how he was to die. Fear shot him to his feet, knocking Barker on his back. With the half-pound of cocaine in hand, Trick took off through the high weeds toward 159th Street as the June bug buzz of a bullet whistled past his right ear. He was suddenly hit with the worst headache he ever felt, starting at the base of his skull and traveling to his temples. With a thud, he fell on his stomach when he tripped over the uneven ground causing him to drop the bag of cocaine. Trick tried to remember how many shots were fired and lurched to his feet. Putting the plastic bag in his coat pocket, he continued running, glancing over his shoulder through the tall growth searching for Barker. Finally making it to 159th out of breath, he put out his thumb and stumbled backward in a daze.

"Hey, take a bath, you bum." A young guy flying past in the passenger seat of a Mustang threw a Wendy's drink cup, hitting Trick on his tan chinos. Crushed ice scattered and cola soaked his already dirty pants. The Mustang continued on its way and Trick inspected his appearance. He tried brushing himself off but it didn't do much good. He looked back in the direction of the model house and continued walking backward with his thumb out.

Several cars honked and flew past before he heard the screech of tires. Trick spun around to see a car stopped in the right-hand lane with the rear passenger door open, so he ran up and jumped in.

"Hey, Cutie. Where ya going?" a young bleach blonde behind the wheel asked.

"Anywhere," Trick managed between heavy breaths. He scanned the occupants of the vehicle to see three teenage girls with similar hair and makeup all chattering at once. The blonde in the backseat asked, "Are you bleeding?"

"I don't know. Am I?" Trick put his hand on the back of his head, then held it in front of his face. "Yeah, I guess I am."

The blonde in the front passenger seat opened the glove compartment and handed Trick a McDonald's napkin which he placed on the back of his head. She asked, "What's your name?"

"Jack," Trick uttered the first thing that came to his mind, "Jack Paar."

"What happened, Jack?" they chimed. "Did you get in a fight?" "Do you want us to take you to the hospital?"

"No … no. Tell you what." Trick inspected the napkin which was already wet with blood. "Drive me to my car. Turn around up here, anywhere, and go back that way." He motioned with his thumb and a nod of the head.

"I'm Kimmi," the driver said making eye contact though the rearview mirror. "This is Jenni," she said, motioning to the front passenger.

"I'm Kelli," the girl in the backseat said, touching Trick's leather clad arm. "How old are you?"

"About twice your age, kid."

"We're not kids. We're sixteen," Jenni said.

"I'll be seventeen in December." Kimmi turned her head from the road.

Jenni turned around and got on her knees facing Trick. "We're like so bored, Jack. Got any suggestions?"

"Hell, I don't know. Try bowling."

"Boooring," Kimmi complained.

Kelli leaned closer to Trick. "Let's go somewhere and get you cleaned up. Whadda ya say, big boy?"

"Just better get me back to my car."

"Which one of us is the cutest?" Jenni asked.

"I've got the biggest boobs." Kelli opened her jacket and pushed her shoulders back.

"Jack." Jenni rested her chin on the headrest and smiled. "What do you call a ménage à trois when it's four people?"

Kimmi shook her head and said, "That's an orgy, dummy."

"We like to have fun." Kelli's hand moved from Trick's arm to his thigh. "Do you like to have fun, Jack?"

"Whoa, kid." Trick pulled Kelli's advancing hand from the inside of his thigh.

"C'mon." Kimmi's blue eyes flashed in the rearview mirror. "No one's home at my house all weekend."

"Look, I got a headache and I think I might need stitches."

"You can take a shower at my place and I can put a bandage on your cut."

"Look, you ladies are just too young for me. I just got out of prison and I'm not looking to go back. OK?"

Kelli backed away. "You're not a murderer, are you?"

"No. I never killed anyone. Jesus." Trick leaned forward and pointed. "Here, this block coming up, turn left."

When they were a block away from his car Trick scooted down in his seat. "Drive by slow up here and turn right," he said, as they went past his car and the house where he was attacked. He noticed the black Buick that had been parked a few doors to the east of the model home was no longer there. "Go around, follow the curve up there and make the first two rights." Trick looked at the paper napkin again, it was soaked with blood. "Slow down ... slow down. Right here. Let me out," he instructed through clenched teeth as they approached his car again. "Oh ... thanks, girls. Stay out of trouble."

"Here, Jack." Kimmi quickly jotted her phone number on a small piece of paper and handed it to Trick. "Think about it," she said with a wink.

Trick took the paper and stuffed it in his pocket as he slowly got out of the car looking around. He threw the bloody napkin on the street and took his keys from the pocket of his leather bomber. As the girls pulled away beeping, Trick heard pounding as he held his aching head. Muffled sounds of Bob's voice were followed by more pounding.

"Bob," Trick said, putting his hands on the trunk of his car. "Is that you?"

"Who the fuck else would be in here?"

Trick looked around, not seeing any sign of Barker. "What are you doing in there, Bob?"

"Open the God damn fuckin' trunk," Bob's muffled voice yelled.

"What was that, Bob? I can't hear you. Did you say open the trunk?"

The pounding got louder and Trick opened the trunk. He leaned over and put his hands on his knees as a bit of blood trickled down his forehead. "Good thing I had you come with me, Bob, keeping an eye on my trunk and all."

"Real fuckin' funny," Bob said, as he climbed out of the trunk.

"Where's your gun?" The porch light from the house they were parked in front of went on.

"I don't know." Bob straightened up, holding his back. "He took it."

Trick walked around to the driver door and asked over the top of the car, "Who took it?"

"Santa Claus," Bob said, getting back in the car. "Who do you think? The guy who put me in the trunk."

Trick heard the blare of sirens to the north. "Did this guy happen to give you a name?"

"No. We didn't exchange pleasantries."

Pulling away, Trick looked over at Bob and asked, "Well, what's this guy who puts people in trunks look like?"

"Black guy. Big black guy."

"Black guy? Not a white guy? A black guy?"

"Yes! I know the difference between a black guy and a white guy. The Jheri curl was a big clue, you fuck."

"OK. Tell me what happened with you and your big, black, Jheri curl friend."

"I was sittin' in the car, checking my gun to make sure it was loaded."

Two Tinley Park Police cars flew past them, with their emergency lights and sirens on, heading in the direction they came from as Trick asked, "You brought a gun but didn't know if it had bullets?"

"Yeah … no. I know my gun had bullets. I was just checkin' to be sure. You know."

"OK. Proceed." Trick turned right on 159th

Street.

"I had my window open, checkin' to see if my Colt had bullets. No … makin' sure it had bullets. All of a sudden I had a gun up against my temple. I heard a voice, sounded like James Earl Jones, say, "I like your piece.""

"So, you're saying James Earl Jones put a gun upside your head."

"No. Of course not, Mr. Funny Fuck. I said he sounded like 'im. James Earl Jones don't go around with any damn Jheri curls. He's too dignified."

"All right, you're a James Earl Jones fan. What happened next?"

"He took my gun. Put it in his pants."

"Wait. What do you mean he put it in his pants?"

"You know, he stuck it in his waistband."

"Why didn't you say waistband?"

"Do you want to know what the fuck happened? I could have been killed."

"Oh, *you* could have been killed. Yes, I want to hear what happened."

"I heard gunshots and he told me to get out of the car. He grabbed my ear and yanked me around to the back and made me get in the trunk. That's all."

"Oh. That's all?"

"Yeah. That's all. I waited a long time, then you let me out."

"I'm glad that's all, Bob. I'm glad no one knocked you on the back of the head with a pistol and shot at you."

"Are you OK?"

"Why, yes. Thank you for asking. I'm great, Bob. Except I probably need stitches, I'm filthy dirty from running through a prairie, dodging bullets and I've got a splitting headache."

"Did you get the money?"

"No. As a matter of fact, I didn't get the money."

"You still got the blow?"

"Yes, I have the blow."

"Well, that's good, anyway."

Trick drove the rest of the way in silence until they pulled up to Bob's trailer home off Southwest Highway. He put it in park, looked at Bob and asked, "You don't still expect me to pay you, do you?"

Chapter 22

"I'm sorry, Pat." Trick knelt and put his hands on his son's shoulders. "I can't take you to the carnival today."

As Pat ran to his bedroom crying, Ginger said, "I hope you're happy with yourself, breaking your son's heart. That's all he talked about all week."

"Look." Trick stood and noticed the gauntness of Ginger's face. "I'm sorry but there's things that I need to take care of right away."

"I thought you wanted to spend time with your son. Where've you been, getting laid?"

"No. That's what I ought to be doing after being locked up all that time." Trick's voice softened. "You know Pat's the most important thing in the world to me. Things are real crazy right now."

"Things are always crazy with you. Ever think things are crazy because you make them that way?"

"Ok, whatever you say. I don't want to fight. Please tell Pat I love him and I'll be by next week. Tell him Daddy's working and I'm going to buy him a new bike."

"I never knew anyone like you." Ginger shook her head. "You don't have any close friends. You don't trust anyone. I don't get it. How does that feel?"

"I trusted you." Trick zipped up his jacket and looked out the second story window and watched a lone robin trying to catch up to a flock flying south. "Look where that got me."

"That's different. I was your wife. Things just didn't work out." Ginger poked Trick's chest. "Just because you were rejected as a child doesn't mean you have to reject everyone else. Sooner or later, you're going to have to trust someone. Otherwise you'll always be alone."

"I don't need any amateur psychoanalysis right now." Trick started for the door. "I have to go."

"Yeah, go on. Get out. I had plans with Petros. Now I gotta find a babysitter. Go fuck yourself!"

***

Unable to finish, Trick pushed the rest of his late morning breakfast omelet away at the El-Dorado restaurant, listening for the payphone in the entryway to ring. After placing a five-dollar bill under his water glass, he went back to the payphone feeling light-headed from lack of sleep. He stood looking at the phone for a couple minutes and then dialed again. "Where is that son-of-a-bitch?" Trick slammed the receiver down after his sixth call to Joker's pager in the last two days. Not liking his options, he drove to Joker's house in the nearby suburb of Chicago Ridge. Joker's El Camino was in the driveway but his Harley was nowhere in sight. He pulled into the drive, walked to the side entrance and rapped on the aluminum screen door, feeling a chill in the air after eight straight days of unseasonably warm weather.

"Trick. My God, what are you doing here?" Joker's barefoot wife, Brenda, pushed the screen door open a couple feet while a toddler in a droopy diaper clung to her leg.

"Is Joker around?" Trick's eyes darted back and forth. With her hand over her head gripping the door, he tried not to stare at the bottom of Brenda's breast which was partially visible in her cut-off

Harley-Davidson sweatshirt.

"No. That bastard took off Friday night, right after Brandi's birthday party." Brenda wiped her wet hands on frayed Daisy Duke shorts, keeping the door propped open with her foot. "Joker, that's a good name for that alley cat because he's a joke of a husband."

"I need to get hold of him," Trick said, looking over the top of his sunglasses. "It's important."

"Get in line." Brenda scowled as she brushed aside blonde frosted wisps of hair that had fallen loose from her rubber band hair tie. "I wish that mother fucker would die on the road."

"Beautiful, just fucking beautiful." Trick stopped talking when he realized the towhead baby boy sucking on a bottle watched him closely with wide eyes. "I don't suppose he left any money here for me."

Brenda's laugh sounded hollow and raspy as she pulled a pack of unfiltered Camels from her back pocket and lit a cigarette. "Are you kidding? If he left any money here, I'd be gone."

Trick looked deep into Brenda's gray eyes that were adorned with last night's stale makeup. "Does he know about us?"

"You mean, does he know you used to ball my teenage ass on a blanket at Bullfrog Lake?"

"Well … that's not the way I would have put it … but yeah."

"I never told him shit but when he gets drunk enough he needles me about you. Probably heard some talk." Brenda blew smoke out of her nostrils. "Why?"

"Just trying to figure out what's going on." Trick massaged his forehead with his fingertips. "When do you think he might be back?"

"I have no idea. He usually manages to show up when there's barely anything left to eat around here and gives me grocery money." Tears welled up in Brenda's sad eyes that appeared old before their time. She took a deep drag off her Camel then flicked it at Trick, bouncing it off his leather bomber. "Why don't you get the hell out of here? You big prick. Did you ever give two shits about me?"

"I … I, what do you mean?"

"You knew I was in love with you. But you tossed me aside like a used rubber when a new bit of fluff came along. What happened? Did you just get tired of screwing me? Is that it?"

"I didn't realize." Trick hid his hands in his pockets. "I'm sorry. That was a long time ago. I …"

"Did you know that the day I married Joker I kept looking back at the church door? I prayed that you would walk in and stop the wedding, tell me you loved me and take me out of there." Brenda's eyes revealed a hurt that ran deep. "You didn't show up at all." Her lips quivered and tears blackened from eyeliner trickled down her cheeks. "And now you're here after all these years looking for money."

"Look, I was a young guy," Trick said, staring at the ground, pushing a small stone around with the tip of his crocodile boot. "I guess I didn't think."

"Oh, you thought. It's just that the only person you ever thought about was yourself. Being young is no excuse." Brenda raised her voice and pointed a shaky finger. "Go on … get the fuck out of here, will you?"

***

Seeing Bob's Cadillac in the parking lot of the Back Door Inn, Trick pulled over and walked in the rear entrance. Bob didn't notice as he approached from behind. Trick spun Bob's barstool around to face him. "Hey, I told you I was on a deadline. It's three in the afternoon and you're sitting here getting shit-faced."

"Whoa. What the fuck. Don't surprise me like that." Bob put his hand on the pocket of his suede fringe jacket. "I coulda stabbed you."

"What the hell is the matter with you?" Trick looked around the sparsely filled bar, gave Bob a light slap on the face and said quietly, "You got coke all over your nostrils and moustache. You're supposed to be selling the shit, not going through all of it."

"I was just headin' out to collect some moolah. Square business."

"Collect? What did I tell you? I don't want you fronting this shit out."

"Look, man, I been doin' this long as you … longer even. This is the way I operate. And I never been busted. I got two words for you, quit fuckin' worryin'."

"Don't tell me not to worry. You have no idea what I'm up against, you dizzy buzz-head."

"So what's a few days … a week? The world's not goin' anywhere. It'll still be spinnin'."

"You don't understand. This is serious shit." Trick grabbed Bob by his jacket. "I need that money by tomorrow at the latest."

"What do you want me to do? Go round with my gun threatenin' customers? These people are my friends. They're loyal."

"I don't care how you get it, just get it."

"I don't need any of your shit." Bob shoved Trick's grip off his lapel. "You think you got problems, you don't know. While you were in the pokey, fuckin' playin' cards and liftin' weights, I lost one of my nuts."

"What are you talking about? Where'd you lose it?"

"Oh, you're gonna be a comedian now?"

Trick spread his hands out in front of him. "I don't know what the hell you're talking about."

"Cancer. I lost my left nut to cancer. Had to get radiation on the other one. Might never have kids." Bob downed a shot of tequila. "So, don't try to rain a shit storm on me."

"Hey, I had no idea. I'm sorry for your loss. But you stumbling in and out of bars with one walnut rolling around in your nutsack has nothing to do with business."

"You're a cold mother fucker." Bob guzzled his bottle of beer and slammed it on the bar. "You know that?"

"How'd you like a swift kick in that one kiwi you got left? Don't fuck with me … not now. I'm telling you, get that money together, quick."

Bob rolled his eyes, stroked the braids in his goatee and said, "OK, Daddy. The lecture over? Can I go now?"

"Just make sure nothing goes wrong," Trick called after Bob as he walked out, then ordered a shot of Johnnie Walker Black before leaving. He got in his Lincoln and started heading to Top Notch to grab a burger but got delayed by a freight train at a railroad crossing on 95th Street. He turned the music down, leaned back and thought about little Pat, wondering what he was doing right then.

"Come home," he could hear his foster mother calling to him. "Come home, I put clean sheets on your bed. Take a little nap before supper," she cooed. "I'm making your favorite, pot roast and hot rolls right out of the oven."

150

Trick wondered why she was rapping her rolling pin on the kitchen table. He was getting annoyed because the tapping was drowning out her words.

"Hey, wake up!"

Trick shot up in his seat, disoriented, and saw an Oak Lawn Police officer hitting his window with a billy club. "Step out of your vehicle, sir," the officer ordered, with the billy club now patting into his open palm. "Sir, do you understand me? Step out of your vehicle."

The patrol car was parked behind Trick's Lincoln and off to the left a few feet giving the officer room to stand without getting hit by the slow moving traffic filing past, ogling the scene.

Letting himself out of the car, Trick stood as the police officer moved in uncomfortably close.

"Have you been drinking, sir?"

"No ... no. I must have dozed off," Trick answered back, trying to sound more awake than he actually was. The taste of Scotch lingered on his tongue so he backed up a step.

"No kidding, Captain Obvious. Is that how you got the black eyes, falling asleep at the wheel?"

Locking eyes with the officer, Trick replied, "What was that?"

"I'm Officer Petak. I need to see your driver's license, registration and proof of insurance."

Without saying anything else, Trick retrieved his insurance and registration cards from his glove compartment, stood and handed them to the officer. He reached into the inside pocket of his jacket for his wallet and felt a handful of loose cocaine packets. He hesitated, being careful not to pull any out along with the wallet.

Officer Petak noticed Trick fumbling around in his pocket and asked, "Do you have anything in your

151

pockets that I should know about? Do you have any weapons on you?"

"No … no weapons," Trick quickly responded. "Here's my wallet."

"Remove your license from the wallet and hand it to me, sir."

The officer looked at the license, looked at Trick, then back at the license. "Mr. Halloran, why are you asleep at the wheel on 95th Street backing up traffic?"

"I've been working two jobs," Trick lied. "Trying to stay ahead on child support."

"Where were you heading when you fell asleep?"

"On my way to Top Notch to grab a beefburger."

"Would you mind opening your trunk for me?"

Trick felt his heart skip a beat. He hesitated and looked at the ground thinking about the cocaine and cash in his trunk.

Officer Petak put his hand on his sidearm and demanded, "Mr. Halloran, I'd like you to open your trunk."

"Look, Officer. I'm running late. I'm starving and I got to get to my second job."

"I can hold you here till I get a warrant to search your vehicle."

Trick knew that he had nothing. He was holding a bum hand, not even a low pair. All he could do was bluff. "Go ahead. Get your warrant. I haven't done anything wrong. Anyone could fall asleep waiting for one of these long-ass freight trains to go by."

"You have something in your trunk you don't want me to see? Drugs? Weapons?"

Pulling himself together, Trick stood his ground, realizing the officer didn't have substantial evidence to get a judge to sign a warrant. "If I'm under arrest, take me in. Otherwise I'd like to be on my way."

Petak stood looking Trick in the eye. Trick held his stare for several moments and wouldn't blink. The officer finally handed the license back but held onto it tightly as Trick tried to take it. "Have a nice day, Mr. Halloran," he said, releasing his grip.

Chapter 23

Pulling out of Ginger's parking lot after dropping off a new bicycle for Pat, Trick saw the Mexicans' Oldsmobile 98 parked in the street. Having them know where his son lived sent a shock of fear through him. He turned right onto the Midlothian Turnpike and put the visor down to block the blinding late afternoon sun while considering his options. He wished there was somewhere he could send little Pat for a while. The boy had no living grandparents and there weren't any close family members for him to visit. He didn't think Ginger would consider pulling him out of school and sending him away anyway. And telling her about the Mexicans would only result in her cutting him off from seeing his son. Dreams of being a father to Pat again were what kept him going those slow, miserable years in prison.

He knew that going to the police wasn't an option. Being involved with drugs and drug money would put him right back in prison. He considered making an anonymous call to the cops describing the four and the Oldsmobile but he had no proof of anything. Knowing how law enforcement operated, there just wasn't enough for them to go on. It could indirectly put him under scrutiny and he didn't need the attention right now. He was unsure of what to do. Try to outrun them? Hide somewhere until he figured things out? If he left town, his enemies could retaliate by going after his son. He had to face them.

The Olds pulled up next to Trick's Lincoln as he headed west. The big guy, still in his red and black Bulls jacket, shouted at Trick from his open passenger window, "Follow us!"

Trick trailed behind as they pulled into the parking lot of Rubio Woods, a short distance ahead. He parked beside them, waiting to see what would happen next. He stayed in his car as all four of the Latinos got out of their Olds and approached his open window.

"I've got part of it." Trick squirmed in his seat, looking up at the four. "I just need a little time. I'll get all of it. I promise."

In the sunlight, the four men looked younger, maybe early to mid-twenties. The short, stocky guy in charge started laughing and the other three followed suit. "He promises," he cackled. "I like that. I promise, I promise. You give me a good laugh. Everybody should have a good laugh every day. Good for your soul."

"Enough funny stuff." The big guy grabbed Trick by his hair. "Where's the money?"

"It's in the trunk." Trick pressed his trunk release button. "In the tool box."

"Don't make us count it," the big guy threatened. "How much is there?"

"$43,000," Trick spoke up. "The $20,000 that was missing plus $23,000 toward the balance. I've been running around night and day, barely sleeping to round this up. I just need more time."

"Remember what I told you about telling me things I don't want to hear?" The leader stroked the patch of black hair growing under his lower lip. "Better get out of the car."

Trick reluctantly opened his door and got to his feet. As the two brothers took him by the elbows

156

and led him into the woods, Trick looked back to see the big guy put the toolbox full of cash in the trunk of the Olds. The tall Chicano quickly caught up and they kept walking until there was nothing but trees surrounding them. He grabbed Trick around the neck from behind while the brothers locked their arms tightly through his.

The leader grabbed Trick by the nose. "You want me to break it again?"

"No … come on." Trick winced in pain.

"Tie him to the tree," the leader ordered.

The big guy released Trick's neck, walked around to face him and pulled a handgun from a shoulder holster hidden under his jacket. He ordered, "Open your kisser," then stuck the barrel in Trick's mouth and backed him up against a big elm tree. The two brothers forced his arms behind the tree and tied his wrists tightly with a heavy cord before the big guy removed the pistol from his mouth.

The leader pulled a Polaroid photo from his shirt pocket and put it in front of Trick's face. It was a photo of little Pat walking out of Nathan Hale elementary school. "Cute little albino. If I cut his balls off, he'll never make you a grandfather."

"Hey, man. This is between us. I said I'd get everything I owe you. C'mon. Please."

"I'm feeling generous today. I'm giving you one more week. Seven days to get the rest of the money."

"Hey, man, can't you give me a break on the price," Trick pleaded, "how about fifty a ki?"

The leader pulled a pair of tin snips from the pocket of his long overcoat with a sardonic expression that Trick wished he could punch from the young gangster's face. "OK. Hey, let's be reasonable," Trick tried to renegotiate, "sixty, man. Sixty a ki." Trick knew he couldn't come up with the balance even if it was fifty a piece for three kilos, not in one week.

"This is for making me wait." The leader put on a pair of latex gloves as he walked around to the back of the tree and grabbed hold of Trick's left pinkie finger.

A tiny fireworks display exploded on the inside of his closed eyelids. "Aaaggghhh!" Trick cried out as he felt tugging and excruciating pain. It was worse than anything he had ever experienced. "Ahh, ahh!" The agony seemed to be everywhere at once. It was bigger than his body, like an aura of hurt.

The leader walked around to face Trick. He held a portion of Trick's finger up for him to see. "The first knuckle. Every time you make me wait, you lose another knuckle." The young sadist calmly dropped the tip of the finger into a plastic bag. "A present for my python."

Trick's stomach convulsed as he dry-heaved.

"Cut him loose," the big guy told the brothers.

One of them pulled a switchblade knife from the back pocket of his Sedgefield jeans and cut the cord with one swift movement. Trick dropped to his knees and inspected his bloody stump of a finger.

"Here." The leader threw Trick a handkerchief. "Oh, *cabrón*," he laughed, "I might have blown my nose on it."

"*Adiós*, stubby," one brother said, putting the switchblade back in his pocket as they walked away.

The pain grew with every breath. Trick prayed to go into shock. He prayed to God. He prayed to the Devil. In that instant he wished for death, anything but the misery that gripped his burning finger. With his right hand, Trick wrapped the hankie around the severed finger, holding one end in his right hand and the other end in his teeth. Almost passing out, he kept pulling tighter until the bleeding slowed, then awkwardly knotted it.

He made his way back to his car, drove to Cicero Avenue feeling dizzy and turned left. With one hand, he steered into the parking lot of St. Francis Immediate Care Center a short distance ahead, wondering if he should go in. "What choice have I got?" Trick began talking to himself deliriously, "cauterize it?" He stared at his finger that throbbed with every beat of his heart. "I hope they don't ask too many questions or call the cops."

Walking in, a combination of smells that didn't register in his memory made him want to vomit. Sights and sounds took on a dreamlike quality. The white walls seemed to pulsate. He shuffled further holding his left hand, the white handkerchief now red with blood.

"Oh my! What happened to you?" A young lady behind the admissions desk exclaimed.

In a voice that seemed to come from someone else, Trick muttered, "I was changing a flat tire and the jack slipped."

"When did this happen?"

"Just now, ten minutes ago."

A doctor walked in from the hallway and said, "Let me see." He pulled on a pair of latex gloves and inspected the end of Trick's little finger. "That looks like a clean cut. Where's the rest of your finger? There's a possibility it could be reattached."

Trick didn't like the way the doctor looked at him. He thought this must be what it's like when an insane person receives unwelcome, scrutinizing stares. He hesitated, trying to wake his brain up. Almost believing his own lies, Trick finally responded, "Oh … there was a sewer grate." Trick felt lightheaded and thought he might lose consciousness. "It fell in."

The doctor continued staring at him incredulously. "I hear a lot of stories here but this … this is bizarre." He took hold of Trick's chin and moved his head side to side, examining his face. "Did you break your nose recently?"

Trick stepped back and vomited on the floor. "I'm in a lot of pain here," he yelled. "Forget about my nose. Just take care of the finger." Trick pulled a few hundred dollars from his pocket that he held back from the Mexicans. "I got cash."

Less than an hour later, Trick walked out with a prescription for pain killers, his finger pumped full of Lidocaine, stitched and bandaged. He eased into his car, still sick to his stomach. "Patrick, my little guy," he sighed, resting his head back, "what's your dad going to do?"

Chapter 24

"Never mind what happened to my finger and don't try to change the subject. I'm serious as ass cancer." Trick pointed at Bob. "I needed that money yesterday."

"Patience, patience. You'll live longer." Bob held his green bottle of Heineken like it was a trophy and shook his head in a condescending manner. "When you bake a cake, you mix the ingredients and put it in the oven. You can't tell the batter to cook faster. You can't tell the oven to bake quicker. You sound like a little kid who can't wait for Christmas."

"Fuck you and your cakes. This isn't home economics, Nancy." Trick slammed his rock glass on the bar. "I'm not fucking around."

Bob hopped backward off his bar stool at The Wall lounge at 112th and Harlem and said, "I'd love to stay and discuss high finances but I'm middlin' a deal in a half hour."

"Monkey in the middle? Sounds about your speed." Trick's finger still throbbed, even with the Vicodin he was taking. "How much you making?"

"One G for an introduction." Bob bit at his jagged fingernails.

"That's not what they're paying you the grand for. They're buying safety … protection. They want to know the other party isn't a cop or there to rip them off. Hope you did your homework and not doing something half-assed like usual."

"I know what I'm doin'." Bob waved his hand as

if shooing away a fly.

"Just be careful," Trick said, trying to sound sincere. "How much is this person buying?"

"A kilo. I swear, doin' business with you isn't worth it, havin' you up my ass all the time." Bob swigged some beer. "Tell you how I operate. I don't like anyone knowin' where the deal's goin' down till the last minute so I got both parties waitin' close by for my calls." Bob did a cheesy impression of Steve Martin and dragged out his words, "Excuuuse meee!"

Sipping his Jameson whiskey, Trick watched Bob disappear around the corner toward the washrooms and payphones. He read 8:24 pm on his watch and followed in Bob's direction slowly, hoping he wasn't being too conspicuous walking past him while he talked on the phone. He had no trouble hearing Bob's usual loud, high-pitched tone setting up the deal. After entering the bathroom, Trick stood with his ear at the crack of the door, listening as Bob continued.

By the time Trick made his way back to the bar, Bob was already at his stool. "I'm taking off," Trick said.

"Stick around." Bob patted the bar stool next to him. "One more quick one."

"No. One's enough. I'm on painkillers." Trick picked up his half empty glass and swirled his ice. "You need liquid courage to do this thing? Maybe you should find another line of work."

"Then who would you have to move all that primo nose candy for ya?"

"Got to fly." Trick gulped the rest of his Irish whiskey. "See you tomorrow for breakfast, and don't come empty-handed."

Once out of view, Trick jogged to his car and

sped north on Harlem to the thrift store at 90th Street. He rushed in and paced up and down the aisles, feeling woozy from the whiskey and Vicodin. "Perfect," he said under his breath, picking up some football shoulder pads. He threw them over one shoulder and located an oversized, dark topcoat, a hooded sweatshirt, sweatpants, and combat boots that looked as though they could have stormed the beach at Normandy. Walking with his arms full of musty smelling clothing, he headed toward the toy graveyard.

He plopped everything into a nearby empty shopping cart when he saw something silvery beckon him. "Damn, if this thing doesn't almost look real," he said, slurring a little as he tossed the metal toy pistol on the pile of clothing. His mind was becoming fuzzy but he knew he needed three more things.

"You work here?" Trick got the attention of an olive skinned, middle-aged woman walking by, bedecked with an ample amount of costume jewelry.

"I'm the owner. How can I help you?"

"I need a pair of gloves, a ski mask and sunglasses. I'm in a hurry."

Trick followed the pear-shaped woman as she picked up various things for him to examine. After securing his final items, he glanced at his watch and asked, "How much do I owe you?"

"Follow me. I'll ring you up."

"Don't got time." He held a couple bills up. "How about forty bucks and we call it even?"

"Yes, sir," she said, snatching the money from Trick's hand like a seagull swooping up a carp.

"You got someplace I can change?"

"Sure. There's a fitting room right back there, behind the appliances. But Halloween's not for nine more days. Who are you supposed to be?"

Trick wheeled the cart back to a tiny stall that had a cloth curtain for privacy and saw his reflection in something that had the makings of a funhouse mirror. Slipping out of his jacket and shoes, he put the items on over his other clothes as quickly as possible. He walked out of the changing area with the life-size toy gun in one coat pocket, sunglasses, ski mask and gloves in another. With shoes in one hand and jacket over his arm, he sprinted out to the Lincoln.

Continuing north on Harlem, Trick wove in and out of traffic trying to make the green lights. He turned on the radio in an attempt to distract him from his pounding heart. He flew through the yellow at 84th Street, then cut a sharp right on 83rd. After making the fourth left onto New England Avenue, he headed north and slowed down, turning off his headlights for the rest of the way. Pulling up to the curb, he had a good view of Newcastle Park's parking lot. He put the wool ski mask on, raised the hood of the faded black sweatshirt, looked in his rearview mirror and put the tinted glasses on.

Breathing heavy with excitement, he turned off the engine and got out of the car. Relieved that there wasn't anyone hanging around or walking by, he tugged the work gloves over his hands and bandaged finger. He was just in time to see Bob pulling into the parking lot on the opposite side of the park and shutting off his lights. Bob got out of his Cadillac looking in the other direction toward residential Newcastle Avenue, lighting a cigarette. Trick walked over to one of the chain-link backstops and crouched down, estimating Bob to be about fifty yards away. There were at least thirty other cars in the parking area and the back door of the clubhouse cast a glowing shaft of light onto the grass behind the one story brick building. Trick carefully moved closer while a square dance caller's voice echoed in the cool night air, "Star through, circle top, left allemande."

Trick noted 9:02 pm on his watch as a cream-colored, older model Mercedes slowly pulled into the parking lot then wheeled into a spot near Bob's Caddy. The driver got out and walked up to Bob. They grabbed one another's hand and pulled each other close in a one-shoulder hug.

Maneuvering himself all the way to the end of the parked cars, Trick peeked around a tire. Recognizing the Kentucky based drug dealer standing with Bob, Trick whispered, "Rebel." He could hear their voices but couldn't make out what they were saying.

While Trick crept closer in the dark, another car entered and slowed down next to Bob and Rebel who were standing behind the Cadillac. The power window of a custom-painted green Mercury Grand Marquis went down and Bob walked up to it. He motioned with his hand toward Rebel, nodding his head.

The Mercury parked at the end of the line of cars and two imposing black men got out, one looking bigger than the other. One was wearing a lime-green suit, the other a full-length black leather coat. As they swaggered over to Bob and Rebel, Trick silently made his way to a minivan near the four.

Trick was hoping there would only be three dealers to contend with and wondered if any of these guys were packing guns. He had second thoughts, reaching into the pocket of the overcoat and fingering the replica revolver. The voices were clear now as the four men made bravado conversation, trying to impress one another.

The man in the lime-green suit, who did most of

the talking, asked Rebel, "You got the whole fifty Gs?"

"Yeah, it's in the car," Rebel replied. "I'll get it."

"OK, go get the package," the ebony eyed man in charge told his leather clad bodyguard.

When the tall, portly man made his way back to the other three, Rebel was standing next to Bob with a brown paper bag.

"Let me see the money," the lime-green suited man called out in a deep voice that resonated in the brisk, damp air.

"No problem." Rebel tossed the bag of money to the man in green. "Hand over the shit."

"Here 'tis." Leather coat flipped a Burger King sack to Rebel and pulled an automatic handgun from his waistband.

Trick jumped up from the cover of the minivan and ran up behind the pistol wielding man in leather. Flashing his toy revolver, he said in a mock Irish accent, "Drop the gun, or the last thing you'll hear is a loud pop." Trick stood close behind him with the cold metal barrel against the dark blue script tattooed on the side of the man's brown neck, fearing his own life could end any second.

"OK. Don't shoot." The big guy tossed the automatic pistol onto the asphalt, landing with a thud. It went off sending a bullet in the direction of the clubhouse, making everyone flinch and Trick gasp.

"Kick the gun away," Trick ordered, with the toy pistol pressed into the bodyguard's neck. The big man trembled and kicked the gun, sending it skidding under a nearby car. "You," Trick continued, directing his attention to the man in green. "Throw the bag behind you or I'll spring a leak in chalky's neck."

"Fuck you and the IRA, you potato eatin' mutha

fucka. You shoot him and I'm gonna lunge atcha ass."

Trick looked to his left to see two men peering at them through the open back door of the field house, the music and voices from within now silent. "This is a .357 Magnum. Bullet'll go right through his neck and into your Moon-Pie face," Trick bluffed, nearly paralyzed with fear.

"Quit fuckin' around, Beasley. Give 'im the money." The big man visibly shook. "I don't want to die, Lord. Please don't let me die!"

"We live through this, I'm gonna kill ya myself, you big pussy-ass coward. You just told them my real name!"

"You two sweethearts can have a lover's quarrel later." Trick tried to sound as menacing as possible. "Toss the bag!"

Beasley looked up at the torrent of swift moving clouds in the night sky, let out a moan and dropped the bag of money behind him.

A slow-moving Burbank Police vehicle stopped at the entrance of the parking lot facing north on Newcastle Avenue. A uniformed arm stretched for the spotlight through the open driver's side window. Trick reached down, grabbed the bag and ran behind the minivan again. He now wondered how he was going to get away with the police there and open fields surrounding the area.

The spotlight hit the other four men still standing there and a voice rang out over a loudspeaker, "Stand where you are! Hands above your heads!"

Two Burbank Police officers exited their vehicle and walked toward Bob, Rebel, Beasley, and his bodyguard with flashlights in one hand and the other on their holstered pistols. Rebel dropped the Burger King sack and put his hands over his head along with the other three. One of the officers shined his flashlight on the hamburger sack at Rebel's feet. "What do we have here? A late dinner?" The officer picked up the bag, opened it and pulled out a handful of new athletic socks while Trick crept toward Newcastle Avenue along the other side of the parked cars.

"Socks?" Rebel looked at Beasley and his muscle.

"I just been robbed!" Beasley shouted, pointing at the row of cars next to them. "A big Irish Mick in dark clothes and a ski mask just stole a bag of money from me."

Rebel yelled, "What do you mean, *you've* been robbed?"

"We received a report of gunshots in the area," one of the officers said, drawing his weapon and looking at his partner with a confused expression.

Trick stood and ran full speed toward the idling police vehicle with the bag of money, jumped behind the wheel and floored it toward 79th Street four blocks to the north. Tossing the sunglasses out the window, he looked in the rearview mirror to see the two officers running into the street, flashlight beams scattering in the night.

Turning west on 79th Street, Trick looked back toward the parking lot to see Beasley's Grand Marquis also driving west, right through the expansive lawn of Newcastle Park toward New England, where he left his Lincoln. Trick knew he had to double back and get his car before Bob recognized it, and avoid Beasley and the police at the same time. He continued past New England one block, turned left on Sayre, drove up a block, pulled over and shut off the lights. Taking the bag of cash with him, he threw the keys under a car parked in a driveway, removed the ski mask and put it in a curbside mailbox. He cut between two ranch style houses and continued back toward his car by scaling a six-foot chain link fence, where he received an unfriendly welcome from a German Shepherd running at him full speed. Trick moved as fast as he could toward the back of the yard, where he threw the bag of cash over the fence and tried climbing over, wincing in pain from his severed, stitched finger. He was almost over the top when he felt a tug holding him back. He looked behind to see the bottom of the long topcoat lodged firmly in the teeth of the growling canine. With his feet planted high on the fence, he removed the toy pistol from his pocket and threw it at him, bouncing it off his head. This just made the dog angrier, so he slipped out of the topcoat one arm at a time. Now free, he swung his body over the top, landing safely on the other side as he watched the large dog just inches away thrashing the coat side to side. It was then he realized his key ring, which included his car and condo keys, was in the pocket of the coat.

"Let go," Trick commanded as he reached under the silvery metal fence and grabbed the collar of the coat. Putting his feet up against the fence, he pulled with all his might but could not dislodge the coat from the canine's teeth. He stopped and looked at his left gloved hand, blood was seeping through the tan canvas material.

Trick stood and tugged the hooded sweatshirt over his head, dangled it over the top of the fence and called to the German Shepherd, who still shook the coat in his incisors like a ragdoll. "Here, doggie, take the nice shirt," Trick coaxed. The dog ignored him so he got a foot hold on the fence, reached over further and began swinging the hood, hitting him on the head with it. The dog lunged at him and he dropped it. His four-legged tormentor grabbed the worn shirt in his teeth and glared at him. Trick jumped down, reached under the fence and yanked the coat to safety. He put it back on and stuffed his hand in the pocket, happy to feel the cold metal of the keys.

Creeping through the damp grass behind a row of neatly trimmed lilac bushes on the residential side of New England, Trick looked for Beasley's Mercury, which appeared to be long gone. Beasley was wisely nowhere in sight as were Bob and Rebel, although their cars were still in the parking lot. The two autoless police officers remained in the middle of Newcastle Avenue joined by another Burbank patrol car. Trick could make out frantic explanations and arm waving from the obviously embarrassed officers.

A third patrol car slowly motored south on New England so Trick jumped behind a thick cottonwood tree. The police car suddenly picked up speed and flew past him. Trick peeked around the tree to see Bob running as fast as his plump legs could carry him through the park, heading toward 83rd Street. The police car at the entrance to the parking lot also raced in pursuit of Bob.

Ducking down, Trick ran toward his own car, got in and started it. He glanced in his rearview mirror to see Bob over a block away in the middle of 83rd, surrounded, with his hands over his head. Trick left his headlights off and drove slowly toward 79th, where he turned right, put his lights on and took off. He put the bag full of money on his lap, opened it and removed one of the stacks of cash held together with a wide red rubber band. He brought it to his nose and took a deep whiff, smelling the dirty history of the bills.

"So, Bob." Trick buttered his toast, watching the shapely waitress walk away from their table. "How did your middleman deal go last night?"

"Oh, fuck, man." Bob slapped his forehead. "You wouldn't believe it."

"Try me." Trick broke a yolk with his toast and took a bite.

"One of these clowns I set the deal up with must have had loose lips because some Irish fuck knew where the meet was. He was disguised and robbed my buddy, took off with fifty Gs."

"How do you know he was Irish?"

"He had a thick brogue." Bob dribbled egg yolk into his goatee, talking with a mouth full of food. "In fact he sounded a lot like you, if you grew up on the Emerald Isle."

"Sounded like me?" Trick looked up from his breakfast with one eyebrow raised.

"Yeah. But he was a lot bigger." Bob put his hands out for emphasis. "Had shoulders like Schwarzenegger."

"You must have …" Trick dropped his fork into his hash browns and burst out laughing. "You must have pissed your pants."

"Hey, man, it's not funny. The cops showed up so I took off. But they caught me. I was in Burbank lockup for three hours. Finally let me go after a shit load of questioning because I didn't have any weapons or drugs on me."

Trick howled with laughter. "Bob, I could just picture those chubby legs of yours running down the street." Tears rolled down his cheeks. "Oh, my God, Bob," Trick managed, almost out of breath, laughing and slapping his hand on his leg.

"What the hell?" Bob shook his head. "You got one weird sense of humor, dude."

Wiping his face with his napkin, Trick let out a big sigh and asked, "Where's the money you owe me?"

Chapter 25

"You look like you could use a drink," Trick said to his reflection in his rearview mirror, "but don't take all day. You're behind schedule." He felt like going to one of his previous haunts, an old school tavern, not some fancy cocktail joint. So he headed over to the Delta Lounge on 87th Street.

Walking into the bar, there was little clue it was late afternoon. Once inside, it could have been just about any time of the day or night. It smelled exactly as it did three years ago. Probably the same as it did in the 1950s. Just like a tavern should. "Give me a short draft, Bert," Trick said, recognizing the bartender. "Old Style, my good man."

"Hey, pardner, der's nuttin' good 'bout me." The old guy chuckled, the wattle of his neck jiggling. "Just ask my wife." He brushed the last wisps of his oily hair to the side with his fingers. "Long time, no see."

Trick tossed a few bucks on the bar, took a stool and watched Bert tilt the glass under the tap as the golden lager filled it, forming a nice thick head. Bert wiped the suds that trickled over the side on the once-white apron tied around his ample belly, then slid the glass across the bar. Trick took a sip of the cold brew and set it down on the cardboard beer mat that Bert tossed in front of him. He kept his left hand in the side pocket of his bomber jacket to avoid questions about his bandaged, still throbbing finger. Glancing around, he took in a young guy down to his right with an empty shot glass in front of him, his hand wrapped tightly on a can of Blatz beer. Awful young to have such big bags under his eyes, Trick observed, and no wedding ring. He seemed to be married to the bottle. "Till death do they part," he mused.

Two older guys, seated down to his left near the pool table, were having a friendly but animated argument about the Cubs and White Sox. Trick tuned them out and thought about Pat, his innocent, confused face haunting him.

Bert went to the phone behind the bar and talked quietly, glancing back at Trick. He hung up the phone, returned and leaned his hands on the bar, raising his eyebrows. "Getcha 'nother one der, chief?"

"Fill 'er up. I'm about a quart low," Trick responded.

"Wish I had a buck for every time I heard dat one," Bert retorted, refilling the glass.

Trick took the bottle of Vicodin from his inside jacket pocket and tried reading the instructions, but he couldn't concentrate. His mind wandered back to the day his son was born. It was the happiest he ever felt. He remembered how he vowed never to let Pat feel alone and unloved as he did. He washed one of the painkillers down with cold beer and looked at his watch. Pushing the rest of his drink away, he got up from his backless bar stool.

"Hey," Bert called out, "yer not leavin' already, are ya?"

"Yeah," Trick said with a nod, reaching for his change, "got things to do."

"Here." Bert grabbed Trick's glass. "Let me top ya off. For da road ... on me."

"Yeah, OK." Trick left his money on the varnished wooden bar and eased back onto his stool.

"Guess I got time for one more quick one."

"Don't make it too quick." Bert grinned, showing a broken front tooth. "Gotta stop and smell da hops once in a while."

Several minutes later, the front door flew open. Late afternoon sun glinted off the glass door hurting Trick's eyes that had become adjusted to the darkly-lit saloon. A tall, good looking guy dressed in dark blue work clothes walked in and took the stool to Trick's right. He wondered why this middle-aged man sat right next to him when there were plenty of other bar stools available.

"Bertie," the guy next to Trick called out. "I'll have a seven/seven and get anyone else who wants one."

Before making the Seagram's Seven and 7 Up, Bert grabbed Trick's glass and started filling it up again.

"No. Wait." Trick waved his hand to the side. "I was just leaving."

"Don't be silly," Bert said, without looking up. "Chevy here just bought ya a beer."

Chevy pivoted on his stool toward Trick and extended his hand. "The name's Stanley Krupnik but friends call me Chevy ... 'cause that's all I ever owned." Chevy ran grease stained fingernails through his salt and pepper, wavy hair. "Please. Have a drink with me. It's gonna change your life."

"Damn, look at you two sittin' next to each other." Bert extended his neck toward them for emphasis. "I can't believe it."

"Bertie, give us a few minutes," Chevy appealed, pointing his chin at Bert, "will ya?"

Trick picked up his glass, looked at it, then set it back down. "What are you selling, Stanley ... Chevy."

"Not sellin' nothin'. Only giving away good news. This face look familiar to ya?" Chevy tilted his head to the side not losing eye contact. "It ought to."

"What're you driving at, Chevy." Trick slapped his hand on the bar.

"Hey, that's a funny one. What're ya drivin' at, Chevy. Ha ha." Chevy dropped his smile. "I'm gonna get right to it, boy. I'm your father, the one that brought ya into the world. Whacha think 'bout that? Huh?"

Unable to say anything, Trick just looked at Chevy with his right hand wrapped around his glass.

Bert walked back over to them and exclaimed, "If yous two don't look like a couple bookends, I don't know what. Like a mirror image. Younger and older. Just like you looked around that age, Chevy. Pretty near just like 'im."

Trick caught Chevy shooting Bert a dirty look. Chevy nodded his head to the right and said through a clenched jaw, "Go get me a Slim Jim. Will ya, Bert?" He rubbed his graying whiskers with his palm and returned his attention to Trick. "So Patrick, I hear they call ya Trick."

"What kind of proof you got?" Ignoring Chevy's last comment, Trick continued, "What makes you think you're my real father?"

"I wouldn't be tellin' ya I was if I wasn't damn sure." Chevy splayed his extended fingers. "I did a lot of askin' around. And now I finally tracked ya down."

"Look, you're a perfect stranger to me." Trick leaned away onto his elbow. "You don't expect me to start calling you Daddy? Do you?"

"I understand this is a shock." Chevy nodded slowly. "Give it time to sink in."

"I need to see some kind of proof. A birth

certificate naming you as my father … something."

"All in good time. First, I wanted to meet ya face to face." Chevy stared at Trick. "Yeah, I can see a lot of your mother in you." Chevy tapped his index finger to his nose then pointed at Trick. "Yep."

"Something about this … doesn't feel right." Trick tried not to stare at the ample amount of curly, graying hair growing out of Chevy's ears. "I've had to rely on my gut instincts all my life to survive."

"Perfectly understandable, especially given your choice of profession … sellin' drugs."

Trick turned to face Chevy. "How do you know about that?"

"No secret." Chevy turned both palms upward. "Word is ya made a lot a dough before ya got locked up. Still have a lot stashed somewhere."

"You heard wrong. All the money I made back then is gone." Trick tightened his right hand. "Like trying to hold onto a fistful of sand."

"I can understand ya wantin' to have people think you're broke. Otherwise ya might have 'em followin' ya 'round, hopin' to get their hands on it. But, hey, 'nuff about that for now." Chevy gulped down his drink and rattled the ice toward Bert. "Probably have a million questions."

"For argument's sake, let's say you're my real father. Who is my mother? Where is she? Why did I grow up alone?"

"Your mom, sorry to say, is gone." Chevy threw a twenty-dollar bill on the bar. "Dead."

"Dead? Of what?" Trick surveyed Chevy's greasy engineer boots. "What was her name?"

"Sally. Sally Smith. Yeah, Hodgkin's took her a while back. Good old gal, Sally. Pretty too. Don't know what she ever saw in a hotrod hooligan like me. Drinkin' and fightin' … fightin' and drinkin'."

Chevy picked up his fresh drink, swirled the ice with his finger and took a sip. "Sorry for abandonin' ya but I was in trouble with the law back then. It was either go to jail or go in the Army. Never had a chance to marry Sally. Didn't even know she was pregnant when I shipped off to boot camp." Chevy pulled a Lucky Strike from his pack on the bar and struck a match. "She was only sixteen at the time."

Trick sat silent for several moments, rubbing his forehead. "Krupnik. That's Polish?"

"Yep. Polish and proud of it." Chevy waved his cigarette as he spoke. "You should be too, boy."

"Always thought I looked more Irish than anything else." Trick glanced across the bar at his reflection.

"Well, Sally was Irish some, I suppose."

"I've got to digest all this. And I'm real busy right now." Trick shot to his feet. "How do I get hold of you?"

"Wait, don't run off. Let me buy ya dinner. We could go over here to the Ground Round."

"Maybe some other time. I've got a lot to do." Trick rocked from his heels to his toes. "We'll talk. OK?"

"I tell ya I'm your father and ya want to leave? What's a matter with ya, boy? Ya get dropped on your head when ya were little? I been lookin' for ya for a couple decades and I finally find ya." Chevy talked with the cigarette in the corner of his mouth, one eye squinting from the smoke. "Doesn't that mean anything to ya?"

"Yeah, sure it does, of course but … I'm in an awkward spot. Shouldn't even have stopped here." Trick grabbed his cash off the bar leaving the coin change. "I can't explain but I'm under a lot of pressure, on a tight schedule. I'd be happy to get caught up in a couple weeks and figure out what's what."

"You're a peculiar one. Must've been raised by some queer folk. All right, run off. Do whatever it is that's more important than gettin' to know your own father." Chevy's long cigarette ash dropped on his pants. "Thought ya'd be as tickled as me."

"Look, this is a lot to take in. I always wondered what it would be like to meet my real parents … and … it wasn't like this," Trick's voice trailed off, his left hand never leaving his pocket.

"Take my number and call me. Hear? Soon as ya settle your nerves." Chevy's face tightened into a smarmy smile. He held out a bent business card. "I love ya, boy. Want to get to know ya."

"Yeah, sure." Trick took the grease smudged Krupnik's Service Station card and looked it over, avoiding eye contact. "OK, I'll call you in a few days."

Chapter 26

"I thought Pat would be here." Trick glanced around at his son's toys strewn about Ginger's living room carpet. "I haven't seen him all week."

Ginger turned her back to Trick and continued folding her lingerie. "His friend's mother took them to the show. He'll be back in a couple hours."

"Damn it. I've been super busy and I set this time aside to see him." He motioned with his hand toward the picture window. "And it turned out to be a beautiful day, seventy-one out there."

"Plans change," she said over her shoulder. "Should have called."

"Well, here. Take this anyway." Trick nudged Ginger on the back of her yellow tube top and handed her a folded stack of bills, keeping his left hand in his jacket pocket.

"What's this for?" She dropped the cash on the coffee table and continued folding and stacking her laundry on the couch. "You're caught up on child support and you already bought me a new car."

"This is for back support." Trick looked Ginger up and down and was concerned that she seemed to have lost even more weight in the past week. "For when I was away."

"I hope you don't think you can buy me back." Ginger bent over in her terrycloth shorts and picked up a see-through negligee from her laundry basket and hung it around her neck like a scarf. "None of this is for sale."

"Look, I'm trying to be nice here. Will you stop that for a minute?" Becoming annoyed and aroused at the same time, Trick continued, "Why do you have to make everything so hard?"

Ginger turned to Trick and raised her voice, "Oh, *I* make things hard? Are you serious? You left me with a two-year-old to raise by myself. You made things hard, Patrick. *You.*"

"I didn't leave you. They locked me up. I had no choice."

"Yes, you did!" Ginger screamed. "You made a choice to break the law. Making a lot of money was more important than your family. I didn't need expensive clothes and flashy cars." She threw a lacy lavender bra on the floor. "I needed you."

Trick's head dropped. "I ... I was trying to provide for you and Pat."

"Don't you know? Don't you remember me telling you back then ... over and over? We don't need all this," Ginger cried. "I would have been just as happy if you worked at a gas station and was home every night ... instead of running around all hours with scumbags like that goofy Bob and Eddie Starnes. Taking stupid chances."

"I wanted financial security for us." Trick stepped closer. "I didn't want to live week to week, always worrying about what would happen if I got sick or lost my job."

Ginger placed her fingertips to her chest. "You didn't do it for me and Pat. You did it for you." She poked at Trick. "Had to be a big shot. Where did it get you?"

"Look, I paid for my crimes. Lost nearly three years of my life. Quit punishing me already."

"You think Pat and I didn't pay too?" Ginger's lips quivered. "You know how difficult it was for us?"

"Being separated from you two was agony. The only thing that kept me going was knowing I would be with my family again when it was all over. Then I get divorce papers delivered to me … in prison."

"It wasn't an easy decision. But now I know I did the right thing." Ginger shook her head. "Soon as you get out, you're right back to your old tricks."

"It's more complicated than that. You don't know. Look, tell Pat I'll try to get by to see him tomorrow."

"No. If you're coming to see him, make it definite, or forget it." Ginger wiped a tear away with the back of her hand. "I'm not going to let you hurt him any more than you already have."

"All right, all right." Trick put his hand on her bare shoulder. "You been to a doctor?"

"Going to see him in a few days." Ginger took his hand from her shoulder. "I think you should leave now."

"Yeah. I'll go." Trick felt her hand slip from his. "But there's something I want to talk to you about next time I see you. Really weird," he said, heading for the door.

Chapter 27

"Have a seat ... anywhere," Bob said with a sweeping hand motion.

Trick looked around the small kitchen in Bob's trailer home. Felines occupied every available seating area. He counted ... four, five cats. Two more crept in while another exited through a clear plastic trap door. Trick stepped over a Calico with a Hitler moustache, then brushed an American Shorthair from a red vinyl chair. "I'm a little out of touch. Who do you see about getting a heater these days?"

"Heater? You mean a gun? Who are you, Jimmy Cagney?" Bob picked up a gray kitten by the scruff of his neck, pulled it close and nuzzled it. "What do you need a gun for?"

"Never the fuck mind. You know someone or not?" Trick felt queasy from obnoxious odors permeating the air. "Obviously, I can't go to a gun store, got a Class X felony on my back. I can't legally own a gun."

"You never shot anyone." Bob looked up from the green eyed kitten. "Did ya?"

Trick stared at Bob. It was not a look that spoke of patience.

"All right, yeah, I know a guy." Bob crossed his feet on the kitchen table, accidently knocking over an open box of Meow Mix, sending his menagerie scrambling for the morsels. "What're ya lookin' for?"

"A revolver. Something that's not going to blow up in my hand." Trick formed his right hand into the shape of a handgun. "Something that's going to hit what I'm aiming at."

"Yeah, gotcha. I'll make a call for ya. Make an introduction. But I don't want to get in the middle of things. Know what I mean?"

"Pick up your phone," Trick said, waving his thumb. "I'm not talking about next week."

Bob got up, stepped over one of the many litter boxes scattered about and took the phone from the wall receiver. "What did you say you were gonna be aimin' at?"

"Dial." A Bengal kitten resembling a miniature leopard walked across the kitchen table like he owned it, put his face within an inch of Trick's and stared into his eyes. "Now."

After punching in the numbers, Bob took the phone by its long curly-cue cord into the living room while Trick watched the gang of cats wander around the kitchen, jumping up and down off surfaces as though playing a feline version of king of the hill.

Bob re-entered the kitchen, reminding Trick of one of the cats, a bigger, rounder one with a Cheshire grin. He hung up the phone, picked a bit of Meow Mix from the kitchen table and popped it in his mouth. "My guy's gonna call you. I gave him your number at the condo."

"What did you do that for?" Trick jumped to his feet. "I don't want some gun runner knowing where I live."

"Whadja expect?"

"I expected you to get the ball rolling, put me on the phone with him or get me a number. Damn. When's he going to call? I've got a million things to do. Can't be hanging around the condo waiting."

"Do ya a favor and ya complain." Bob lifted his leg and farted loudly.

"Damn, Bob. It smells bad enough in here already." Trick waved his hand. "Call him back. Tell him anything. Say you gave him the wrong number. Let me talk to the guy."

"Not gonna happen. I'm not callin' him back. You'll make me look stupid." Bob scratched his spiky dark mullet and burped, sounding like a bullfrog in spring. "This's the way he does things."

"OK, what's his name?" Trick headed for the door, holding his nose as one of the cats relieved itself in a litter box that was already in need of cleaning.

"Don't know his real name, goes by Sun Bin. He'll call you sometime tonight."

***

Trick parked further away than usual in the condo complex and looked around for Starnes and Moogie, or worse yet, his south-of-the-border tormentors. He let himself in the back door of the building and entered by the kitchen door. After closing the living room drapes of the first floor condo, he went back to the kitchen and poured a few fingers of Jack Daniel's into a rock glass. He changed his clothes and sprayed on some Aramis cologne, feeling as though he still smelled like ammonia from Bob's cats.

Sitting on the carpet, sipping his sour mash and leaning against the couch, Trick dozed off. In the grips of a nightmare about being surrounded by banditos with machetes in the Mexican desert, he stirred when he heard muffled voices. Disoriented, he blinked a couple times and saw shadows on his drapes.

"These drapes were open before," the familiar sounding voice travelled through the wall-unit air conditioner. "I'm sure of it."

No mistaking, Trick thought. It was Moogie's voice followed by Starnes saying, "He might be in there." Trick crouched down and made his way to the bedroom just as the phone rang loudly. "Not now," he thought, picking up the phone from the nightstand.

Trick didn't say anything; he held the phone to his ear until he heard, "This Trick?"

"Yeah, it's me," Trick answered, keeping his voice low, "you Sun?"

"Affirmative. Where do you want to meet?"

The voices and shadows moved to his open curtained bedroom window. Trick crouched next to his bed and whispered loudly, "There's a place, Juke Box Saturday Night, 159th and Laramie."

"Yeah, I know, Oak Forest. I'll find it. But I can hardly hear you. Speak up."

"Sorry, I got laryngitis." Trick glanced at the illuminated clock on the nightstand. "Give me an hour."

Sun Bin asked, "What do you look like?"

"Five eleven, hundred seventy-five, dark blond hair. What about you?"

"How many Chinese guys are gonna be there?"

"Oh, yeah. Gotcha."

Trick sat in the silence of his bedroom for forty-five minutes, hoping that Starnes and Moogie got tired of waiting around. He crept to his back door, cracked it open and glanced around. The coast looked clear so he jogged to his car and drove to Juke Box Saturday Night. He walked under the front end of a 1957 Chevy mounted over the entrance and into the 1950s and 60s music bar. Trick made his way through the large, dimly lit room. At the far end of the rear bar was a short but rough looking young man of Chinese descent in a silvery silk suit with a white patch taped over one eye.

Trick walked straight to him, nodded and pointed at his drink. "Can I get you another?"

Sun Bin shook his head no and replied, "Your voice problem cleared up quick."

"Comes and goes. Where do you want to do this?"

"Outside, in the van." Sun downed his tall red drink and wiped his wispy black moustache with a purple silk pocket square.

They walked through the dimly-lit rear parking area and up to a white van that was adorned with Chinese and English lettering for a noodle company. The van was running with its lights off and Trick was surprised when Sun opened the sliding side door. It revealed two more Asian men sitting across from one another at a small round table, playing a board game he wasn't familiar with.

The man with his back to the rear of the van had a large stiletto in a sheath, belted across his wide chest. The knifeman got up and said, "Sit here," before moving out of view behind him. Trick sat on the small folding chair, suddenly feeling caged. The man sitting across from him wore a black fedora with a white hatband. At first, he appeared to be in his twenties, like Sun. But he seemed to age a couple decades when he removed his green tinted glasses and spoke in a commanding sing-song accent, "You copper?"

"Me?" Trick brought his fingers to his chest. "No, no. I just got out of prison a couple weeks ago."

"Give me wallet," the man in the fedora commanded.

Looking to Sun, who was crouched on one knee, Trick raised his eyebrows as if asking an unspoken question.

"Give Laoban the wallet. He needs to know you're not with law enforcement." Sun flashed a quick staged smile revealing a gold tooth. "Go on, relax. He's not going to rob you. As long as you're who you say you are, you'll live another day."

Trick removed his wallet from the inside pocket of his lambskin blazer and handed it over to the hat-wearing man in charge.

Laoban removed Trick's driver's license and tossed the wallet onto the table. "Patrick Halloran. Irish." He looked up at Trick again. "I knew a Halloran in New York. Ran heroin from Malaysia. You know?"

"No, never been to New York."

"I not ask where you been. I ask you related."

"Not that I know of." Trick shook his head. "No."

"Where you go prison? What for?"

"Well, I started out in Cook County, after that Joliet, then I got shipped to Vandalia. Went in on a cocaine beef." Trick picked up his wallet and said, "I'll take that license."

The knifeman behind Trick moved close enough that he could feel his hot breath on the back of his neck.

"Maybe you get busted again. Want to set me up to reduce your sentence." Laoban's voice took on a menacing tone, "Huh? You wear wire?"

The man behind Trick reached around with his knife and in short order sliced two buttons off his shirt. He pulled Trick's shirt open, revealing only his brown-haired chest.

"Look." Trick hated the unexpected quiver in his voice. "I'm not a cop." He looked to Sun. "Ask Bob. He'll vouch for me. You think he'd send me to see you if I was a cop?"

"Bob is a piece of shit," Sun spoke up. "I'd slice his throat and set him on fire for fun. His only worth to us is moving heroin."

"All I'm looking for is a gun. A revolver. That's it. I'm not looking to get in the arms business or anything else."

"What you do with gun? You just get out of jail. If you caught, it parole violation." Laoban crossed his fingers across his chest and scrutinized Trick's face. "They ask you where you get gun. What you say?"

"I'll say what I always say to the cops ... nothing. I'm not a rat. When I got busted I kept my mouth shut and did my bit." Trick stood, hoping to leave without any trouble. "What I do with a gun's my business."

After an uncomfortable silence, Laoban said, "I just fuck with you, my man." The three Chinese men laughed. "If you rat, we just kill you and family. Sit down, Irish," Laoban continued, holding out Trick's driver's license.

Trick snatched it, sat back down and stared at Laoban straight-faced. "What've you got for me?"

Laoban opened an ornately painted wooden box that sat on the table next to him. He removed a Ruger .357 Magnum and pointed it at the roof. "You OK-Joe. I hear good things about you on street," he said, setting the gun on the table between them.

"You heard about me?" Trick said, with surprise in his voice. "Why did you fuck with me like that?"

"I need to see for myself, look in your eyes, if you man of rock or paper." He reached across the small table, grabbed Trick's forearm, nodded in approval and said, "Gun business not important. I need man in southwest suburbs to move product for me. Sun, give Trick new shirt. Large."

Sun reached into a bag and pulled out a neatly folded silk shirt wrapped in a paper band with Chinese lettering. Sun handed it to Trick and said, "Here. Sorry about your shirt but I think you sweated it up pretty good anyway." The Chinese men laughed again.

"I'll let you know about the other thing," Trick said diplomatically. He opened the cylinder of the Ruger and spun it, counting six empty bullet chambers. "Right now I've got a problem … six of them." Taking an educated guess at the street price, Trick held out a folded stack of twenties. "Two hundred?"

"For you, one eighty." Laoban handed Trick a small carton. "I throw in box of bullets. You give me answer about important powder business. One week. Sun call you."

Chapter 28

Trick brought a steak knife, thumbtacks and Super Glue into the condo bedroom and knelt in front of the smoke-mirror covered wall. With each mirror being one foot square, he carefully worked the blade under a corner mirror on the lowest row. He cautiously maneuvered the knife further under and side to side. After removing the mirror, he glued a thumbtack onto each corner on the backside. He then used the serrated knife to cut a hole in the drywall about eight inches around, giving the glue time to dry. Next to him sat the $50,000 he robbed from the drug deal between Rebel and Beasley. He took stacks of rubber-banded cash and put them through the hole, reaching in and piling them up behind the wall. After he was through, he pushed the mirror back using the thumbtacks to hold it in place, then cleaned up the telltale drywall residue. Trick grabbed a light jacket and headed out the door into the warm Indian summer weather, driving the short distance to Ginger's apartment.

"You're early," Ginger said, opening her door. "Pat doesn't get home for another ten minutes."

"I wanted to talk to you first," Trick said, brushing past her, "about something important."

"I already told you; forget about us getting back together." Ginger lit a cigarette, then coughed.

"No," he said, with a wave of his hand. "It's about something else." The calming scent of a lit vanilla candle took Trick back to earlier days with

Ginger and he absentmindedly removed his left hand from his jacket pocket. "I don't have anyone else to talk to."

"Oh my God!" Ginger exclaimed, dropping her lit cigarette on the carpet. "What the hell happened to your finger?"

"Oh, that." Trick looked at his bandaged finger, trying to act nonchalant. "It was an accident. I was walking down the street, minding my own business when this huge Doberman attacked me." He slid his hand back into his pocket. "He only bit off a little bit."

"What? Oh no." She picked up her cigarette, rubbed her bare foot over the scorch mark and studied Trick's face. "First it's your nose, now it's your finger. What's going on with you ... really?"

"Nothing." Trick looked out the picture window and studied the multicolored leaves, avoiding eye contact. "Nothing's going on."

"Well, trouble seems to follow you around and I don't want it touching Pat."

"I would never let anyone or anything hurt our boy. I'd give my life to protect him." Trick expelled a lungful of air. "I got to tell you about something. I met a guy in a bar. He claims to be my father."

"No! What's his name? What's he look like?"

"Name's Stanley Krupnik. A little taller than me, about six foot. Thick, dark graying hair. Good looking, kind of. I don't know, late forties maybe. Blue eyes like me. Otherwise, I don't see any resemblance."

"Did he say anything about your birth mother?"

"Yeah." Trick wrinkled his brow. "Said she died."

"Oh, I'm sorry."

"It's all really weird." Trick shook his head. "Don't know what to think. I need to see some kind of proof."

"Well, yeah, of course." Ginger looked around the room then tapped cigarette ash into her open palm. "But how do you feel about it?"

"I'm not sure. I got mixed feelings. On one hand, I always wanted to meet my parents but something about this … I don't know, doesn't sit well with me."

"So, you're saying you don't trust this guy. No surprise. You don't trust anyone." Ginger took a drag and exhaled smoke from round, pursed lips. "I don't know what to tell you. Something you'll have to figure out for yourself." She paused and pointed at Trick, raising an eyebrow. "But don't let him meet Pat unless you're one-hundred percent positive."

"Of course. Wait, that sounds like him now." Trick heard footsteps coming up the apartment stairs and opened the door for Pat. "Hey, pal. Good to see you."

Pat read his mother's serious expression and frowned, sensing the heavy mood in the room. "Are you and Mommy fighting again?"

"No. Mommy and me were just talking about how much we love you." Trick called to Ginger as she doused her cigarette and ashes in the toilet. "Right, Mommy?"

"Righty right." Ginger walked up to Pat and knelt on one knee, pulling him close. "Daddy's going to take you to Chuck E Cheese." She kissed Pat, then stood facing Trick. "Well, good luck with that thing."

"Yeah. I'll figure it out." Trick looked her up and down. "Thanks for having some clothes on today."

"Oh, real funny." She motioned with her thumb toward the door. "Scram."

Driving west on woodsy 143rd Street, Trick admired the changing leaves. He wished for a change in himself but felt like he was in emotional limbo. He thought of the way so many men in prison are frozen in time emotionally, while girlfriends and wives on the outside go on with their lives and continue to change and evolve. And now that he was out, he was still in limbo, unable to move forward. He knew it was unrealistic to date or try to develop a new relationship while dealing with the dangerous situation he was in. He hoped he could pull off a miracle and get the Mexicans and Starnes paid off and get away from the drug business altogether. Then maybe, he could move on with his own life.

Chapter 29

Trick dropped a quarter into the payphone at the Clark gas station on Ridgeland Avenue and Route 83. He punched in the numbers and heard, "Bob's Butcher Shop, no one beats my meat."

"Yeah, that thing we talked about." Trick ignored Bob's tired gag. "Meet me at Cattle Company."

"Like when?"

"Like fifteen minutes or soon as you can." Trick hung up the scuffed black phone without another word.

He headed north on Ridgeland and pulled into the Chicago Ridge Mall parking lot on the west side of Sears. He walked through the store and came out the east entrance. Continuing through the parking lot straight to the Cattle Company steakhouse, he took a seat at the sparsely filled bar and ordered a Perrier with a lemon wedge.

Bob strolled in several minutes later wearing a beat-up, pinstriped suit, a tight fitting Bruce Springsteen t-shirt barely covering his big belly, sandals and a Panama hat, hiding the top of his exaggerated mullet.

"That's what I like about you, Bob, always inconspicuous." Trick picked the lemon wedge off the napkin, squeezed it into his sparkling water and dropped it in.

"What'chu talkin' 'bout, Willis," Bob chuckled, looking pleased with his own low-level wit. He pointed at Trick's bandaged finger. "Talk about me bein' conspicuous. What about you? Looks like you fingered a mummy."

Trick swung his stool around and leaned back on his elbows. "So this guy, your other connection. You know him a long time?"

"Yeah, man. He's big time. Doesn't fool around with anything under a kilo."

"I'm in the market for two kis." Trick felt phantom pains from his missing fingertip and reached for his bottle of Vicodin. "Damn, I hate meeting new people. I need to know, one-hundred percent that this guy's OK. Gotcha?"

The pretty, mid-twenties bartender put down the glass she was polishing, walked over to Bob and asked, "What can I get you?"

"Gimme a double Sambuca, neat, three beans. And bring me an order of mozzarella sticks, pronto. See this dollar?" Bob waved a bill in the air. "I got more of 'em in my pocket for you little lady if you get that fried cheese out to me real quick." Bob waited until she was out of range and continued, "This dude's connected, man. That's how he gets the deals."

Trick turned around and poured the rest of his bottled water into the large glass of ice. "I especially don't like getting too close to the Outfit."

Bob stroked his scraggly black goatee. "Quit fuckin' worryin'. He's not a made-guy, he's an associate. But in real tight with the big goombas."

"What's his name?" Trick washed down his first pain pill of the day.

The bartender placed a cocktail napkin in front of Bob and set his drink on it. "Your mozzarella sticks will be up soon. Anything else, guys?"

Bob shook his head and waited for the bartender to walk away. "Gene. I heard his real name's Hale but he goes by Ciccone, Gene Ciccone. From around Midway." He motioned northeast over his shoulder with his thumb. "Over by there."

"Go ahead and get the ball rolling," Trick said out of the side of his mouth, "then give me a call. Don't say any more than you have to over the phone. Let's set up the place to meet right now. Less said later the better."

"He owns a piece of the Baccarat, you know, on 79th. Probably be OK if we meet there."

"I know the place." Trick poked at the floating lemon wedge with his straw. "Greeks, right?"

"Yeah, but Ciccone owns a piece off the books. Havin' a silent partner with mob ties is good for biz. Less problems with deliveries, or yahoos comin' in to make trouble. And God forbid someone tries to rob the joint. They'd hunt 'em down and torture 'em."

The bartender returned with Bob's order. "Was that quick enough for you?"

"Perfect." Bob pushed his hat back, licked a five-dollar bill and stuck it to his forehead. "Go ahead, sweet teats, that's all yours."

She rolled her eyes and started walking away.

Bob called to her with the five still on his forehead, "Do these things have cholesterol?"

"I don't … I can check for you."

"That's all right. I love cholesterol." Bob turned his attention to Trick. "You know they put that stuff in food to make it taste good?"

Trick just shook his head.

"Wait, little lady," Bob said loudly as the bill dropped from his head onto the bar. She walked back and he asked, "Do you ever wear panties with little ducks on 'em?"

She dropped the practiced smile and put her hands on her hips. "What? That's none of your business."

"I was just wonderin'." Bob wiggled his tongue at her. "Do you ever pet the ducks?"

"You jagoff." She spun around and walked away.

"Why the fuck do you pull that shit?" Trick looked at Bob incredulously.

"What?" Bob chuckled and straightened up. "I'm just being friendly. Makin' with the jib-jab. I like to brighten people's day."

"Do me a favor, don't brighten mine." Trick reached for a cheese stick. "I'll try one of those."

"Uh uh, wait." Bob put his hands together in prayer. "Gotta say grace first." Bob cleared his throat and called out, "Oh, Jesus. I'm so damn hungry and this bounteous meal smells heavenly. Can't wait ta dig in. So, without further ado ... uh ... say hi to your dad. Amen."

"What the hell kind of grace was that? You didn't thank anyone, or humble yourself to God in any way." Trick frowned, looking at Bob sideways. "Say hi to your dad?"

"He knows what's in my heart." Bob grabbed a mozzarella stick and dipped it in the marinara sauce. "Go ahead, dig in."

"No, that's OK. Knock yourself out. I'm out of here." Trick swirled the ice in his Perrier then took a long sip. He looked around and said quietly, "When you give me the day over the phone, say it's for the day after. I'll know. Make the time two hours after the real time. If I'm not home, leave it on my answering machine."

"I know the drill," Bob said with a mouthful of food.

"First, I need a price. Second, it has to be pure. See what you can find out."

"I'll put my ear to the ground."

"Good, good." Trick stood to leave.

"Then I'll get up, wash my ear off and make a couple phone calls."

"Yeah, right. You do that, Bob." Trick left enough cash to cover his drink plus a healthy tip for the bartender's trouble. He glanced over at her and smiled but she shot him a dirty look.

Trick headed toward the exit and didn't look back as Bob called out, "Later, tater!"

Chapter 30

After making his rounds for the night, dropping off premeasured amounts of cocaine and collecting cash, Trick stopped for a drink at the Godfather Lounge on 111th Street. Sitting at the bar, memories of better days with Ginger and Pat from 1981 came flooding back. He ordered a second Chivas Regal and saw something that jolted him.

Chevy, dressed in an expensive looking suit and tie, walked in the door and straight up to Trick with a big grin on his smoothly shaved face. "How are ya, son?"

Trick's face tightened into a squint. "What are you doing here?" he asked over the music and loud conversations coming from all around. "You following me?"

"Naw. Saw your car in the parking lot." Chevy plopped into the seat to Trick's left. "Thought I'd stop in and say hi."

"You know what kind of car I got?" Trick noticed not only Chevy's freshly cut and styled hair but his ample ear hair was neatly trimmed away.

"Sure. I know a lot about you. Been doin' my homework." Chevy patted Trick's shoulder. "That's a good thing. Right?"

"Well, I don't know. It's a little creepy to tell you the truth," Trick answered, looking straight ahead. "You come here much?"

"I stop in once in a while when I'm in town. Come here to give these horny old divorcées a thrill up their thighs," he said, throwing his head back in an open-mouth guffaw.

"Yeah, I bet," Trick said, straight-faced. "That's a nice suit. I know quality."

Chevy nodded and placed clean, manicured fingers on Trick's cash and pulled it closer. "Put your money away. It's no good when I'm around. I'm loaded, kid."

"You're loaded? Why the dirty work clothes the other day? Krupnik's Service Station?"

Chevy removed a metal tube from his inside suit coat pocket and unscrewed the top. "Oh, that's just a hobby. Love foolin' around with cars, especially Chevys." He tapped a cigar from the tube. "I don't need to work, but I think every man should have a livelihood. Shows character."

"You not only look different, you sound ... I don't know, more polished or something." Trick pushed an ashtray toward Chevy. "Who's the real you?"

"I'm like a chameleon, boy. I become whatever I touch." Chevy took a cigar cutter from another pocket and snipped the tip. "When I'm in Monte Carlo at the roulette tables, you'd think it was Sean Connery sittin' there." He pulled a silver lighter from yet another pocket and lit his cigar, turning it as he held the blue flame under it.

Trick read H. Upmann on Chevy's cigar band and remembered it was the same brand JFK used to smoke. "So, how'd you make your dough?"

"After I got outta the army, I took a real estate class on the G.I. Bill." Chevy blew a smoke ring that spread out, becoming larger and uneven as it headed in Trick's direction. "Struggled at it for a while, then began movin' some houses. Later, started pickin' up some fixer-uppers. Eventually, I became a general contractor and built a lot of apartment buildings. I'm retired now at forty-nine. Live off the income from my properties."

"Sounds great." Trick patted the bar. "But, what's this proof you have that says you're my real dad?"

"Got all the paperwork in a safe deposit box in Indianapolis. Drivin' out there in the morning to pick it up. Be back with it tomorrow night." Chevy's demeanor turned authoritative. "That soon enough for you?"

"Sure, sure," Trick said, letting down his guard and actually feeling good about the situation. "I don't know what to say. Just want to be sure, that's all. Know what I mean?"

"Of course I do. You should be careful, especially 'bout somethin' important as this. I wouldn't expect anything less, not from any kid I brought into the world."

"All right," Trick responded. Cigarette smoke hung in the air as the bar became more crowded while they talked. "Glad you understand."

"Hope I'm not bein' too nosy." Chevy motioned toward Trick's left hand. "What happened to your finger?"

"That's a private matter, rather not talk about it. Not right now anyway." Trick moved his conspicuous looking hand to his leg under the bar. "Let's keep it light."

A burly guy with a black handlebar moustache pushed his way between the two of them, put his cigarette out in Chevy's ashtray, then disappeared back into the crowd without a word.

"Sure. I understand. You need a little time to get to know me." Chevy tossed his cigar in the ashtray. "Hey. Let's say we get outa here and go somewhere more private we can talk."

Trick sat silent for several moments, then replied, "I suppose we could go back to my place."

"Perfect." Chevy rubbed his hands together. "How 'bout I follow you over there?"

***

After a couple more drinks and conversation, Chevy said, "Thanks for lettin' me stay over. No sense in goin' back to the hotel tonight. I'll head out early for Indianapolis, turn around and come right back with all the paperwork."

"Why don't you take my bed?" Trick stood and motioned toward the bedroom. "I'll sleep on the couch."

"No, no, I insist. You sleep in your own bed. I'll be just fine right here." Chevy sat deep in the sofa with his stocking feet on the coffee table. "Besides, I get up real early. Like to go out for coffee. Then I'll hit the road."

"I've been running for a couple weeks with barely enough sleep. So, don't wake me. Got a lot to do tomorrow." Trick settled back on the lounger and finished his drink. "I can't get over all this," he said shaking his head. "Always wondered what my real dad would be like. And here you are sitting in my living room."

"How 'bout one more?" Chevy got up and took Trick's glass from his hand. "You sit there and relax. I'll get the next round." Chevy returned from the kitchen a few minutes later and handed Trick a fresh drink and clinked glasses. "I can't tell you how wonderful it is to get to know you. I want you to come out and visit me at my winter home in Malibu."

Trick sipped his drink, listening to Chevy go on about a mint condition 1957 Bel Air he had back in

California. His lids got heavy and Chevy's face became dim as though dark clouds were rolling into his living room. Chevy's mouth was moving but the words were muffled and seemed to be coming from a deep well. Trick fought to stay awake and tried to speak but couldn't get his mouth to co-operate.

**

Trick shot up in bed from a bad dream, the same nightmare he had been having since he got out. In it, he was back in prison, in yet another confrontation or dangerous situation. He didn't remember going to bed. His mind was foggy and he was fully dressed. Looking at his watch, 7:53 am, he realized he must have slept several hours straight, the most he had in the last couple weeks. Walking to the living room, he noticed the bathroom door was open. Chevy was already gone. He went back into the bedroom and pulled the mirror he rigged from the wall and put his hand through the hole, relieved to feel the pile of cash. He slid the bedroom closet door open and removed the shopping bag that contained his scale and cocaine. Everything seemed to be there, untouched.

Toweling off after his shower, Trick walked back into the bedroom to get dressed and noticed his keys and the watch his foster father gave him were gone from the nightstand next to his bed. His mind was still fuzzy and tried putting the pieces of the previous night together. Then he remembered the $33,000 he hid in the trunk of his car from last night's collections. Zipping up his jeans, he felt the sting of cool, damp morning air on his bare chest as he hurried to his car, relieved at least to see the Lincoln still parked where he left it. The car was unlocked so he hit the trunk button and walked back to inspect it.

Lifting the spare tire where he left the cash, he knew he had been had. Chevy wouldn't be coming back; he got what he was looking for. The keys were in the trunk, the money was gone.

***

Trick removed the business card for Krupnik's Service Station from his wallet, gulped some morning coffee and dialed the kitchen phone.

A bubbly female voice on the other end answered, "How can I help you?"

"Yeah, I'm looking for Stanley Krupnik. Chevy?"

"I can take a message."

"Is this Krupnik's?"

"No. This is his answering service."

"Yeah, big fucking surprise." Trick threw his coffee cup in the sink, shattering it. "Tell him Patrick Halloran called. Tell him … tell him I'll see him."

***

Trick drove to the Oak Forest address listed on the business card but noticed right away that the sign read Rizzo's Service, not Krupnik's. He got out of his car and started for the door when a lanky, Italian looking man walked out to meet him.

"I'm looking for Stanley Krupnik." Trick approached across the gravel lot. "They call him Chevy?"

"Oh, that guy. If you're looking for a car, he already pulled them off my lot."

"He doesn't own this place?" Trick held out the card Chevy had given him.

"Of course not. I let him park a few cars here on consignment." The man scrunched up his face reading the card then pointed his thumb at his chest. "This is my place."

Trick breathed in a combination of gasoline and decaying leaves from nearby Bachelor's Grove Cemetery. "You know where I can find this thief?"

"Nope. He came by yesterday and pulled a Camaro off my lot, that was the last of them." Rizzo motioned around the corner lot with a wrench in his hand.

"He leave you a number?"

"Sorry. Don't really know much about the guy." A customer pulled up to one of the Union 76 pumps. "Gotta get back to work, sport. If you need any service work done, let me know."

"He give you a forwarding address, anything?"

"Nope." Rizzo headed toward the pumps. "Can't help you."

Walking away, Trick crumbled the card in his fist. "First Joker, now Chevy," he muttered.

Chapter 31

Five days after being severed, Trick's finger still throbbed with pain as he steered with his right hand into the parking spot. He pulled the bottle of Vicodin from the pocket of his camel hair sport coat and flipped the top off with his thumb. Swallowing a pill dry, he got out of his car and watched an Oak Lawn ambulance roar by on 95th Street. He walked in the front entrance of The Rusty Nail looking for Bob a little past four in the afternoon. The local lounge and divorcée hunting ground was known for the smell of stale cigarette smoke and stale pick-up lines. "As long as I'm in The Rusty Nail, might as well try one," Trick called to Claus, the bartender.

"One nail, very rusty, it is," Claus replied.

Trick folded a five-dollar bill into the shape of a paper airplane and sailed it into the receiving hands of Claus who just set down his drink. Savoring the smoky flavor of the Scotch mingling with the sweetness of the Drambuie, Trick spotted Bob at the other end of the bar and carried his drink down to talk to him. "Bob, you hear anything from Ciccone yet?" Bob didn't answer, so Trick spoke louder, "Hey, man. What's going on? You don't look too good."

Bob's hanging head came up slowly and his bleary eyes focused on Trick. "Found out my girlfriend's been cheatin' on me."

"No." Trick took the stool next to Bob. "You know who the guy is?"

"Yeah." Bob looked around and spoke in tones just loud enough to be heard over the jukebox. "That dago son-of-a-whore, Joey DeBonarino."

"Oh, Joey the Boner. That's no big surprise." Trick swirled his drink and took a sip. "Who hasn't he screwed?"

"How could she do this? I don't know what's gotten into her."

"Well, obviously Joey DeBonarino."

"You prick." Bob grimaced and pounded his fist on the bar. "I'm really fucked up over this."

"OK, I'm sorry." Trick tried to suppress a smile. "Just can't resist a great straight line."

"Shit! I don't know what to do." Bob downed his Sambuca and rubbed his forehead. "I'm gonna kill that wop bastard."

"Your problem isn't Joey. If it wasn't him, it would probably be some other guy. You can't go around killing people. There's too many men in the world who'd screw your girl if they had the chance. Got to get to the root of the problem."

"Ah, bullshit." Bob lifted his glass for another sip but there was nothing but three coffee beans stuck to the bottom of the snifter. "Hey, barkeep. I'll have another, just like the other."

Trick raised his eyebrows, smirked and asked, "How many of those you have?"

"Lost track a couple hours ago." Bob reached into his pocket and threw more cash on the bar.

"You're going to get diabetes ingesting that much sugar."

Bob took a big gulp of his fresh drink and coughed out a coffee bean. "Gotta die of somethin'."

"That Joey's always screwing around on his wife." Trick heard giggles and turned his head to view a table of thirtyish looking ladies at a small table

212

nearby. They were gabbing with animated hands and sipping foamy drinks garnished with orange slices and cherries speared on miniature plastic swords. "But I'm not going be the one to tell her and end up in the middle."

"Yeah ... Joey's wife. That's one good lookin' lady, a bubble head but sweet ... and what a rack." Bob's head swiveled around like a gyroscope. "I know a way to fix him."

"What're you going to do?" Trick's light mood disappeared.

"Don't worry." Bob flashed a silly, crooked smile. "I got somethin' in mind."

"You better be careful. Joey may not be a real bad-ass but he always carries a shiv. He isn't someone to play games with."

Bob slapped his hand on the bar. "He was game to fuck my girl and now I'm game to play some games."

"You're not going to break the guy code and tell his wife, are you?"

"Nope." Bob drained his glass again. "It'll be good though." Bob leaned over and put his hand on Trick's arm, breathing licorice smelling alcohol on him. "And hey, the place for the meet with Ciccone's been changed. I'll let ya know."

Chapter 32

His mind racing, Trick got out of bed with only a few hours of sleep. After getting ripped-off by Joker and Chevy, and Bob late on payments, he knew there was no way he was going to come up with enough money to appease the Mexicans and not lose more body parts. He looked at his hands. It was bad enough he was missing part of a finger, he liked the rest of them just the way they were.

He walked to the bathroom and studied his face in the mirror. There was no trace of the black eyes and the bump on his nose wasn't going to be as noticeable as he thought. He searched the cabinet under the sink, took out Reggie's clippers and plugged them in.

"Good bye, old friend," he said to his reflection and slowly buzzed off his moustache. He examined his new face, then removed his sideburns too. Going through the clipper attachments, he picked one that he thought would do the job and trimmed his bushy hair down to approximately two inches all around. After lathering up his face and getting a close shave, he went to Reggie's bedroom closet and located a tweed newsboy style cap and tried it on. "That'll do," he said, looking in the closet mirror.

***

"I'm glad you're home." Trick walked in as Ginger leaned against the open door, looking tired. He let out a big breath, then removed his tweed cap and sunglasses.

"What in the world?" Ginger scrunched up her face, seeing Trick as she never had. "What happened to you?"

"Just thought it was time for a change." Trick rubbed his smooth face.

Pat ran into the living room, shouting, "Hi, Daddy," then stopped in his tracks with his mouth and eyes wide open.

"OK, let's have it." Trick ran his fingertips through thick freshly cropped hair. "What do you guys think?"

"Well, you do look younger." Ginger giggled. "I'll give you that."

"You look weird, Daddy." Pat fell down laughing, kicking his feet.

"All right, joke's over. Let me take you two to breakfast." Trick looked out the large picture window. "Get out of the area, take a ride to Indiana. What do you say?"

"Sorry. Petros is coming by in a couple hours to take me and Pat to Greektown."

"You're still seeing that Durante nose, olive picker?"

"Of course I'm still seeing him." Ginger coughed a few times. "We plan on getting married, soon as I get better."

"What is it you think you got?" Trick walked closer to the window and looked down at the street.

"Probably just the flu." Ginger rested against the wall.

"I hope you're right, but I got to tell you, your eyes are starting to look yellow and you're way too skinny."

"I just don't have an appetite and I'm tired all the time. I'm sure I'll kick whatever it is. Always do."

"I can't hang around." Trick glanced out the window again.

"What's with you? Why are you so fidgety?"

Trick knelt next to Pat. "Hey, pal. How'd you like to draw me a picture?"

"OK, Daddy." Pat got up and ran into his bedroom.

"Damn it." Trick rubbed his temples. "Just make sure you know where Pat is at all times. Don't let him out of your sight."

"Oh, no. Patrick, what did you do?" She stomped up to Trick, grabbed his lapel and slapped his face. "What have you done now? Is our son in danger because of you?"

"No." Trick grabbed Ginger's wrists. "Not if I can help it. I'll kill anyone who tries to harm him." Trick put on a brave face and tried to hide how afraid he really was. "Just don't let him play outside for a few days, till I figure things out."

Ginger cried and put her head on Trick's chest. "Why can't you stay out of trouble?"

Her knees buckled and Trick scooped her up in his arms with an ease that alarmed him. He laid her on the couch and knelt beside her. "When's the last time you ate?"

"I tried eating something last night but I threw up. Don't worry about it. I'm not your concern anymore. Petros'll take care of me."

"Just because we're not married anymore doesn't mean I'm not concerned." Trick's voice trailed off when he realized Ginger had suddenly dropped off to sleep. He stayed on the floor next to her, stroking her cheek and watching her breathe the way he did when they were married.

Pat entered the room a few minutes later and held out a crayon drawing of the three of them on a roller coaster. "Is Mommy going to get better soon?"

Trick took the colorful artwork and rubbed Pat's thick blond hair. "I sure hope so."

Chapter 33

Bob weighed an ounce of cocaine, then dumped it from the scale tray into a Ziploc. He drove to Field's Supper Club at 104th and Cicero and pulled into a spot behind the building at twilight, looking around for Joey DeBonarino's red Corvette. He tapped out a line of white powder from a vial onto the back of his hand and snorted it through a rolled up twenty-dollar bill. Bob sniffed a couple times, then pinched the bottom of his nose. He sighed and opened his eyes as Joey nosed his Corvette into a parking spot and flashed his brights before stepping out.

Bob licked the residue off his hand and hopped out of the car like a kid on too much Ovaltine. "So, Joey. Joey, my buddy," he said, walking up to greet him. "You got the cash on you?"

"Yeah. Right here." Joey pulled a folded stack of hundreds and twenties from the back pocket of his Lee stone-washed jeans. "Sixteen hunnert."

"You know you're the only one I sell an ozzie to for this price?" Bob handed over the cocaine. "I don't step on it either. 'Cause you're my trusted friend. Right?"

"Yeah, sure thing. Buddies." Joey extended his hand. "*Mio amico.*"

Bob gave Joey's hand a tap and locked eyes with him. "Stay out of trouble." Bob turned and walked back to his car.

Joey threw the ounce of cocaine in his trunk and watched Bob leaning against his old Caddy as he pulled away. The evil smirk on Bob's round face prompted Joey to head straight to the nearest payphone.

Trick picked up the condo phone. "Yeah, who is it?"

"Hey, yo, it's Joey. Joey DeBonarino. Zat you, Trick?"

"How did you get this number?"

"Reggie told me you were gonna be stayin' dere." Joey hopped from one foot to the other like he was walking on hot coals. "I was doin' things with Reggie till he quit. Now I'm goin' through Bob."

"Yeah." Trick didn't try to hide the annoyance in his voice. "So?"

"So, I know he's gettin' his stuff through you. He told me. I wanna cut out the middle man."

"I don't step on no one's toes, especially an old customer."

"Let me tell ya, dis guy's no one ta waste your loyalty on." Joey used hand gestures for emphasis even though he was on the phone. "If ya heard da shit he says 'bout you behind yer back."

"You've said too much already. I was just heading out the door. How soon can you meet me in the parking lot behind the El-Dorado?"

"You kiddin'? I'm right down da street."

Trick grabbed his supply of cocaine to be delivered that night and walked out the door into the cool dusk. He threw a paper bag full of ounces, half ounces, quarter ounces and 'eight balls' into his trunk and headed for the El-Dorado Restaurant up the street on the northwest corner. He pulled into the parking lot off the Midlothian Turnpike moments before Joey turned in from the Cicero Avenue entrance. There were four semitrailers and tractors parked behind the family-style restaurant so Trick used them as cover from passing traffic. Joey was experienced enough to know the moves and pulled close to Trick's Lincoln in the large gravel lot surrounded by trees to the north and west.

They both got out of their cars and instinctively looked around. Joey stuffed his hands in the pockets of his denim sport coat, his head bobbing like a Jack-in-the-box as he walked toward Trick. With the sounds of traffic and dinging from a nearby gas station in the background, Joey retorted, "Whadaya hear, whadaya say?"

"Got a lot of running around to do. No offense." Surrounded with the aromas of garlic and onion coming through the rear screen door of the El-Dorado, Trick shrugged and turned his palms upward. "But let's get to the part where you tell me exactly what you want."

"Cool your jets, Trickster. Been a long time." Joey extended his hand.

"Maybe not long enough." Trick ignored Joey's waiting hand. "Look, I already told you, I don't cross people in business. Always comes back to bite you on the ass."

Joey pulled a joint from behind his ear and fired it up with a long pull. He held it out toward Trick as he suppressed a lungful of the odiferous dried weed.

"You know I don't partake." Trick shook his head. "OK, you got my curiosity up. What's Bob saying?"

"I can't repeat it. You're gonna be pissed."

"I'll be pissed if you *don't* tell me," Trick said, raising his voice.

"OK, but don't kill da messenger. Bob said you were a punk in da joint. Did most of yer bit on yer knees." Joey took a drag off the joint. As he let the marijuana out of his lungs, he said raspily, "Said yer ass is so loose, every time ya fart ya shit yourself."

Trick glared at Joey. A rage started somewhere in his gut and slowly rose up his body and exploded out of his mouth. "Mother fucker! I'll kill that prick!"

Joey jumped back, dropping the joint on the stones at his feet. "Whoa, dude." He turned to the sounds of commotion and looked behind them. "What da fuck?"

Two squad cars and an unmarked gray Caprice pulled in off Cicero and flew at them, skidding to a stop and throwing gravel every which way. Joey picked up the joint and flicked it off his thumb with his middle finger, sending a tiny orange arc that burst into a small flicker several feet away. Four police officers and two plainclothes detectives piled out at the same time and converged on Trick and Joey.

"What's going on, boys?" one of the uniformed Crestwood officers asked, his hand on his holstered sidearm. "Smells like someone's been smoking some good shit."

"Don't say any more than you have to," Trick said to Joey out the side of his mouth.

An officer with a thick rust-colored moustache walked up uncomfortably close to Trick. "Any weapons or anything else in your pockets we should know about?" Not receiving an answer, he shoved Trick, then Joey toward the Corvette. "Up against the car. Hands on the hood."

A heavyset older officer, with a nameplate reading Officer Shadowsky, wheezed heavily when he yelled, "Spread 'em." He kicked Trick's legs further apart as he patted him down from behind. He went through Trick's pockets, throwing the contents on the warm hood of Joey's car. "If I cut my hands on any razor blades, I'll personally cut your balls off." Shadowsky moved on to Joey and threw an elbow into his kidney from behind sending the late-twenties drug dealer to his knees in pain. "Oh. Excuse me. Did that hurt, Joey? My daughter told me to tell you hello, if I should ever run into your low-rent Casanova ass."

Detective Frank Murray approached Trick and said, "Keep your hands right where they are." He turned to his new partner, Jimmy Garcia. "Meet Patrick Halloran. We know each other. Don't we, Trick? Yeah, I remember that Lincoln. See the bullet marks?" Murray waved a finger toward Trick's car. "I was with Oak Forest when we put 'Mr. GQ' here away a few years ago. Him and his buddy had to do it the hard way, turned into a gun battle." Turning his full attention back to Trick, Murray continued, "I don't know what you're up to but I could report you to your parole officer just for associating with a known felon like Joey the Boner here. Get you sent right back, lickity split."

Back on his feet with his hands stationed on his hood, Joey interrupted with, "Yous guys didn't suddenly appear because ya smelled pot from Cicero Avenue. Whadda ya want?"

Shadowsky barked, "What do we want, he asks. We want to lock your ass up for a long time. Take your *braciole* out of circulation till it's useless." He took both Trick's and Joey's keys and opened the trunk of the Corvette. "Well, well, looks like our tip was right." Shadowsky held up the ounce of cocaine Joey just purchased from Bob. "I'm buying first round at Murphy's Law. OK, let's check Halloran's car."

"Let me have Trick's keys," Murray said with a wave of his fingers. He snatched the keys out of the air and handed them to Trick. "Get out of here. We got what we came for."

"What're you doing?" Shadowsky yelled and

shook his fist. "He might be dirty!"

"You set me up?" Joey shouted as Trick walked to his car.

Trick got behind the wheel thinking about the several ounces of cocaine in his trunk and dropped his set of keys on the floor mat. He picked them up and steadied his right hand with his left to get the key into the ignition. He turned the engine over and put it in drive, praying the cops didn't change their mind. As he pulled away, his relief turned to dread. Something wasn't right. A lot of things weren't right. Why did the cops show up when they did? More importantly, why did Frank Murray let him go without checking to see if he was holding? As he pulled onto the Midlothian Turnpike heading west, he passed Bob, who was parked on the side of the road facing east, looking onto the El-Dorado parking lot with a wicked smile.

***

When Trick was through with his deliveries and pickups for the evening, he went back to the condo, quickly packed up what little he had and loaded it into his Lincoln Continental. A short time later, driving north on Western Avenue on Chicago's southside, Trick surveyed the multitude of used cars shining under florescent lights. He pulled into one of the used car lots and got out of his car with the title in hand. Less than an hour later, Trick drove away in a nondescript looking white Pontiac with temporary plates and his belongings in the backseat and trunk.

Parking behind the brick wall at the J.C. Motel at Southwest Highway and Harlem Avenue, Trick recalled the times he took Ginger there when they first started dating and couldn't keep their hands off one another. He went to the registry office and signed in under the name Harry Callahan. Slipping an extra fifty under the glass divider to the middle-aged man in a slicked up, 1950s jellyroll hair style, Trick appealed, "I don't have my driver's license with me. Are we cool?"

"Yeah, dad," the old greaser said, in a Southern accent with a lit Raleigh cigarette situated in the corner of his mouth. "We cool." He reached for the cash with a hand that bore a crude India ink tattoo of the ace of spades. "We very cool."

Trick dragged his tired body up the outside metal stairway to his room, unlocked the door with the oversized key, then flopped on the bed fully clothed. Hearing the muffled din of traffic from Harlem and an X-rated movie coming through the wall from the next room, Trick tried tuning everything out. But nothing could tune out his thoughts of the four Mexicans. He only had a fraction of the $277,000 he owed them but thought, if he could dodge them for another week, score two more kilos and sell it all in time, he might be able to come up with the money. Then he would only have Starnes to deal with. The lesser of two evils, but not by much.

Chapter 34

"Hey, what's with the new image?" Bob hopped out of his Cadillac with the radio blasting. "You look like a damn game-show host."

"Fuck you." Trick yelled at Bob. "Did you do that? You set Joey up?"

"Who me?" Bob laughed, dancing an awkward boogaloo, his ample t-shirted belly bouncing over the waist band of his hip-hugger jeans.

"I saw you, man." Trick grabbed Bob by the collar of his open jacket with both fists, forcing him to stand still. "I saw you parked by the El-Dorado with that pussy eating grin on your fat face."

"Let go of me! Don't ever put your hands on me." Bob shoved Trick off and backed away. "You think you're Mr. Scary Guy now that you been in the joint? I'm not afraid of you."

"I was holding! I could have gone back to prison for a long time!"

"I didn't tell you to start sellin' drugs again. Don't blame me if you get locked up. You got your own free will. I got mine."

"If I find out for sure you ratted out Joey, you're through in this business. Don't think I won't spread the word." Trick held out his hand. "Where's my money?"

Bob handed him a sealed envelope and got back in his car muttering something Trick couldn't make out. Trick hollered over the music, "What was that, Bob? Huh? There's some other shit we're going to straighten out when this deal's done."

***

"Sit the fuck down and don't touch anything on my desk," Oak Lawn Detective Sam Carlsbad ordered Bob. "What have you got for me? Better be something good this time. Otherwise you're gonna find your mangy ass sharing a cell with Big Dick Willie."

"Don't worry." Bob waved both hands. "I got plenty this time."

"Worry? Do I look like I'm worried?" Carlsbad leaned back in his padded office chair. "I'm not the one looking at twenty-five years. Regardless of what you have to say, I'm going home to my color TV and a cold bottle of beer."

"I can give you Trick Halloran wrapped up in a bow. Not just that, I got info on some psycho dealer named Barker. Now, I don't know his first name or where he lives but he works with a big black guy. Wouldn't be surprised if he hooked up with him in the joint." Bob picked up a clear acrylic paperweight with a horsefly inside of it.

"Put it down!" Carlsbad yelled. "You got a description of this Barker? You even know if that's his real name?"

"Well … no and no. But he's a bad mammer jammer. Tried to rip-off Trick. Whacked him on the head with a pistol. His partner robbed me and stuck me in a car trunk."

"Sounds like I'd be doing you and Halloran a favor by locking you up. You two tough guys are liable to get killed trying to be drug kingpins." Carlsbad slammed his palm on his desk, making Bob flinch. "Forget about this Barker for now. Give me some specifics on Halloran."

"First of all, he just changed his appearance. Cut his hair short, no moustache, wearin' a round snap-cap. He's drivin' a different car too, a white Bonneville with temp plates."

"Keep going," Carlsbad said, not looking up from taking notes.

"Here's the big thing, he's movin' some heavy product. Wants me to set him up with someone to buy two kilos from."

"Really?" Carlsbad's scowl turned to a grin. "You better not be bullshittin' or you can kiss your virgin ass g'bye. So long freedom, hello baloney sandwiches and lights out at ten."

"I'm not shittin' you. How 'bout I set him up with you guys to make the buy? He thinks he's coppin' from Gene Ciccone. Doesn't even know what Ciccone looks like."

"I'll do the thinking around here." Carlsbad threw his size twelve shoes up on his desk in Bob's face. "But that's not a bad idea. Yeah. Halloran and I never met." Carlsbad ran a hand over his short spiky hair. "Set it up for tomorrow night. Tell Halloran the deal's going down tomorrow or he'll have to wait a few weeks. I'll let you know the time and place in the morning. I want this guy *now.*"

"It's not that simple. Besides, I want somethin' in writin' givin' me immunity."

"Tomorrow! Get the hell out of here before I send your goofy butt over to County for the night. Just for the fun of it." Carlsbad grinned at Bob and patted his sidearm. "I'll say you went for my gun."

Bob jumped to his feet and stuttered as he strode out of the room, "I'm g-gonna get right on it, t-tonight!"

***

Trick felt groggy, something wasn't right. His eyes were heavy, felt like his lids were glued together as he slowly forced them open. Through blurred vision he saw something sparkling in the air, then movement and geometric shapes. As his eyes focused he realized the luminous object was a crystal chandelier, with people milling around tables beneath it in an upper-scale banquet room. He couldn't move and looked down to see his shirtless body chained to one of the round support pillars in the vast room. He knew everything had finally caught up to him. It was over. It was all over. He scanned the faces of guests standing around making small talk and filling their plates with shrimp, crab claws and steak tartare from long tables covered in white linen.

He viewed at least thirty people. The group included Starnes, Moogie, Bob, Joker, Todd Wickerstock, his parole officer Arthur Patoremos, Ginger, Petros, Collette, Chevy, Charles Brummerstedt in his wheelchair, Joey, even some of his teachers from grammar and high school. Occasionally, one of them would smile at him as they ate with their fingers, talking and laughing. Trick tried calling out, but only emitted unintelligible garble.

Then he noticed the four Mexicans strutting around with machetes and carafes of sangria. They walked up to him and one by one silently cut slices off his stomach, chest, shoulders and arms, putting them on their plates with the rest of the assorted meats. He looked around frantically for someone to stop them as he desperately tried to scream in pain. Blood ran down his body and saturated his tan slacks.

Starnes and Moogie were next. Brandishing silver steak knives, they walked up and shaved off more slices of skin. Starnes gave Trick one of his usual sneering expressions and said, "Got a tip for you in the last race. Don't put your money on Patrick the Dreamer. He's a longshot."

Trick's heart beat so hard he could barely breathe, the pain so excruciating he thought he'd pass out. One at a time they approached making small talk and hacking off bits of his body. Before taking his slice, his high school wrestling coach said, "You never tried hard enough. Might have made something of yourself."

Collette walked up next. She cut off one of his nipples and giggled, "You're like way old anyway. Might get ptomaine poisoning from this old piece of meat."

After Collette walked back to her waiting girlfriends, his former foster father, Charles Brummerstedt, wheeled up. He pulled up a bloody pant leg and carved off a piece of Trick's brown-haired calf. Trick thought he might vomit from the pain, then Charles said, "Remember your lessons, boy. A pound of flesh, 'tis mine and I will have it." He put the skin between his false teeth, blood dripping down his gray chin whiskers and wheeled away.

Ginger was last. "I suppose this means I won't be getting any more child support?" She unzipped his blood soaked pants, now completely red, took out his cock and began cutting.

Trick shot up in bed, covered in sweat, screaming the scream he couldn't in his sleep. His heart pounded like a jackhammer. He grabbed his fifth of Jack Daniel's from the motel nightstand and drank straight from the bottle. It was going to be another night in a long row without enough sleep. Using the remote, he clicked on the TV and scanned the channels, settling on *CBS News Nightwatch*. He got up and opened his suitcase, took out his scale, cocaine supply, Ziplocs and began weighing out his deliveries for later that day.

Chapter 35

"OK, I'm at a payphone now." Trick glanced around the tight metal-framed enclosure, surrounded by cigarette butts, candy wrappers, and dried gobs of spit on the acrylic windows, being careful not to lean against anything. "What's so urgent?"

Bob's raspy soprano voice sounded higher than usual as he excitedly explained, "The meet with Ciccone's on for tonight at the Oak Lawn Hilton, nine o'clock, room 1004. Got that?"

"Yeah, nine tonight, 1004. You're going to be there, right?"

"Uh, no." Bob cleared his throat. "Wait, yeah. I'll try to make it."

"I want you there," Trick's voice changed to a commanding tone. "Never even met this Ciccone before."

"All right, all right. I'll try to get there before you. Just go up and knock on the door."

***

Trick entered the Oak Lawn Hilton Tower at 93rd and Cicero with $70,000 he stacked in an old briefcase that he found in Reggie's closet. Smelling chlorine and feeling humidity from the indoor pool area, he paused and scanned the lobby, looking for anything out of place. Three casually-dressed men sat on chairs reading newspapers. Two of them peered up at him, then went back to their papers. Trick looked back as the automatic sliding doors opened with a swooshing sound. In walked four men in polyester suits and ties who headed straight toward the first floor bar. Apprehension tugged at him, pulling him back toward the door. He had the strong urge to abandon the deal but didn't have a plan-B. Checking his watch, he thought there was time for a quick drink and still be on time.

Walking into the upper-scale lounge, Trick had a feeling people were watching him and felt his neck and shoulders stiffen. As a two-piece husband and wife lounge act performed, he wondered if people were looking at him because he displayed nervousness or they were watching him because they were undercover officers. He walked to the bar and set the briefcase on the barstool next to him. Standing with an alligator loafer on the chrome foot rail, he pulled out a ten-dollar bill and waved it at the bartender.

The thirtyish, bosomy bartender sashayed up to Trick, running her hands down the front of her ruffled tux shirt. She pulled at the ends of her black clip-on bowtie and smiled. "What can I get you, sir?"

"Cuervo Gold, straight up," Trick spoke up, loud enough to be heard over the entertainers performing *Love Will Keep Us Together*. He watched her tight black shorts as she walked away, then noticed eyes darting at him from across the bar from two men in fresh barbershop haircuts. He wasn't sure if he was being paranoid but everyone looked like a cop to him that night.

Long false eyelashes batted at him when the bartender set a shot of tequila in front of him. "Would you like lime and salt?"

"Don't be silly," Trick said, waving his hand to the side. He downed the shot and set it down hard on the polished resin covered bar. "Hit me again."

A man in a silver Schwarzenegger *Commando* haircut and neatly trimmed moustache walked into the bar scanning faces, then walked out again.

When she returned with another shot, Trick asked, "Do you know that guy who just walked in and out of the bar?"

"What guy?" she asked, raising her dark penciled-in eyebrows.

Trick threw his head back and swallowed the ounce of booze in one gulp. "Never mind." He dropped the ten on the bar, walked back into the lobby and stood looking at the door. Breathing heavily, he glanced down at the briefcase and decided to leave. He walked into the parking lot and looked up to the tenth floor of the cylinder shaped hotel, then at his recently purchased Pontiac about thirty feet away. His watch read 9:04 as he made his way back to his car. Hearing the lock buttons pop up, he opened the door listening to the dings. He peered up again, studying the thirteen story building, the tallest in the area. The dinging was like an alarm telling him he had to decide, either run away and be a victim or face his problems. He couldn't stand the annoying dinging anymore and slammed the door. The effects of the tequila suddenly made him feel gutsy and he turned back to the hotel.

The doors parted and Trick reentered, ignoring the inner voice warning him of danger. His heart beat harder as he walked the circular hallway, located the elevators and pressed the button. As he waited, two men in suits passed slowly behind him. They paused, then kept walking. Clutching the briefcase to his chest, Trick rode the elevator to the tenth floor. Practically everything he risked his freedom for over the last two weeks was stuffed in the faux leather case.

He stepped out of the elevator, made his way around to room 1004 and knocked. The door swung open and Trick looked up at a man with a salt-and-pepper crew cut who towered over him. Behind him, sitting on the dresser, was a younger, thick-muscled guy with short, neatly parted hair.

"You're a little late. Thought you might have changed your mind." The tall man, in an inexpensive sport coat and open-collared shirt, stood back, allowing Trick to walk in. "You are Trick, right? Patrick Halloran?"

"Yeah, that's me." Trick craned his neck and entered. "You Ciccone?"

"I'm Sam. Ciccone works for me." The big guy shut the door and extended his hand. "You can deal directly with me from now on."

"Where's Bob?" Trick felt the vice-like grip and added, "Thought he'd already be here."

"We sent him out for some beer. He'll be right back." Sam motioned with his thumb. "This mope over here's my partner, John."

John hopped to his feet and shook Trick's hand. "We do a lot of business with Bob. Never screwed us and knows how to keep his mouth shut. He tells us you're someone that can be trusted."

"I never ratted on anyone." Trick glanced back and forth between the two. "Kept my mouth shut and did my own time when I got busted."

"That's what we want to hear," Sam bellowed. "You have it all with you? Seventy thousand?"

"Yeah." Trick opened the briefcase and held it in front of him. "You want to count it?"

John took the case, closed it and set it on the nightstand. "That's OK, we trust you. Bob wouldn't send someone stupid enough to try and rip us off." John glanced at Sam, then back to Trick. "We want to make sure we're on the same page. You're here to buy two kilos of cocaine, right?"

"Two kis, yeah. Where's the stuff?" Trick looked around the room. "You got it here?"

"Sit down." Sam motioned toward the bed.

John walked behind the bed, returned with a small suitcase and set it on Trick's lap.

Trick looked up at Sam and John standing next to him. He opened the suitcase and immediately knew something was wrong. Inside the case were two large Ziplocs filled with loose white powder. "What the hell is this?"

Sam's and John's demeanors suddenly changed. Both reached behind their backs and drew pistols that were hidden under their sport coats. Sam yelled, "Put your hands behind your head! You're under arrest!"

The hotel room door and the adjoining room door burst open simultaneously with three more men from each bearing down on him with guns drawn.

Trick felt his heart sink as he realized Bob had set him up. It was all over. His freedom, relationship with his son, everything was gone. "How could I be so stupid?" Trick berated himself internally. "What's going to happen to Pat?" he thought, looking down the barrels of pistols.

"You're lucky we're not the bad guys," Sam said with annoying glee, taking the suitcase containing the phony kilos of cocaine from Trick's lap. "You might be dead right now. I'm Detective Samuel Carlsbad. Patrick Halloran, you're under arrest for Intent to Purchase a Controlled Substance. I'll take your wallet."

Carlsbad instructed Trick to stand and put his hands behind him. He cuffed Trick, then pulled the car keys to his Pontiac from his leather jacket. Trick felt his stomach convulse when Carlsbad threw the keys to his partner and said, "Check out the car."

Carlsbad read Trick his rights and added, "We'd like to ask you a few questions."

Uniformed and plain-clothed officers walked in and out of the room getting a good look at Trick. They joked around looking very pleased with themselves while burning off adrenalin.

With handcuffs pinching his wrists, Trick walked to the window and looked down at the southwest corner of 95th and Cicero where the Lorelei Restaurant used to be, before the Oak Lawn tornado leveled it in 1967. His mind went back to younger days when he rode to the restaurant on his bicycle. After he swept up, the owner would let him sit at the counter and order a banana split. The only words that came out of Trick's mouth were, "I'd like to speak to a lawyer."

Dreading further bad news, there was nothing Trick could do but wait for the other shoe to drop. Several minutes later, John rushed back into the room holding a brown paper bag in the air. He laughed as he called out, "Jackpot!"

Carlsbad grabbed Trick by the collar of his jacket. "Halloran, looks like you're double fucked."

***

At the Oak Lawn Police Station, Trick couldn't remember his lawyer's number so he dialed his ex-wife's phone. "Ginger," he blurted out, "I need your help. Call my lawyer."

"Oh shit," Ginger answered, the disappointment in her voice painful to hear. "Are you kidding me?"

"Look up his number and tell him I'm at Oak Lawn. I need to talk to him as soon as possible."

"You're only out a few weeks and you're already

in jail. Oh, let me guess. Is it drugs?"

"Look, I don't need any lectures right now," Trick pleaded. "Please. Just tell him to get someone over here right away."

"And you wanted to get back together, have a normal life. This is how you were going to do it? Did you think about your son when you decided to deal again?"

An older uniformed officer walked up to Trick and yelled in his ear, "OK, time's up!"

"I've got to hang up, just …"

The officer pushed the receiver button down and grabbed the phone out of Trick's hand. "Let's go. Fingerprint and picture time. Did you want a comb and mirror, pretty boy? Those big bubbas are gonna love you over at County."

Chapter 36

His lawyer never showed up and Trick spent several hours in Oak Lawn lockup before he was transported to the infamous Cook County Jail the next morning. Trick dreaded what was ahead, processing at County, one of the roughest, most dangerous jails in the U.S.

Still in his street clothes, Trick was herded from one holding area to another at County with hundreds of others brought in that day, where they were evaluated physically and psychologically.

He hated the eyeballing from other inmates sizing him up, the fierce stares and intimidation tactics. He knew to look someone in the eye when being challenged but not get into a staring contest. He couldn't control this world, just do his best to get along and stay alive. Get the wrong person angry and you could get a shank in your ribs while being distracted.

"Hey, man." Trick turned to see a short, aggressive freckly white guy, who appeared to be a few years younger, barking at him. "What's your name?"

"Halloran," Trick replied, pushing his shoulders back and lifting his head. "What's up?"

"I'm Bulldog," he said in an overly practiced tough voice. "What're ya in for?"

"Drug charges," Trick replied reluctantly. "Cocaine."

"Stick with me and do everything I do and no

one'll fuck with ya." Bulldog's head bobbed when he spoke, causing his exaggerated rusty-colored pompadour to bounce too. "I'm with the Gaylords."

"This isn't my first time coming through here." Trick turned away. "I don't need protection."

"You look like a first timer." Bulldog smirked, rolling up his black T-shirt sleeve. "Like you're lost."

"I'm OK." Trick looked at Bulldog sideways. "I know the ropes."

"Stay close to me," Bulldog ordered, shooting challenging looks around, his body language overly aggressive and exaggerated.

***

Trick managed to ditch Bulldog when he had to stand in line for the sexually transmitted disease checkup. This was the part he hated most. After about forty-five minutes in line, it was his turn for the barbaric penis torture.

"Let's go," the man in a white coat, sitting on a stool in front of him, ordered, "take 'em down."

Trick unzipped his pants and pulled them down along with his boxers and stood for the examination. After having his testicles fondled, it was time for the intrusion. He wondered whether the man was an actual doctor or just some reasonable facsimile. The man in the white coat held Trick's penis so it faced straight toward him. Trick knew that the worse thing he could do now was flinch. It could lead to serious injury. The man shoved what resembled a thermometer inside his penis and pulled it back out. He remembered when he went through this procedure three years earlier. It was going to burn for a few days when he urinated.

When Trick ran into Bulldog again, he looked like a different person. His would-be protector appeared smaller and paler. The stern expression on his boyish face was gone, replaced with a look of defeat and fear, making him appear even younger.

"Halloran," Bulldog said in a trembling voice, visibly shaken. "I just vomited blood. The doctor said I'm having a nervous breakdown."

Trick walked away shaking his head. "Tough guy."

***

Trick stood naked with about fifty other guys, lined up along the cinderblock wall in a vast cold hallway, their street clothes in a pile behind them. He knew the drill, turn around, bend over, spread your cheeks and cough on order as the mountainous black guards filed passed. If they found someone keistering anything, they'd knock the hell out of you.

The guard captains' voice boomed, "Stand with your arms at your sides and both feet on the ground at all times. Do not fold your arms. Do not cross your legs. Do not speak unless answering a direct question from a guard."

As the captain continued, a thirtyish black guy to Trick's left absent-mindedly folded his arms in front of him. One of the guards immediately got in his face and shouted, "Drop your arms!"

Instructions went on for several more minutes and Trick cringed when the guy to his left forgetfully folded his arms again. The same guard, that warned him previously, busted the inmate hard over the head with his billy-club. The man went down with a thud, his head bouncing off the hard cold floor like a basketball. The guard stated matter-of-factly, "That's what happens when you don't follow instructions."

Facing straight ahead as ordered, careful not to move his body, apart from the heaving of his chest and direction of his eyes, Trick glanced down at the injured inmate. The man lay still except for involuntary spasmodic twitching. He was out cold. A pool of blood formed at his head which lay less than a yard from Trick's bare feet. As the jailhouse directions continued to boom off the gray walls of the corridor, Trick spied the blood forming a tiny stream and heading toward his left foot. He knew that moving away from it would mean the same brutal treatment so he stood at attention looking at the wall in front of him.

A few moments later, he glanced down to see the unwelcome body fluid a few inches away. He'd heard rumors that the new AIDS disease was carried through blood and saliva and that intravenous drug users were at greater risk from sharing needles. Trick saw the telltale track marks on the man's arms. The red stream was now less than an inch from his left foot. He carefully and slightly moved his foot away from the stream of crimson which continued creeping toward him. Standing still for a long time was proving tougher than it seemed and his lower back began to ache. With the dark red fluid dangerously close, he moved his left foot up against his right, making it even more difficult to stand with his weight less distributed. Again the blood gained ground and Trick felt he had no choice but to move both feet slightly closer to the young Puerto Rican man to his right when the guards were not watching him directly.

Trick heard commotion coming from the hallway to his left. A black trustee, in blue Cook County Jail clothing and white jacket, rolled a wheelchair up to the injured man. Trick couldn't tell if the prone inmate was alive or dead. Even the spasms stopped. The orderly in latex gloves, along with the head-cracking guard, scooped the limp man into the chair and he was wheeled away with his head bobbing to the side.

To his relief, Trick heard the captain of the guards announce, "Put your clothes back on."

Trick stepped over the tiny river of blood and turned around to retrieve his clothes. After everyone quickly dressed, they followed orders and proceeded to the next level of hell.

***

After Trick received his Cook County-issue clothing, his own things were put in a clear plastic zipper bag to be returned when and if he was no longer incarcerated. When a person walked into this jail, getting out alive was never guaranteed.

Groups of inmates were taken to various holding areas waiting to be assigned to divisions within the immense jail system which housed over 5,000 men and women. Trick was one of the last ones left in his group when a guard called out, "Patrick Halloran. Division 6. Come with me."

Division 6, Trick knew that was the high bond and no bond division. Since cocaine charges had recently been reclassified as a more serious offense, he would be housed with the most dangerous of all the inmates. With his bond set at $300,000, he would have to share overcrowded conditions with those charged with murder, rape, home invasion, kidnapping and other heinous crimes.

The Illinois state courts allowed inmates to be released by posting 10% of their bond. Trick didn't have $30,000 and realized it might be several years before he was on the streets again. He imagined his son as a teenager and how Pat might react to seeing him again. He could not picture a happy ending. Instead he envisioned a sixteen-year-old kid, nearly as tall as him, disappointment and hate in his sky-blue eyes. A version of himself at that age, with a chip on his shoulder, daring someone to try and knock it off.

Hit with the smell of body odor and Lysol while walking into the thunderous noise of G Block, Division 6, the heavy steel gate rolled shut with a loud clang behind him. The lone television, turned up full blast, was mounted high in one corner near the chain-link fenced guard shack. But it could barely be heard over the commotion of men talking, arguing and playing cards.

Trick was somewhat relieved to see that most of the men in this tier were adults, thirty and older. This meant less daily fighting and confrontations compared to being locked up with younger guys. He glanced around, not making eye contact. He knew the protocol and didn't want anything he did to be misconstrued as challenging. Don't go around acting like a tough guy, there's always someone tougher. Don't start any shit and don't take any either. Just be yourself, learn the rules, but mostly, just try and get along. This place was filled beyond intended capacity with vicious men forced to live with one another in brutal, overcrowded conditions. It was a situation where just a little friction could turn into fire.

Groups of inmates, the majority of them black, watched Trick as they leaned on the rail in front of the upper row of cells. There were forty cells, twenty upper and lower, two men assigned to each one. But with the overcrowding, at least fifteen more slept on the floor each night.

Wanting to attract as little attention as possible, Trick got out of the line of view and leaned against a support beam in the far corner under the upper deck where it was quieter. Surveying inmates seated at the steel tables and benches bolted to the floor, and others standing around talking, he couldn't help but notice a short guy in his late twenties with pasty colored skin and black hair making eye contact with him. The guy slowly made his way over and asked, "You hooked up?"

"No," Trick replied, knowing that he was being asked if he belonged to a gang.

"You're neutron, that's OK. About a fourth of the guys in here are. But watch yourself, *People* run this deck. There's a lot of *Folks* up in here too but they're outnumbered. The real dark guy up there in the dago-t, that's Chili, he's barn boss. Fair guy, keeps things in order. Hates thieves."

Trick thought how confusing it would be for some average Joe Citizen to end up in Cook County Jail for the first time. Neutron meant you were neutral, not in a gang. The People Nation was an association of various criminal groups including the El Rukns, Vice Lords, Latin Kings and others. Their adversaries, the Folk Nation, consisted of street organizations such as the Black Disciples, Gangster Disciples and Spanish Cobras. Yeah, this guy was being helpful. An inmate offering you something, even if it's just advice, was someone to be wary of.

The young man pointed to the crude tattoo of a crown on his forearm. "I'm with the Kings."

Trick knew that meant the Latin Kings and sized him up. "You Latino?"

"My father's German. Mother's Spanish." The young man spoke in low, surprisingly gentle tones. "What's your name?"

"Halloran," he answered, not wanting to mention the nickname Trick because of the jailhouse connotation of someone who's a snitch.

"I'm Mike. Mike Weidmann. Whatcha in for?"

"Drugs." Trick glanced down at the cheap

commissary-purchased shower shoes Mike was wearing. "Got set up on a buy."

"You got busted buyin'? Dealers usually get popped sellin'." Mike pointed a thumb at his chest. "Shoulda come to my people. You wouldn't be in here right now. I can set you up on the outside."

"Don't know if I'll be seeing the outside for a while," Trick sighed. "Anyway, I'm through with that dirty business for good."

"Uh oh," Mike said under his breath, turning his attention to the large, muscular inmate being brought into their housing unit. "Not good. This guy's serious trouble. Goes by Shabaz. He outranks Chili. Meet the new barn boss."

"He's a big son-of-a-bitch." Trick glanced at Shabaz, then quickly looked away.

"Stay the fuck out of his way. Don't want to be on his radar."

Trick looked around at the L-shaped tier of cells and the one big dayroom they were all squeezed into. "How am I supposed to do that? I don't even have a cell to go to."

Mike didn't say a word. He just stared ahead as though deep in thought.

***

A paunchy white guy, who appeared to be well into his forties, struck up a conversation with Trick. The new arrival introduced himself as Pete and after some small talk, revealed he was in jail for murdering his wife. "Walked in on her fucking my best friend." Pete put his face in his hands. "I don't know … I just went crazy."

Dinner consisted of tasteless mostaccioli with tiny bits of something rubbery resembling meat. Also on the tray was a slice of white bread with a pat of butter, a shriveled orange and a carton of milk. Sitting next to him was a twenty-year-old black guy, who called himself G-20. The thin young man relayed his story of how he ended up in jail. A teen from his neighborhood was unable to pay him $200 for some pot that he fronted him. So G-20, his girlfriend and his partner drove the unlucky kid to the forest preserve, tied him to a tree, tortured and killed him.

G-20 giggled like a schoolgirl. "Boy shit himself he was so scared."

Trick nodded as the young man continued, doing his best to act nonchalant and not reveal the horror he felt at the total lack of human compassion.

"Only reason I got caught is that goofy bitch I was goin' out with. Heard I fucked her little sister so she turned me in." G-20's tone turned sinister. "Stupid cunt didn't know she'd be charged with murder as an accessory. She's over in juvie right now."

As nighttime approached, Trick found there weren't enough thin foam rubber sleeping pads to go around so he had to sleep on the cold, hard floor. He could only get his hands on a thin, smelly pillow with no pillowcase that seemed to be seeped in decades of facial oil. The small, scratchy, wool blanket wasn't much better. He hoped there were no bedbugs or other parasites living in the olive-drab blanket as he lay on half of it and did his best to pull the remaining part over his body.

The sound of the gate opening announced another late night arrival. The skinny, young inmate being brought in seemed to be looking everywhere at once with wild, dark Puerto Rican eyes darting in every direction.

G-20, who was hanging in front of the TV with

fellow gang members, made his way back to Trick and Pete. He filled them in on the new arrival who would be sharing floor space with them. "Crazy ass mutha fucka strangled his mama in her sleep."

Pete's head shook with a slight palsy. "C'mon. Let's pull up next to each other in case he tries to get one of us while *we're* sleeping."

After the main lights went out, Trick lay sandwiched between murderers Pete and G-20, realizing the absurdity of the situation.

He had a horrible nightmare of being in jail, only to awake to the real life nightmare of his new world.

Chapter 37

The next day, Trick noticed that Mike Weidmann, who was friendly the day before, was avoiding him. Not an easy thing to do in such a confined area. Trick approached him and said, "Hey, what's up?"

"Walk it off." Mike flicked his cigarette ash on the floor. "I can't be seen with you no more. Go on, go."

"What're you talking about?" Trick spread his hands out like a pastor giving a sermon.

"You owe the wrong people a lot of money." Mike finally made eye contact. "Right now they're waitin' to see what happens to you. If it looks like you won't be able to pay them, you're dead. Either in here or the penitentiary. But it'll happen."

"You know who these guys are? Are they with the Latin Kings?" Trick reached out. "I need to know."

"Don't ever approach me again. If you do, I'll shank your ass." Mike turned and walked away.

***

While Shabaz talked with fellow gang members A.D. and Chili, Trick couldn't help but notice the way their eyes intermittently darted toward him. Later that night, Trick was surprised he was assigned a cell so soon. The usual waiting time was about a week. When he found that he would be sharing a cell with Shabaz, his insides ached.

***

Trick stood at the locked cell door looking out through the bars at the darkened, relatively quiet dayroom. He heard Shabaz get off the lower bunk and walk up behind him. Not knowing what he wanted, Trick considered swinging his elbow hard into Shabaz's throat. He hesitated, then regretted it when Shabaz grabbed him around the neck from behind with a heavily muscled arm. He knew not to struggle when he felt the cold steel of a homemade shank against his lower throat.

"What do you want?" Trick gasped through the tight grip.

"I want what ya got, mutha fucka," Shabaz whispered in his ear with breath that smelled like rotting crabs.

"You'll have to kill me. Go ahead." Trick's body stiffened. "The only way you'll have me is dead and lifeless."

"What ya think? I'm gonna rape ya? Don't flatter yaself. Ya got money on da street and ya gonna hand it ova ta my people."

"You heard wrong." Trick struggled for breath. "I'm broke. What I made after I got out was ripped off, the rest the cops confiscated."

"Don't gimme dat shit. Ya got bread out dere."

"Do what you got to do," Trick bluffed with his life. "If I do have money, you can't get secrets from a dead man."

"Neva said I was gonna kill ya. I stick this in yo spine far nough, it'll paralyze ya. How'd ya like ta spen da rest of yo white-ass life in a wheelchair, huh? Think I won't do it? I'm already in for murder. I'm neva getting' out again anyway."

Shabaz took the blade from Trick's throat and pushed it against the back of his neck. "Think I'm playin' whicha?"

Feeling the sharpened metal puncture the back of his neck, Trick's heart pounded and thought he'd pass out as he wheezed, getting just enough oxygen to keep him alive.

"Ya try goin' ta da guards, I'll know 'bout it. Dese are my people. Ya dig? We one big family. Dey get a taste too." Shabaz breathed heavily into Trick's face. "Tomorra ya gonna git on da phone and make some calls. If it's in yo house, we send someone ova ta pick it up. If it's in a car, we go git the car. It's in a safe, ya gonna tell us the combination or where da key is. Undastan?"

Trick felt the sting of the blade push harder into the back of his neck and thought about the few thousand he had stashed in Reggie's condo. He knew Shabaz was expecting a lot more than that. How could he give them something he didn't have? How could he convince Shabaz his money was gone?

Trick lay awake tossing and turning most of his second night in jail. He considered attacking Shabaz in his sleep but knew it would end up in a life or death struggle. And if he did kill Shabaz, he'd never get out. When he did sleep a little, again it was filled with nightmares.

Chapter 38

With Shabaz out of the cell for breakfast, Trick was finally able to doze a bit more, but was jarred awake. "Patrick Halloran!" From behind the eight-foot tall gate, a voice yelled out over the raucous jailhouse commotion, "You're goin' home!"

Trick was in shock. He had a hard time believing anyone would bail him out. Was it a fluke? Maybe there was another Patrick Halloran in the system he was mistaken for. Whatever the reason, he couldn't clear out quick enough.

The process of getting out was almost as lengthy as getting in. After a couple hours of red tape, he walked into the immense lobby of Cook County Jail to find Starnes and Moogie standing there waiting. As they approached, Trick said to Starnes, "You're the last person I expected to spring me."

"Surprise, surprise." Starnes laughed. "I'm retiring from the drug trade. Gettin' too hot out there. Everyone's snitchin' someone else out. No integrity left in the business."

"Yeah," Trick responded, "I know exactly what you're talking about."

"Come on, let's move this outside," Starnes said. "You and me have had our differences but you always came through. You were into me deep but you paid me back. Which is exactly what I expect you to do now, with interest, including the forty Gs you owe me for the kilo I fronted you. I'm goin' into the loan shark business. I got enough to retire on.

Gonna put my money on the street to keep up with inflation."

Trick walked down the concrete steps with Starnes and Moogie crowding him and caught the aroma of grilled onions coming from the sandwich truck parked out front. "What kind of juice we talking?"

"I'm givin' you a special deal since you didn't ask me to do this." Starnes rubbed his stubble, pausing as if still deciding. "Straight ten-percent. Payments start thirty days from tomorrow. Due the first of every month." Starnes poked Trick's chest. "You gotta stay out. Promise your lawyer your first born. Turn rat. I don't care but stay on the street and keep earnin'. You end up doin' time and we got a problem. Easier to have you stabbed in the joint than it is out here. We got an understandin'?"

Trick tilted his head back, the late morning drizzle needling his face. "I hear what you're saying."

"You're gonna start collectin' for me too. You're gonna be workin' with Moogie till you get me paid off. That means you're gonna be leanin' on people, breakin' bones if you have to. Got it?"

"Yeah, yeah. I got it," Trick answered in order to buy time.

"That little boy of yours could bring in a good buck on the black market. Grow up suckin' dick in Bangkok. Imagine a bunch of dirty, sweaty degenerates strokin' that blond hair while he gobbles their cocks. Once he disappears into the underground he'll never resurface."

Trick stepped closer to Starnes, leaned in and growled, "I told you once before, if you ever threatened me with my son again I'd kill you."

Moogie grabbed Trick by the sleeve of his leather jacket but he shook him off. "Anything ever happens to my boy, I'll finish you off," Trick said, glaring at Starnes, walking backward toward the row of taxicabs.

***

Ginger's phone rang ten times. Trick hung up and hopped in the shower at the Cloud 9 Motel to wash the smell of Cook County Jail out of his hair and pores. He quickly dressed and drove to Ginger's apartment. Seeing children walking in the misty rain, dressed up as witches, cowboys, Elvira and Hulk Hogan, made him realize what day it was.

As Trick walked to Ginger's door, the wet wind blew against his neck, stinging the puncture wound from Shabaz's shank. Her car was in the lot so he rang the buzzer and looked up to her second story window. It appeared dark in the late afternoon, gray light. He rang again and heard tapping. He looked up to see Ginger's next door neighbor, Karen, waving to him from her second story picture window. The entry buzzer let him in and he bound up the steps two at a time. Karen opened her door with little Pat bouncing up and down behind her.

"Hi, Daddy!" Pat waved, hopping around on a pogo stick.

"Come on in," Karen said, shaking her head. "Ginger already knows. It was in the *Southtown Economist* and the *Sun-Times*."

"Where is she? Working?"

"Working? She's in Christ Hospital. You didn't know?"

"Christ?" Trick's expression quickly turned to one of concern. "What's going on?"

"She passed out at the top of the stairs last night. I called an ambulance. She didn't look good at all."

Trick grabbed his short cropped hair with both

hands. "I got to get over there."

"What about Junior? I've been watching him since last night. He's a little cutie but I got things to do. Why don't you take him with you?"

"I don't think that's a good idea. I better see how she's doing first … you know, just in case. I don't want to scare him," Trick said low, as Pat dropped the pogo stick and watched intently.

"What the hell were you thinking? Getting involved with that shit again. Are you that greedy that you'd risk your freedom for a buck?" Karen motioned toward Pat. "With a precious little guy like this? I don't get you at all."

"Pat, go wash your face and hands." When his son left the room, Trick continued, "It's not what you think. There's always more to a situation than meets the eye and I don't have the time or the inclination to explain it all." Trick reached into the back pocket of his creased designer jeans. "Look, here's a little dough. Please, get some kind of costume together and take Pat trick-or-treating. Keep an eye on him while I see what's going on."

Karen took the cash and counted it in front of Trick, flipping through the bills with her lips moving.

"Come here, Pat," Trick called, then got down on one knee. Pat ran back into the living room clutching a hand towel, his face dripping with water. Trick pulled him close. "I'll be back as soon as I can. I love you big bunches."

Pat didn't say a word. He just looked at Trick with sad eyes and nodded.

***

Driving by the main entrance to Christ Hospital and Medical Center, Trick saw Ginger standing out front. He did a U-turn on Kostner Avenue and pulled up near the revolving doors. He put his window down and called, "Hey. What's going on? You need a ride?"

Ginger looked around, then got in his car. "Petros was supposed to pick me up but he never showed."

"Told you he was an asshole." Trick looked at Ginger who just stared ahead as the wiper blades kept time with Broken Wings by Mr. Mister playing low on the radio. "How are you?"

"My stomach and back hurt. I got a prescription for some pain meds."

"Did they say what's wrong with you?" Trick put his signal on then turned right onto 95th Street.

"No. They're running more tests. I'm surprised to see you back out so quick. Did you go see Pat?"

"Yeah. I gave Karen some dough to get him a costume and take him trick-or-treating."

"I wanted to take him," Ginger's voice quivered.

Trick saw a tear roll down her cheek and touched her shoulder. "You can take him next year."

"If there is a next year."

"Come on. Don't talk like that. I'm sure you'll get better once the doctors figure out what's wrong with you."

***

After getting Ginger's prescription filled, they continued south on Cicero. She remained quiet most of the way home. Trick broke the silence as they passed the Condesa Del Mar restaurant and banquet hall. "I was wrong."

Ginger opened the paper bag and looked at the label on the brown plastic bottle. "What are you talking about?"

"Everything. I was wrong about everything." Trick cleared his throat. "I'm sorry."

"That's a switch." She put the bottle back in the bag. "I never heard you talk like this."

"You were right. I should have never taken the chances I did back then, selling drugs … when I had a wife and a little boy at home waiting for me."

"You don't have to do this, not now."

"I do have to. I made excuses. Told myself I was doing it to provide for you and Pat, to set us up, buy a nice house, financial security … all that. I was really doing it to fill a void, an empty spot I had inside. Turned out to be a bottomless pit, caused by the abandonment I felt growing up, not understanding why a mother and father would just ditch me. Spent many years wondering. What was wrong with me? Wasn't I a cute enough baby?"

Ginger reached over and squeezed Trick's arm. "Oh, Pat."

"Guess I always felt like I wasn't good enough. But all the money, fancy clothes, jewelry, didn't solve my problems. They were just band aids. I know what's important now. I hope you can forgive me."

"Of course I can. I guess I've been pretty hard on you. I'm sorry too."

When they pulled up in front of Ginger's apartment, Trick asked, "You think I could come up for a while?"

"I'm really tired. Maybe we can talk tomorrow." The interior light went on when she opened the door, illuminating her gaunt cheeks.

Chapter 39

Since the Oak Lawn Police confiscated Trick's last two ounces of cocaine, there wasn't much to do but collect money from his customers. So he spent the day gathering as much cash as he could. It wouldn't be enough to appease the Mexicans and not even close to paying Starnes back. Trick sat and looked at wads of bills in his open glove compartment and thought. The money he collected wouldn't do him any good if he were back in prison. It would be even less helpful if he was dead. He purposely missed his meeting with his parole officer and knew he could be locked up again any day now, any hour. He knew what he should do with the money.

Driving south on Cicero Avenue, Trick saw the Latinos' Oldsmobile 98 pull out of Hot 'n Now Hamburgers as if waiting for him to come by. He wondered how they knew he was in a different car now and floored it, darting in and out of traffic when the Olds sped up behind. Horns blared as Trick swerved back and forth between lanes dangerously close to other vehicles. He looked in his rearview mirror to see the four gang members keeping up with him. Accelerating to eighty miles an hour, he looked around for police cars. A minivan changed lanes in front of him and Trick hit the brakes. With the smell of hot tires and grinding brake pads heavy in the air, he swerved, gripping the steering wheel hard, trying not to lose control. He couldn't stop in time and pulled to the left, bouncing over the median and into oncoming traffic. His glove compartment popped open, spilling cash onto the floor and passenger seat. Reaching over and slamming the glove compartment shut, he cut back into his own lane of traffic, almost clipping the front end of the Olds.

Someone screamed at him from an open car window. He couldn't make out what they were yelling and didn't care. He floored it again, zigzagging in and out of traffic. With his neck muscles aching from tension, he slammed on the brakes just after he flew through the yellow light at 147th Street and did a U-turn, bouncing over the median. Gunning the engine, he ran the red light, narrowly missing a Fasano pie truck that was heading west.

With the Olds now sandwiched in traffic at the red light, Trick nodded to the driver as he drove past. He continued north on Cicero and pulled into the Crestwood Police Station, parking in the rear of the lot behind rows of other cars. He stuffed handfuls of cash in his pockets, got out, locked his car and circled around the back of the building to 138th Street. He walked the short distance to Lamon Avenue and went south past the dead-end, cutting through the half-bare trees and shrubs. Twigs and leaves crackled under his shoes, high tension lines hummed as he passed under them in the drizzle. As he approached the dead-end side of Leonard Drive, he saw the coffee-colored Olds circle around from Char Lane. He ducked behind a gathering of damp smelling saplings, crouched in the wildflowers and waited. After they pulled off Leonard and onto the Midlothian Turnpike, he ran as fast as he could to Ginger's apartment building and pushed the buzzer.

"C'mon, Ginger," he pleaded into the metal-framed intercom, "answer."

A garbled voice asked, "Who is it?"

"Ginger, it's me." Trick huddled under the canopy with his collar up. "Please let me in."

She looked out her living room window, then asked, "Where's your car?"

"I can't explain. Buzz me in!"

After racing up the stairs, Trick's hearing dimmed. Then his vision started going black as he braced himself against the door jam in view of the peephole.

Ginger opened the door scowling. "What are you doing here? I just got out of the shower." She held her terrycloth robe together with one hand and put the other up to shield her face. "I don't even have my makeup on yet."

Trick felt light-headed and leaned against the door frame breathing heavily. He took a moment to compose himself and rubbed his eyes. "You look cute without all that makeup, like the young lady I first started going out with." He thought he saw a hint of blush on Ginger's now gaunt and sallow face.

"Patrick's not here. He's spending the night at his friend's house."

"That's all right. I wanted to come by and give you some money." Trick stood in the doorway feeling dizzy and put his face in his hands. "Can I sit down?"

"Of course." Ginger led him to the living room sofa and sat next to him. "What's the matter with you? I never saw you like this." Her abrasive manner turned to one of concern. "You're so pale."

"Things just keep going from bad to worse. Damn it." Trick pounded a fist on his leg. "I just wanted to be a good father to Pat. But I screwed everything up. Screwed up my whole life." Trick pulled wads of cash from various pockets and dumped it all on the coffee table in front of them.

"Not sure how much is there. Got to be at least fifteen grand. Why don't you get away somewhere with Pat?"

"I can't just take off." Ginger looked at the money, reached for it then pulled away. "What about Pat's school? Where am I going to go?"

"I don't know." Trick rubbed his temples. "I can't think."

"You don't look good. You're shaky."

"I'll be all right. As long as I know you two are safe." Trick held his hands out and watched them tremble.

"Can I get you something? A glass of water?"

"Something stronger. What've you got?"

"Bourbon ... but it's 3:00 in the afternoon." Ginger waited for a reply that didn't come. She studied Trick, who was now sitting with his head back against the sofa cushion, staring up at the ceiling. She left the room and came back a few minutes later with two rock glasses of Wild Turkey on ice. Setting them on the coffee table, she sat closer to Trick. "Now you got me worried." Picking up her glass, she stared at the rich brown color blending with the melting ice and took a sip.

Trick gulped half the glass down on an empty stomach. "I didn't mean for any of this to happen." His words seemed to be coming from someone else, like he was watching a movie. He wasn't sure if it was stress, lack of sleep, the bourbon leaving a warm spot in his stomach or the sweet smell of Ginger's clean wet hair. Reality was harsh. Fantasy felt more welcoming. "I love you and Pat so much." Tears welled up and he turned his head to hide his shame.

"Oh, Pat," Ginger said softly, reaching over and pulling his face toward hers. "It's OK, Baby. It's OK."

Trick looked down at Ginger's tanning-bed browned thighs to see her robe separating, revealing she had nothing on underneath. They met in a soft kiss and the passion they once knew for each other exploded. Trick got on his knees in front of Ginger, grabbed her legs and pulled her forward. They made love fast and hard and Trick climaxed quickly.

With his face on Ginger's bare chest, Trick whispered breathily, "That's the first time since I got out. I feel like a fifteen-year-old who just got laid for the first time."

"What? Are you trying to tell me you haven't been with anyone else? That's a little hard to believe."

"Scout's honor."

"You were never a Boy Scout." Ginger giggled as Trick scooped her up in his arms and carried her into the bedroom.

***

It was dark out when Trick woke with Ginger in his arms. He was forced to think about what he avoided facing earlier; Ginger was so thin he could feel her rib cage. She had lost an alarming amount of weight and the whites of her eyes were tinged with yellow. Disoriented, he glanced at his watch in the dim glow of a nightlight to see it was going on 7:00. He tried getting out of bed without waking her and put his feet on the floor.

Ginger's hoarse whisper called out in the dark, "What time is it?"

"Just about 7:00, at night, I think. Who kept calling?"

"Probably Petros. After you dropped me off last night, I drove over to the restaurant. I walked into the backroom and caught him screwing some new bimbo he hired, right on a banquet table."

"I'm sorry." Trick wasn't sure if he was sorry but said it anyway. "I don't want to see you hurt."

"The way my life is going." Ginger sighed. "What does it matter?"

"The hell with him. That nose of his ... I don't know how you got close enough to kiss him with that huge thing in the way."

"Oh, Pat. You're so bad." Ginger giggled. "It is pretty big though."

When Ginger turned on the lamp next to her side of the bed and sat up, Trick tried not to show shock at the amount of blonde hair on her dark red pillowcase. He pulled his silk boxers on and went to the kitchen, putting his mouth under the faucet, gulping cool water. Ginger followed him into the kitchen tying her robe then turned on her Mr. Coffee.

Trick wiped his mouth on his forearm and walked in the dim light to the living room as Ginger called out, "Do you want a cup?"

Trick finger-combed his cropped hair back and looked out Ginger's large living room window for signs of trouble. "Yeah, sure." He sat on the sofa in a shaft of light from the corner streetlamp that backlit his hair in a halo-like glow.

Ginger joined Trick and set a hot cup of coffee in front of him.

He wanted coffee to taste as good as it smelled, but with every cup he drank, it never did. Pouring the remaining bourbon from earlier into his coffee, he asked, "How are you feeling?"

"A little loopy ... numb." Ginger's eyelids fluttered. "The pain stuff I'm on is pretty strong."

"I want to explain all the craziness that's been going on. I lied to you because I didn't want you to worry. But you deserve the truth." Trick rubbed his fingertips over the scab on the back of his neck. "About three weeks ago, right after I lost my job selling cars, I found a bag full of money and cocaine. I owed Starnes $60,000 so I gave him the cocaine to settle our score. Thought I was on easy street with $285,000 in my kit. Then the guys that the bag belonged to somehow caught up with me. They threatened me, took the rest of the cash and broke my nose."

"I *knew* something was going on. Figures. That's when you gave me the money for my new car."

Trick nodded and continued, "They gave me a week to replace the drugs or pay them $300,000. I tried but I couldn't raise that much in that short of time." Trick held up his left hand, showing his little finger with the tip missing. "I've been dodging them ever since."

"Is that why you cut your hair and shaved your moustache?"

"Yeah." Trick brought the cup to his face and smelled the rich aroma. "I knew I couldn't fool you for very long. Not you."

"*That's* why you told me to keep an eye on Pat." Ginger softly touched Trick's leg. "Why don't you go to the police?"

"It's not one of those kind of deals. They'd just lock me up for getting involved with drugs again and I'm even more vulnerable inside than out. There's nowhere to hide in there, not even in seg."

"Well, Trick," Ginger said, with more than a hint of sarcasm, "you finally put yourself in a trick bag."

"I really screwed up this time." Trick shook his head. "I'm sorry."

"What *are* you going to do?"

"I don't know. I tell you one thing, it wasn't worth it. If I could do it all over I would have left that bag on the side of the road and done any kind of work, even if it was digging ditches." Trick sipped his spiked coffee then set it down. "Something's been bugging me. I got to ask. Did Joey DeBonarino ever come around when I was locked up?"

"Oh yeah, sure. He started showing up as soon as you went to jail."

"That rat fuck. Tell me what happened."

"He came around, saying he was concerned for me and Pat. Said he wanted to help. Offered me money."

"Lousy rotten mother ... sure he wanted to help, wanted to help himself to *you*. Did you take any of his dough?"

"No. You think I'm stupid?" Ginger brought a hand to her chest. "It wasn't easy turning him down though. I was worried how me and Pat were going to get by."

"So, you're telling me nothing went on between you two?" Trick pointed a finger. "We were still married at the time."

"Nothing happened. He pestered me for a while and saw he wasn't getting anywhere. He got the hint and quit coming over. That's the whole story."

Trick grimaced and punched his palm, causing his healing finger to sting.

"What are you going to do?" Ginger pulled his face toward hers. "I told you nothing happened."

Pulling away, Trick said slowly, "I'm going to have a little talk with Joey the Boner."

"Oh, Patrick. Please don't. You're on parole. You don't need a battery charge too."

***

Trick called Joey and set up a meeting in the large parking lot of the Southwest Ice Arena. He knew he'd have to control his temper because there was something he needed from Joey before he could get even with him. He also had to set the record straight. Not wanting false rumors spread about him, he needed Joey to know he didn't set him up.

Spotting Joey's Corvette on the outskirts of the lot with the parking lights on, Trick pulled next to him. They got out of their cars and walked up a few feet from one another. "Looks like we both got lucky and made bail," Trick said, trying to read Joey's demeanor.

"Yeah, but I'm fucked. Probably do time again. And I swear, I'll kill the mudder fucker dat set me up."

Trick watched Joey go for the back pocket where he kept his stiletto switchblade. "I'm telling you, Joey, I didn't set you up. You know my reputation. When I got busted in 81, I kept my mouth shut. Never ratted on anyone in my life."

"No one else knew I was gonna be at the El-Dorado, just you. And I never saw cops let anyone walk away from a situation like dat. Tell me it's not fuckin' fishy."

"Think about it. How could I have known you were holding? You called me. Said you wanted to meet." Trick suppressed his anger. "I was holding too. Doesn't make sense that I'd call the cops on myself."

"Yeah, OK. Dat much figures." Joey brought his empty hand back to his side.

"Who else knew what direction you were heading, what kind of car you were in, and that you'd have the shit on you?"

"Yeah," Joey replied, bobbing his head slowly, "dat fat fuck Bob. He was actin' funny when I copped from him … right before I met you."

Just to watch the expression on Joey's face, Trick asked, "Any reason he should be pissed at you? Enough to set you up and lose a customer?"

"All right, let's drop it." Joey backed up a couple steps and waved his hands. "I believe ya. Why'd ya call?"

"Your family's from Bridgeport. You know a guy, a Sal Bianccini?"

"Yeah, I know him. He's in Pontiac, got winged in dat shootout with you and the coppers about four years ago. Why, wazzup?"

"I need to talk to him but I don't want him to know I'm coming. I want you to send word tomorrow morning, have him put you on his visitor's list. I plan to go see him using your name. I'll need to borrow your driver's license."

"Whoa. Forget about it. Dat guy's nutso," Joey said, circling a finger near his temple. "Wouldn't want to end up on his shit list. He may be locked up but he's got a long reach."

"Look, Joey, you do this for me and I'll get even with Bob for you."

Joey ran a thumb across his neck. "Ya mean like do him in?"

"I'll take care of him." Trick's anger rose just thinking of the things Bob said about him.

"Mmm ... *bene*, OK. But how you gonna pass for me? Huh? Ya don't even look Italian, ya mick."

"Don't worry about that part."

"Whadda ya mean? I'm five-nine, ya got a couple inches on me." Joey motioned with his hands like someone juggling oranges. "I got brown eyes, brown hair. You got blue eyes and hair like one of dem soap opera guys."

"I told you, I got it covered. Set it up."

"*Madonna mia*," Joey said to the night sky, then

pulled out his wallet and handed Trick his driver's license.

Chapter 40

In the parking lot of Pontiac Prison, Trick put on a pair of brown-tinted glasses, greased his dark blond hair with VO5, giving it a darker look, then put on a Chicago White Sox cap. Getting out of his car, he slouched as he walked to the entrance of the visitors' gate. After showing the driver's license that read Joseph Vincent DeBonarino, Trick got a queasy feeling walking into the maximum security prison. Passing through correctional center security gates again, he imagined walking into a funeral parlor and seeing his own coffin.

After being patted down, Trick was led through a series of gates and doors. Once inside the large visitor's room, he went to one of the vending machines, inserted a dollar and got back a paper cup with small chunks of ice and bubbling Pepsi. He removed the glasses and hat, took a seat at one of the small round tables, sipped his drink and waited. Prisoners all dressed alike sat at tables with loved ones, family and friends. The spacious, cigarette hazed room echoed with conversation while inmates and their visitors caught up on each other's lives. Some laughed, some cried and some had bitter words while they picked at thin slices of microwaved pizza, ice cream in tiny paper cups, soda and coffee.

Several minutes later, Sal entered the visitors' room scanning faces. Trick stood and motioned to Sal who looked at him harshly. As Sal walked toward him, Trick saw that his right arm was shriveled, scarred and hanging limply at his side in his short sleeve shirt.

"Hey, Lefty, ya got a visitor?" A Puerto Rican gang member mocked Sal, "I didn't know ya *had* any friends."

Sal ignored him and walked up to Trick and stared into his eyes. "That is you, you mudder fucker. What're you doin' here? Get the fuck out."

"Wait. Come on, sit down for a minute." Trick stood and motioned toward a chair. "I drove a long way to get here."

Trick sat back down, looking up at Sal, who hesitated for a few moments, then lowered himself onto one of the brown plastic chairs. He swung his body, landing his lifeless right arm onto the table.

"You like that?" Sal looked at his useless appendage, then back at Trick. "Doctors want to cut it off, said I'll never have use of it again. I won't let 'em,"

"Hey, Lefty, who's your cute friend?" a young man with mahogany colored skin and a plastic bag over his hair interrupted. "Can you set me up?"

Sal raised his fist. "Push on, you gorilla-face fuck."

The young man howled and laughed. "Pontiac builds excitement." Then he danced away like he was moving down a Soul Train line.

"See what I gotta put up with every day?"

"I did time over that deal too." Trick tapped his fingertips on his chest. "Didn't like it any more than you."

"Yeah, but it's your fault I'm in here. You and that greaseball, Benny."

"Wait a minute. Benny was the guy who set that deal up. I was only doing business with him for about six months. Said you and him grew up together."

"Yeah, we both grew up in Bridgeport but I never liked that slime jabonee. Used to steal money outta his own mudder's cash register. Piece of shit." Sal grimaced. "That guinea scum split and went back to Italy, but I'll get him too if I can find 'im."

"I got taken in just like you." Trick put his open hands out. "That deal wiped me out. Spent close to a year fighting my case. Went broke in the process … bonding out, lawyers, appeals. They watched me like a hawk, could hardly make any dough before I went away. I'm out there struggling."

"Why should I give a crap? I don't wanna hear your problems. Got plenty of my own."

Trick sat back and waited several uncomfortable moments. At a nearby table a young woman with her hair in cornrows sat close to her incarcerated man. He had his prison-blue shirttail out trying to hide that she was stroking him under the table. They were caught up in the moment and didn't notice a guard approaching from behind. The uniformed guard hit the table hard with his baton making the couple flinch. She drew her hand back and they both straightened up. Trick spoke quietly, "Word is you're getting out in a few years and plan to kill me."

"Who'd you hear that from?"

"Not important." Trick reached out with both hands. "I came to see what we can do to settle things between us."

"Settle?" Sal motioned with his left hand. "Can you bring my arm back?"

"Come on." Trick leaned in with both palms on the table. "I didn't shoot you."

"I told you I didn't wanna go back and here I am, livin' in this jungle with these animals. Every day I gotta hold myself back from killin' one of these *mulignans.* Then I'll be here forever. I begged you to put a bullet in my head and you wouldn't do it."

"Then I'd have been in here for the rest of my life. You're not thinking right. The coppers investigate these kind of shootings. They pull the bullet out and run ballistics on it. They'd have known it was me."

Sal stood and swung his body, knocking over Trick's Pepsi with his paralyzed arm. "Visit's over. See you in a few years. You'll never know when or where it's gonna happen but I dream about the look on your face when you know it's the end. That dream's what's keepin' me goin'."

Trick's heart beat rapidly as he watched Sal walk away but then stop at the guard's desk by the door and motion back at him with his good arm. He knew it was time to get out of there.

Chapter 41

Trick got out of bed and pulled the drapes closed to seal off the flashing neon from the Rainbow Motel sign. Once again he couldn't sleep and decided to drink himself into a slumber. Walking outside to the ice machine, he was met with the aroma from a nearby pizzeria mingling with the noxious smell of car exhaust. He filled the plastic bucket to the brim then carried it back to his room as noisy night traffic zoomed past on Archer Avenue.

Breaking the seal on a bottle of Woodford Reserve bourbon, he heard the dim pop as he removed the cork, then filled a bathroom sink glass to the top over ice. He turned on the small black and white television and scanned the channels. He settled on an episode of *Alfred Hitchcock Presents* with actress Linda Fiorentino, but couldn't concentrate on the plot.

Trick wondered what he was missing. How his enemies always seemed to be a step ahead of him. Pacing the floor of the small room feeling caged again, he wanted to get out of there, to go anywhere, out of the city, out of the country. Maybe that was the move. But he didn't have a passport and knew they wouldn't issue him one while on parole. He thought about his son, knowing he couldn't leave him again, not if he could help it somehow. He considered running away with Pat but it wouldn't be fair to Ginger. Losing her son would surely destroy her. This left him with one other reasonable option,

277

turning rat. That would probably get his sentence reduced but it was a dangerous gamble. And what if his enemies retaliated by going after his son? Even if cooperating was a safe alternative, he couldn't live with himself after doing that. He couldn't become what he hated.

***

Trick woke the next morning to a maid banging on his door. "Meester! I need to get in!"

Kicking the sheet and cover off, Trick stumbled to the door. "Stop that damned pounding. I don't need my room cleaned!" He slammed the door in the woman's face, grabbed his throbbing head and hurried to the bathroom. Dropping to his knees, he vomited, breathed in the stench of last night's regurgitated gyros sandwich and the urine stained rug around the toilet bowl, then puked some more.

"Oh God," Trick moaned, feeling like firecrackers were going off in his skull. "Please make it stop." He wondered if more people prayed on their knees in front of toilets than they did in churches.

Feeling a little better after a nap, Trick shaved and showered. He poured about a shot of bourbon into a glass of water and drank his hair of the dog with a shudder. With a fresh change of clothes, he headed out into the cool, early November breeze. Driving east on Archer, past a multitude of storefront businesses and apartment buildings, he pulled into Brandy's restaurant on the corner at Cicero Avenue. His hunger was finally overtaking his nausea and he settled on a cheese omelet with wheat toast, washing it down with several glasses of Chicago tap water. His dull headache did not help as he struggled to think of a way to change his luck.

With some food in his belly, he felt straightened

out enough to continue and drove down the street, leaving his recently purchased Pontiac in the long-term parking lot at Midway Airport. He walked to the car rental area and drove away in a two-tone Chrysler Fifth Avenue.

***

Trick pulled his cap down low before getting out of the rental car and walking into Barone's Restaurant at 127th and Central. He looked over the top of his sunglasses to dial the payphone in the vestibule. "Joey, it's me. I got to give you your license."

"Yeah. I want dat back right away. Wanna meet downtown at Faces? Ton a pussy dere."

"No. Tell you what, let's meet at Heritage Park by the cannon. It's more private and there's something I want to talk to you about. Make it 4:30."

***

Driving up on 149th Street in the foggy dusk, Trick could see Joey's red Corvette. He pulled into the small parking area and walked straight up to Joey.

"Hey, Trick. Wuz happenin'? Some bidness ya wanna discuss?"

"Yeah. You could say we got some unfinished business. And don't ever call me Trick. It's Pat to you."

"Uh, OK. Pat?" Joey's hand went to his back pocket. "What's da beef here?"

"You come sniffing around my wife when I was gone?" Trick surprised Joey with a hard uppercut to the stomach, doubling him over. "You pull that knife and I'll snatch the eyes right out of your head."

Trick grabbed him by the hair as Joey put his hands up and wheezed, "Wait, wait."

"*You* didn't wait too long, Joey. Started coming

around soon as I was locked up." Trick gave Joey a right cross, knocking him on his ass.

"Stop, stop! Nothin' happened!" Joey wiped blood from the gash under his eye with the back of his hand. "I jus came around ta see if she needed some help." Joey pulled his knife. "Dat's all."

"You weren't going to mention it though. Were you? Didn't think I'd find out." Trick kicked Joey on the forehead, laying him out. "Don't ever come anywhere near Ginger again, you fuckin' lowlife." Trick threw Joey's driver's license at him and walked away, wishing he could solve all his problems that easily.

Chapter 42

Toying with the paper wristband, that had Ginger's room number on it, Trick rode the elevator up to the seventh floor. The metal doors parted and he stepped into the hallway, remembering the last time he came to visit Ginger in Christ Hospital. How beautiful she looked, her disheveled hair against the mint green pillowcase as she held newborn Pat close, his little blond head resting on her chest.

A chubby young nurse's aide smiled at Trick who looked lost carrying a bouquet of flowers. He walked around looking at numbers on doors, some closed, some open, revealing family members sitting and standing, some with heads hung low. Pushing open the partially closed door, shock hit him when he saw Ginger lying on the first bed, her mouth open, tubes in her arms. Her half open eyes rolled to the side to see Trick holding a dozen roses surrounded with baby's breath, wrapped in green tissue paper. He thought he saw a hint of a smile as she lay there motionless.

"Don't get up," Trick joked, hoping it would lighten the mood and hold back his tears.

Ginger tried telling him something but he couldn't make out what she was saying. He grabbed a chair and pulled it close to her bedside.

No more than a hoarse whisper came from Ginger, who repeated, "Take good care of Pat ... tell him every day how much I love ..."

Her eyes closed and Trick wondered whether she

suddenly fell asleep, passed out or worse. He dropped the flowers on the floor and ran to the nurses' station. "Hey. Who's in charge of Ginger Halloran?"

A woman of middle-eastern descent with thick black hair and thicker eyelashes said, "I'm Doctor Fahri. How can I help you?"

"What's going on with my ... Ginger? I was just with her three days ago. How could she get so sick, so fast?"

"Are you family?"

"Yes, she's the mother of my son. She looks so weak. What's being done for her?"

"We're doing everything possible for Ginger. But we've run out of reasonable options. I'm afraid I have bad news. Would you like to come into the conference room?"

"No, please ... tell me what's going on."

"Ginger has pancreatic cancer. I'm sorry but this type of cancer usually has a poor prognosis, even when diagnosed early. It typically spreads rapidly and is seldom detected in its early stages. Signs and symptoms might not appear until it is well advanced, when surgery is no longer an option."

"Oh, God. No." Trick leaned against a wall.

"The cancer has spread to Ginger's liver and other areas. I wish there were more we could do. Give her anything she would like, candy, ice cream ... whatever will make her happy."

"You're saying she's dying?"

"I'm afraid she doesn't have much time."

"I don't get it. A month ago she thought she just had the flu or something. She was up and around a few days ago."

"Some cancers metastasize at a very rapid rate. I'm so sorry."

Trick went back to Ginger's bedside, picked the flowers up from the floor and set them on the bed. He sat thinking about young Pat. His son didn't deserve any of this. He was just a little boy, never did anything to harm anyone.

Visions of Ginger's younger girlish face kept Trick company as their first conversation replayed in his mind. He recalled the first time he took her to dinner, admitting he was a coke dealer and that she seemed unfazed. Only to realize two dates later that she thought he worked for Coca-Cola.

Trick lost track of time, lost in daydreams, lost youth, lost innocence. Ginger stirred, opening her eyes again and seemed surprised to see him, as though she didn't remember talking with him only an hour earlier.

"I was dreaming." Ginger smiled slightly. "You and me were at the Cape Cod Room, drinking piña coladas."

"You want a piña colada?"

"What?" Ginger weakly shook her head, "Don't be silly. I can't have a drink. I'm in the hospital."

"You want a piña colada?" Trick repeated.

A pretty young black lady pushing a cart with covered trays entered the room and cheerily asked, "How y'all doing? Would you like to feed Ginger?"

"Can someone else take care of that?" Trick replied. "There's something I got to do but I'll be right back." He stood and patted Ginger's foot through the bed covers. "See you soon."

Riding the elevator down alone, Trick let out the tears he had been holding in. Back in his car, he drove to the McDonald's drive-thru just down the street and ordered two large Cokes. He pulled away, opened his door and poured the drinks out onto the asphalt parking lot, then put the lids back on. He then drove to Petey's Bungalow across the street from the hospital and walked in with the paper cups.

"Two piña coladas, easy on the rum. Put them in these." Trick slid the empty cups toward the short burly bartender who had more hair on his arms than the top of his head. "And give me a Chivas neat while I'm waiting," he added. "Got any twenty-four-year-old?"

"Twelve. That good, pal?"

Trick nodded and took the glass barely out of the bartender's fingertips. He brought it to his lips, smelled the oaky aroma and swallowed half of it in one gulp.

The bartender returned with the piña coladas and Trick downed the rest of his blended Scotch whiskey. He put the plastic lids back on, tore the paper off the straws and pushed them through the small slits in the lids. "How much do I owe you?"

"$6.50. But, hey, I can't let ya walk out with those. Ya gotta drink 'em here."

Slapping a fifty-dollar bill on the bar, Trick looked him in the eye. "Try and stop me."

Without looking back, Trick hurried out and got in his car, half expecting the guy to come out the door after him.

He returned to Ginger's room to find her alone again. She seemed a little stronger after her meal and pushed herself into a sitting position. "You get me a shake?"

"Something better." Trick handed her a drink and sat next to her. "Till the world is through with us," he said, tapping his cup against hers.

Taking a sip through the straw, Ginger managed a smile and sang in a raspy voice, "If you like piña coladas and getting caught in the rain."

Trick turned his head and blinked back tears.

"I'm not going home anymore, am I?"

"I don't know. Try to think positive." Trick kissed her hand. "I'll always love you."

"I know, Pat, I know," Ginger said softly. She winced in pain and grabbed her side. "I need to know that Pat's going to be OK. Please promise me you'll do everything possible to straighten out the mess you're in and keep him safe. He needs you now more than ever."

Trick knew he couldn't honestly say everything would be all right. He didn't want to lie to Ginger but felt he didn't have much choice. He couldn't send her to her grave worrying. "I've got everything straightened out. I worked out a deal with the cops."

"Thank you. It's not going to be easy for him." Ginger's eyes rolled back. "You're going to have to love him enough for both of us."

"There's nothing more important to me than our son. I'll do everything humanly possible." Trick caressed her face. "Is there anything else I can do for you? Anything."

"Karen has a key to my apartment. I left the money you gave me in Pat's lunchbox. The title for my car is in my top right dresser drawer, bring it to me." Tears rolled down Ginger's sunken cheeks and her voice broke. "I want to see my son one more time."

A short while later, Ginger was asleep again. Trick got on his knees next to her bed, put his hands together and looked up at the ceiling. "Please God, I never asked for much. Please help Ginger. Don't let her suffer. Please."

***

Trick walked into the condo for the first time in a week to an annoying ring. He went straight to the bedroom and picked up the phone on the nightstand. "Yeah, who the fuck is it?"

"Is that any way to talk to your benefactor?" Starnes growled back. "If it wasn't for me, you'd still be in the can. And where the fuck you been? I been callin' over there the last couple days."

"None of your damn business. Look, I'm not in any kind of mood for your bullshit right now."

"Bullshit? Don't get cocky with me, you paddy nigger. Meet Moogie over at El-Mar bowling alley tomorrow morning at 10:00. Yous two are gonna go pay someone a visit."

Pulling the rigged mirror off the wall, Trick reached in and pulled out his pistol. "I'm not going anywhere with that asshole. Find someone else."

"You and me had a deal. I got you out, mudder fucker. Now you're gonna do what you're told. You know what happens to welchers? Huh?"

"I don't have rules anymore." Trick never felt so low. Hitting bottom changed something in him. He survived things most men hadn't, things a lot of men couldn't. Knowing his situation couldn't get much worse made him feel strange, almost giddy. After everything he went through, he was still here. Left with only choices. Nothing seemed to matter much anymore. Just his son. "The only rules I have are the ones I impose on myself."

"What kind of crazy-ass shit you talkin' about? You understand what's goin' on here? I'll fuckin' kill ya!"

Trick opened the chamber, counted six bullets and snapped it closed again. "Do what you got to do, boy. I'll see you around." He hung up the phone and caught his reflection in the mirrored wall. He sat on the bed and put the barrel to his temple. He suddenly felt tired, very tired. He wanted to sleep, a good long sleep.

Chapter 43

"Sorry I couldn't be there when you got locked up at Oak Lawn. I was in Florida golfing," Trick's lawyer, Paul Grande, said, tapping his Monte Blanc pen on his desk mat. "I have to tell you though, I'm amazed you were released at all, bond or no bond. You could get pulled in any minute on a parole violation. Go hug your son or do whatever else is important to you."

Trick rubbed his face. "I can't believe they'd pull a reverse sting on me. DeLorean just beat a case like this last year. It's entrapment."

"Every case is different. DeLorean had a ton of dough to fight his charges. Besides, even if you did beat the Intent to Purchase charge, there's still the two ounces they found in your car. That's all they need to send you away for a long time."

"Well." Trick's face and shoulders dropped. Life seemed to ebb from him. "Looks like I'm fucked."

"Did you talk with anyone while you were in Oak Lawn lockup?"

Trick splayed his fingers and shook his head. "Just some biker looking dude."

"How much did you tell him?"

"Not too much I guess."

"I hope not." Grande pointed his pen at Trick. "That's one of the cops' methods. They put an undercover officer in with you, usually unshaven, bummy looking. They know when someone's in that kind of predicament, they tend to talk out of nervousness. Think they're talking to someone else in trouble. The cops can't use what they heard in open court but they can tell the judge in his chambers. That's where everything is decided. It's all done beforehand regardless of what goes on in the courtroom, barring some big surprise or you come up with enough dough to grease the wheels. And right now with this Greylord investigation going on, forget about that. They're locking up judges and lawyers right and left."

"You're telling me it's already been decided what's going to happen?"

"Yes. That's what I'm telling you. You're going bye bye. I'm here to try and keep your sentence down as much as I can. Hopefully shave a few years off but we're looking at twelve to twenty-five. They're not going to settle for any less than twelve. If you cooperate I can definitely get you no more than that."

"Forget about me cooperating." Trick waved both hands away. "That's not going to happen."

"Don't be too quick to turn down a deal, especially if you haven't even heard the terms."

"I'm not a rat."

"Just go talk to Detective Frank Murray. That's all I'm suggesting. Hear what he's offering."

"Murray?" Trick cocked his head. "Not Carlsbad?"

"That's right. Murray oversees all the big drug cases in the area."

Trick stood and squinted. "I don't think so." He searched Grande's eyes. "But if I did, you'd go with me, right?"

"You don't need me there. This is all off the record." Grande handed Trick a plain white business card with black lettering. "Call him."

Chapter 44

"Pat, I don't want you to be scared when you see your mother." Trick parked near the corner on 93rd Street and unbuckled his son's seatbelt. He walked around the Hertz rental car and let Pat out as the siren from an ambulance roared past toward the emergency entrance. "She's very, very sick."

"Does she have a belly ache?" Pat hopped to the ground.

"Worse." He took Pat's hand and walked south on Kostner Avenue toward the hospital entrance. The southerly wind brought the aroma from Mama's Cookies factory in Ford City where Trick worked as a teen, leaving a bittersweet taste in his mouth. "Your mom has cancer."

"What's cancer?"

"It's a serious disease." Taking short steps, putting one foot in front of the other reluctantly, Trick never felt as sad as he did at that moment. "Mommy has a very bad kind of cancer."

"When is she coming home?"

"Oh, Pat. I ... I don't know what to tell you." Trick found it difficult to continue with the lump in his throat. The tenderness of Pat's hand somehow made him feel sadder. "She might not be coming home."

"Can I live with her in the hospital if she don't come home?"

"No. You can't do that. Little boys don't live in hospitals."

"You're not supposed to step on the cracks, Daddy," Pat said, walking carefully. "Step on a crack, break your mama's back."

"Sure, Pat." Trick continued, avoiding the separations in the concrete. "Your mom misses you very much. If she cries, that's OK. She might be so happy to see you that she can't help herself."

"It's all right." Pat watched the sidewalk warily. "I saw mommy cry lots of times."

The fragrance of flowers coming from the gift shop masked antiseptic odors as they walked through the revolving door and up to the visitor's desk hand in hand. After getting clearance to continue further, they stepped into the elevator. Riding up, Trick said, "Mommy has tubes in her arms. It's to make her feel better. It might look weird but it helps her. Do you understand?"

"Yeah. Don't worry. I won't say stupid stuff."

Once in her room, Pat ran to his mother's bedside, but when he saw her, he screamed and ran back out.

Trick could see a noticeable difference in Ginger's appearance from just two days earlier.

Ginger's weak voice broke when she cried out, "What was I thinking? This isn't how I want him to remember me. I shouldn't have been so selfish."

"Selfish?" Trick tried his best to console her. "There's nothing selfish about wanting to see your son. I better go after him."

Trick walked out of the room to find Pat plastered against the wall in the hallway. His little face looked white. Trick got on his knees and put his hands on his son's shoulders. "Pat, sometimes we have to be brave. Even when we don't think we can." He put his cheek to Pat's and spoke softly. "Mommy loves you and misses you so much. You think you can be a brave soldier for her? She needs you to make her feel better."

Trick could feel his son's tears as Pat whimpered. "She doesn't look like Mommy. She's skinny and little."

"She looks smaller but her love for you is as big as ever. Do you need a little time or do you think you can go back in now?" Trick pulled his face back and looked his son in the eye. "Mommy needs you, more than anything else in the whole world. Seeing you is better for her than any medicine." He pulled a clean handkerchief from his back pocket and gave it to Pat.

Pat wiped his face, blew his nose and handed it back. "I can be a brave soldier," his voice quivered.

"All right then. You want me to carry you?"

"I'm not a baby anymore."

Unfortunately, Trick knew this was true. His son was never going to be a normal little boy again after this. He would be forced to grow beyond his years in a matter of days. He followed close behind Pat who walked anxiously, as though trying not to step on cracks.

Pat walked up to his mother but stayed a few feet away. "I'm sorry I screamed. I got scared."

"That's all right, Pat. Mommy understands. I'm kind of scary without my makeup."

Pat giggled and cried at the same time. He stepped a foot closer. "You're still the prettiest mommy."

"Oh, sweetie, thank you." Ginger put a hand to her sunken cheek. "Are you behaving yourself at school? No more punching?"

"No more punching. Just Davey, 'cause he pushed me, so that don't count."

"Maybe you can find a better way to settle your problems instead of fighting all the time. You think you can do that for Mommy?"

"OK. But if someone tries to wipe a booger on me I'm gonna hit 'im on the nose."

"Well, it would be better if you told the teacher instead of using your fists."

"I'm not a tattle-tale. I hate kids who rat."

Ginger looked to Trick who just shrugged and shook his head. "Daddy, Mommy's so tired she can hardly stay awake."

She reached out to her son. "Pat, come closer. I have something important to tell you." Pat took her hand and she pulled him next to the bed. "Mommy is always going to love you no matter where I am. I'm always going to be with you even though you can't see me. Do you understand?"

"Are you going somewhere?" Pat's chin quivered.

"Yes. I'm going to a place where I can always see you and love you. I'll be watching out for you."

"Like an angel?"

"Yes." Ginger cried. "Like an angel." She looked to Trick. "I want to hold him."

Trick lifted Pat and laid him next to his mother. She lay holding him, stroking his hair until they both fell asleep.

***

Trick hit the power lock button on the remote as he walked up to the car with Pat in his arms.

Pat opened his eyes as his father set him in the front seat. "I want to go with Mommy and be an angel too."

"Oh, Pat." Trick knelt on the damp grass next to the curb. "You're too young to be an angel. Mommy wants you to stay here and grow into a man and maybe get married, have a little boy of your own one day."

As Trick got behind the wheel, Pat asked, "How

come I never sleep at your house?"

Not wanting to chance a confrontation with his enemies with Pat around, Trick turned to his son and replied, "I don't think it's a good idea." He was soon to be Pat's only parent and wanted to start off on the right foot and be honest. "I would love to have you stay with me but Daddy has something important to do. Something that little boys can't be part of."

"If you have work, I can help you. I'm gonna be six pretty soon and I'm strong," Pat said, flexing his arm.

Trick buckled Pat's seatbelt. "I'm sorry but I'm doing this to keep you safe. You're going to sleep over at Karen's again tonight."

Chapter 45

"Hey, asshole, anytime you're feeling froggy, leap up!" Trick yelled at the man a few stools to his right. Trick jumped to his feet and threw his empty whiskey glass, shattering it against the wall. He turned his attention back to the bartender. "I'll tell you when I've had enough. Don't ever try to tell me what to do. No one gives me orders!"

"Ingo, what are you doing? Get 'im outta here!" the bartender called to the six-foot-seven bouncer.

The musclebound Ingo was leaning in close, rapping on a young lady with Farrah Fawcett hair. He heard the commotion and stomped up to Trick, who looked unsteady on his feet. "C'mon, out the door or I'll throw you out." He pushed at Trick's chest.

"Hey, fuck you, Lou Ferrigno." Trick backed up and raised his fists. "Fuck you and Arnold Whatziznigger. You can both go screw each other in the ass."

"Walk out while you got the chance." Ingo pointed to the door behind Trick.

"Who the fuck you supposed to be, Mr. Clean?" Trick's body swayed. "Is it in the union rules all you clowns got to shave your head and wear a goatee?"

"Look, lame-brain, I'll hit you so hard your daddy'll feel it."

Trick thought about the faceless man who fathered him and came at Ingo swinging. He punched the bouncer on his jaw, then missed with his left.

Ingo hit Trick hard in the stomach, knocking the wind from him and doubling him over. He threw the wheezing Trick over his shoulder, pushed the door open with his foot and dumped him on the gravel parking lot. "You ever come back here, I'll put you in a wheelchair."

***

As he staggered into the condo at four in the morning, Trick imagined his brain to be a bowl of bread pudding, at least that's how he felt. He had never gone so long with so little sleep. Maybe if he could sleep a few hours undisturbed, he'd figure a way out of the maze that had become his life. Pulling off his torn jacket and dropping it on the floor, he made his way to the bedroom. The little red light on the answering machine was blinking. He thought of Starnes' threat to kill him. "Go ahead and shoot me," he mumbled. At least he would be able to sleep. A good long sleep. An eternal sleep. It sounded good right now. Except. Little Pat. He had to keep playing the game.

Trick pressed the button on the machine. "Hello. Mr. Halloran. This is Ms. Gothley over at Christ Hospital. I'm afraid I have bad news for you. Please call us back at your earliest convenience."

Trick lay on the bed, the swirling ceiling fan was a blur through his tears.

Chapter 46

Trick kept glancing in his rearview mirror. A late-model gray Ford with blackwall tires and a spotlight had been following about a block behind on Ridgeland Avenue since 143rd Street. So he sped up and flew through the red light at 107th. He could see the flashing lights ahead, warning that a train was coming. Accelerating faster, he bounced over the railroad tracks just before the gates came down. He slammed on the brakes and made a hard left onto 102nd Street, then made his way to Fireside Drive where Joker lived. There was no sign of Joker's motorcycle and the garage door was closed so he circled around to 102nd again. With the revolver in his pocket, he parked next to the curb, cut through a yard and flipped over a wooden fence to get to Joker's garage. Peering into the side window, he could see Joker's Harley Softail parked there. Trick drew his gun, went to the side door and rapped lightly.

"Trick!" Joker's wife, Brenda, with her toddler in her arms, exclaimed, "What do you want?"

"Is he in there? Don't fucking lie to me."

"He's still in bed. Trick, what are you gonna do?"

Pointing the pistol in the air, Trick ordered, "Start walking. Keep going and don't come back for a half hour."

Brenda hurried down the sidewalk barefoot, crying, holding her little boy close as Trick opened the creaky aluminum screen door. With the gun pointed out in front of him, he crept to Joker's bedroom door. He put his hand on the door handle and turned it slowly.

Trick threw the door open and Joker yelled, "What the fuck!" He jumped out of bed in his long johns and ran to his dresser.

"Don't fucking move another step!" Trick screamed. "I'll goddamn shoot you in the head!"

Joker's hand reached for the top dresser drawer and Trick fired, sending a .357 hollow-point into a large glass jug filled with coins. Quarters, dimes, nickels and pennies exploded around the room, spraying into Joker's face.

"All right! All right!" Joker yelled with his hands up to shield him. "Where's Brenda?"

"She took the kid for a walk. Won't be back for a while. Just you and me here."

With the revolver pointed at Joker, Trick pulled up the edge of his mattress. "Still hiding your money in such a corny spot?"

"You think I'm gonna let you get away with this? Comin' into my house, pointin' a gun at me?"

"You think I was going to let you get away with ripping me off? I just lost Ginger and I don't give a fuck anymore. You think you're man enough to come after me, you do it, big guy." Trick stuffed the rubber banded wads of cash into his pockets and backed out of the room. "I'll be waiting for you." Trick shot the overhead light fixture, showering Joker with shards of broken glass, then ran out of the house.

Chicago Ridge Police cars pulled up to Joker's house with sirens blaring as Trick jumped over the wooden fence in the backyard. He peeked through the slats to see Joker in the driveway with his hands in the air, gripping a pistol. Crouching down, Trick ran to his car, hopped behind the wheel and drove off looking for Bob. But as he pulled away, he passed the same Ford with blackwall tires parked on the side of the street. The middle-aged man, in a jacket and tie, behind the wheel, watched him intently. As Trick drove away, the Ford pulled out after him.

***

"Damn. I got to shake this guy," Trick muttered to himself, "fucking cop." He drove up and down side streets, speeding up, slowing down, cutting through alleys, trying to ditch the Ford tailing him. "Screw this. I'm hungry."

Trick pulled back onto Ridgeland heading north. He continued up to 95th Street and avoided the light by cutting through Fannie May Candies. He drove one block east and pulled into The Dot Spot drive-in. He watched his tail go east on 95th, then turn around and park across the street from him. Trick got out of his rental car and walked up to the counter of the 1950s eatery. After getting a tamale boat and a grape cooler, he sat under the shade of a tree at a picnic table and ate his lunch staring at his surveillance the whole time. Thinking.

After finishing his meal, Trick got back in his car and flew out of the parking lot heading east, going ten to fifteen miles over the limit in order to make the green lights. Approaching Tulley Avenue, he looked in his rearview mirror to see the Ford a couple blocks behind. Just ahead was a railroad crossing, the same one that Officer Petak questioned him at a few weeks earlier. He slowed down and looked both ways on the tracks. To his right he saw a freight train in the distance heading his way. Before the crossing gates had a chance to come down, Trick impulsively made a left directly onto the tracks. With his tires straddling the steel rails, the whole car bounced on the wooden railroad ties as he headed northeast. He looked back to see warning lights flashing, bells going off, and gates lowering, trapping the surveillance car in traffic. But he had a new problem. The train was approaching faster than he estimated.

With Cicero Avenue in view several blocks away, Trick sped up, jarring his entire body. The foul smell of grease, tar and oil from the tracks crept into his car making him gag while the train whistle blew over and over. The chili covered tamale, grape soda with vanilla ice cream he just ingested felt like it was going to revisit his mouth as he bumped along praying not to get rear-ended by the rapidly approaching train. Up ahead he could see the gates coming down on Cicero stopping traffic as the train closed in on him with its deafening whistle becoming louder by the second. Trick hung tight onto the vibrating steering wheel as the train barreled up to his rear bumper with its brakes screeching. Just as the train was a few feet away, Trick cut his wheels to the left, skidding sideways off the tracks and onto Cicero.

With the train roaring by just feet behind him, Trick sat frozen gripping the steering wheel. Breathing heavily with his heart pounding, drivers and passengers stared and pointed at him. From an open window, a man, in a gray car with gray hair and a gray hat, shouted, "What are you? Fuckin' nuts?"

He took a moment to compose himself, thinking maybe he *was* going crazy, then drove north on Cicero going as fast as he could without getting pulled over. He continued north surveying traffic behind him searching for the Ford until he got to Midway Airport. Wishing he could hop on a plane, he pulled into the Hertz car rental area instead, went in and switched out his car for another.

***

Trick walked around the corner of the Mokena townhouse garage in the moonlight as Bob was getting out of his Caddy. "Didn't think I'd find you, did you? I followed your girlfriend over here and waited." Trick backhanded Bob across the face making his cheeks ripple.

Bob punched Trick in the ribs then caught him on the jaw with a left hook sending him back a few feet. "You think I'm someone to slap around, fucker? I used to box Golden Gloves."

"That was a lot of years and a lot of pounds ago, you fat fuck." Trick came at Bob with fists raised and faked with a right. He swung his body to the left and kicked Bob hard on the knee instead, sending him onto his back crying out in pain. Trick pounced on Bob, pinned his shoulders down with his knees and pummeled his face.

"Get off me!" Bob screamed, lying on the cold asphalt driveway, "I'll kill you! I swear to God, I'll fuckin' kill you!"

"You ain't killing no one today." Trick punched Bob in the mouth as hard as he could.

Bob spit out bloody broken teeth and mumbled, "I'll get you for that."

"I'm taking a souvenir for all my trouble with you, Bob." Trick shook off the pain from the punch, then grabbed Bob's left ear and started pulling, feeling skin tear.

Bob kicked his legs, wailing in pain, "Please! Please don't pull it off!"

"Oh my God, Bob. What's that smell? You stinking ass mother fucker, you shit yourself." Trick let go of Bob's partially torn ear and got off him.

"Keep your ear. You're going to need it in prison when some big bubba is whispering in it, ordering you to get on your knees." Trick drew back his foot to kick him in the ribs but hesitated. Almost feeling sorry for Bob, he walked away listening to him blubber.

Chapter 47

Trick went to see the funeral director and requested that there not be a wake since Ginger had no close living relatives and only a handful of friends. Many of the people she thought were friends dropped her when he went to prison and they no longer lived in an expensive rented home and entertained.

The funeral was scheduled two days later. Trick wanted to get this nightmare behind him as soon as possible. It was bad enough that he found Ginger's death almost unbearable; his main concern was for Pat. Losing a mother at such a young age could cripple a person emotionally. His son was going to need all the support he could get. But he didn't know who Pat would get it from since he was facing a long prison sentence.

It was already a week and a half past the date he was supposed to pay the Mexicans $277,000 but he only had a fraction of it. After the police confiscated the $70,000 he brought to the Oak Lawn Hilton, he had less than $20,000 left. To bring the Mexicans such a small amount could lead to disaster. He needed time to sort things out but knew it was already too late.

***

"I'm so sorry for your loss," Karen whispered, standing in her apartment doorway. "She was a good person and I'll miss her."

"Thank you. And thanks for watching Pat again."

Trick smiled at his son, who was putting his jacket on. "He likes you. I can tell."

"Well, I like him too but I haven't been able to look for work and babysit him at the same time."

"Here's a thousand bucks," Trick said, holding out a handful of cash. "I need you to be available to watch him again in a couple days."

"What? A thousand? No, that's too much."

"Take it," Trick said, putting the money in her hand and closing her fingers around it. "I need someone I can trust right now. Now you don't need to look for work just yet. Remember this, when he's with you, it's important that you have him in your sight at all times. You can't let him play outside. Don't ask why."

Trick walked down the apartment building stairway with Pat in his arms, then looked out the window to survey the area before slowly opening the door to inspect further. He saw no sign of Starnes or the Mexicans and hurried to his rental car. Not knowing how many days he had left with his son, he drove to the Ritz Carlton Hotel adjacent to the Water Tower Place shopping mall on the Magnificent Mile in Chicago.

***

Feeling somewhat safe within the confines of the upscale establishment and the adjoining towering mall, Trick got a suite and spent the next couple days with his son, escaping from the world outside.

On their first night away, Trick sat next to Pat in a booth at the lavish, mahogany-paneled Ritz Carlton Dining Room, where he instructed his son how to properly eat his lobster bisque, what fork to use for his salad, and to quit purposely burping as loud as he could. Trick ordered a bottle of Dom Pérignon to go along with his filet mignon as though he might be having his last meal on death row. He slowly sipped the chilled champagne while talking to Pat and taking in the other patrons.

While sharing with Pat his towering concoction of chocolate cake, topped with a chocolate mold containing vanilla ice cream, covered in warm chocolate sauce and fresh whipped cream, Trick nodded hello to actor Richard Romanus, who was having dinner with a lady he presumed to be the man's wife. "Always leave a good tip," Trick advised Pat, counting out hundred-dollar bills, "even though you may never see the person again. It shows class and it's good Karma."

"What the heck is Karma?"

"Me and my big mouth." Trick rubbed his forehead. "Karma is when if you do something bad to someone, something bad will happen to you sooner or later. If you do something good, you'll be rewarded somehow."

"Are you being rewarded for good things you did?"

"Hmm." Trick thought about the good and bad things he did in his life. He liked to think of himself as a fair, compassionate person. He never stole anyone's personal property, never cheated anyone, never went after another man's wife, never hurt anyone that didn't have it coming, never killed anyone. Not yet anyway. But there was the drug thing hanging over his head. Maybe Karma was kicking his ass for that.

Pat sat with his chin resting on his fists, searching his father's face. Trick had to give his son some kind of answer. "The jury's still out on that one, Pat."

***

After a decent night's sleep, room service breakfast and baths, father and son ventured out of their room again and into the city within a building. They walked around, travelled up and down escalators and elevators, played in toy stores and window shopped while working up an appetite.

Trick and Pat strolled through the expansive twelfth-floor hotel lobby and stopped to toss coins into the fountain while Tina Turner, nearby, signed autographs for an enthusiastic, young couple. They had a light lunch at the Ritz Carlton Café, where Pat slowly opened up about school, his friends and favorite toys. Trick tried to recall what it was like being a five-year-old. He couldn't remember friends and toys. Instead, he remembered being punished at school and at home.

After taking the elevator down to the movie theater on the sixth floor, Trick was glad to see a film listed on the marquis featuring his favorite actor, Clint Eastwood. Trick bought two tickets, a box of Sno-Caps to share and walked hand-in-hand into the darkened movie house with the aroma of buttered popcorn heavy in the air.

***

The night before the funeral arrived too soon and Trick knew what he had to do. What he dreaded worse than going to prison. "Pat." He lay on his side in bed next to his son. "We have to do something tomorrow that's going to be very, very hard. It's one of those things you have to do even though you don't want to."

"Like getting a shot?"

"Yes. But a lot worse. So, I just want you to be prepared." Trick touched Pat's concerned face. "Your mother is gone."

"You mean like my hamster?"

"Yes. Like that. But I don't know if hamsters go to heaven."

"Mommy said," Pat cried as he spoke, "my hamster was in heaven."

"Well, Mommy knows more about that stuff than I do."

"I hate it! I hate it!" Pat punched his pillow again and again. "I prayed over and over for Mommy to get better and it didn't work! I'm never going to pray again!"

"Pat, you can't give up on hope." Trick rubbed his son's back. "When you give up on hope, you lose an important part of yourself."

"God didn't help me," Pat managed between sobs. "It's all a fake."

"We can't always get the things we pray for. Sometimes we just don't understand God's plan." Trick pulled Pat close. "Just remember, Mommy's no longer sick. She's never going to suffer again. She's in a better place now."

Pat pulled away and rolled onto his stomach, his back rising up and down as he bawled.

Chapter 48

Trick turned his trenchcoat collar up. The Indian summer was over. Early November brought the seasonably cool wind, fog and rain.

As the pastor finished his eulogy to the handful of people standing graveside, Pat asked, "Daddy, how can Mommy be in there and be in Heaven too?"

Trick felt a cold breeze blow across his sensitive unbandaged finger. "Only God knows."

"If she's under the ground won't it be harder for her to fly to Heaven?"

"I don't know, Pat. Maybe we should pray for wisdom." Holding Pat's hand, Trick watched the coffin being lowered into the ground not far from the cemetery road. He recalled one of his favorite songs as a boy and quoted low, almost in a whisper, "And when the angels ask me to recall, the thrill of them all. I will tell them I remember you."

Trick knelt on the wet grass and did his best to console his son who now wept against him. Directly in his line of view, Trick saw the four Mexicans. They were looking straight at him, sitting and leaning on his car. He stood, held Pat's hand with his left and put his right hand into the inside pocket of his coat to grip the .357 Magnum. It puzzled him how they knew what kind of car he was driving now. Knowing he couldn't walk out of the cemetery, he just stood there trying to figure his next move.

"Daddy, how come those guys are on your car?" Pat whimpered and wiped tears on his sleeve. "Are they your friends?"

"No, Pat. Those guys are definitely not my friends."

"Are we going to just stand here?"

"I'm not ..." Trick stopped midsentence when he saw a car with municipal plates drive up slowly.

The window went down revealing Detective Frank Murray. "Halloran. I want to talk to you." Frank parked and got out. He noticed the Latino gang getting off Trick's car and walking toward their own vehicle. He pointed his chin in their direction and asked, "Something I should know about?"

"No," Trick answered, knowing that any information he revealed about the situation would incriminate him even further. Relieved to see them getting in their Oldsmobile and driving away, Trick continued, "What are *you* doing here?"

"I came to pay my respects and let you know we should talk about your case. I might be able to help."

"No, thanks. I know what you got in mind. You want me to turn rat, become state's evidence against people I know." Trick brushed past Frank. "Not going to happen."

"Don't say no until you've heard what I have to say."

"I already know that tune and I don't sing it. I'm not a canary."

"Don't be stupid. You missed your appointment with your parole officer ten days ago. They can revoke your bond for that. Hit you with a parole violation any day now, any hour." Frank yelled at Trick's back as he walked away, "Come in and talk. Talking's not going to hurt you. You got that boy to worry about. And don't even think about disappearing. I got a tail on you, twenty-four-seven!"

As they approached the rental car, Pat asked,

"Why don't you wanna talk to that man?"

"He wants me to do something I don't want to do, something dangerous, against my principles."

Buckling his son in the front passenger seat, Pat said, "I've got a principal. His name's Mr. Pitlik."

"That's nice," Trick answered, not paying attention. He shot Frank a dirty look, got in and drove away.

Chapter 49

"Get your hands off me," Trick said to the two Oak Lawn Police officers escorting him into Frank Murray's office. He shook his arms free and glared at Frank sitting behind his desk. "I told you, Murray, I got nothing to say."

"You want us to stick around?" one officer asked Frank as he took handcuffs off Trick.

"No. You guys can go." Frank waved his hand toward the door. "Thanks for bringing him in. And close the door behind you."

"Patrick 'Trick' Halloran. You're really a piece of work." Frank pointed at the chair across from his desk. "Sit down."

"I'll stand." Trick squinted at Frank. "I won't be staying."

Frank stood and shouted, "I said, sit the fuck down! You're not going anywhere until I say so. You cocky fuck, I could have you locked up right now. I've had a tail on you this last week." Frank eased back into his chair. "Been a bad boy."

Trick plopped into the metal folding chair. "Those assholes had it coming."

"Joker and Bob. I don't give a fiddler's fuck what you did to those bottom feeders. This isn't about any of that shit. We have more important things to talk about." Frank pointed a ballpoint pen at Trick. "You're in a world of trouble. That Oak Lawn Hilton bust is a second offense. You're looking at twelve easy, could be twenty-five with my recommendation.

Work with us. I can get your sentence cut in half. Otherwise you'll be a stranger to that beautiful boy of yours. By the time you get out, he'll hardly remember you, be calling someone else daddy."

"I can't do it." Trick hung his head. "I'm not made like that. I did the crime. I'll do the time."

"You stubborn son-of-a ... I can really turn the screws if I want. Get you assigned to one of the roughest joints in Illinois. I'm not fuckin' around. You don't have till tomorrow to think about it. Help me set up someone bigger or you're going away for a long time." Frank stood, walked to the door and turned the handle. "Give me an answer right now. The offer comes off the table if I walk out this door, and you go straight back to County."

"You don't give a damn what happens to me ... just trying to help yourself. You care if someone I set up comes after me to settle the score? Who's going to protect my son after I've testified in open court?"

Frank stood in the open doorway. "What if I arrange it so you don't have to appear in court, work behind the scenes?"

"No way. These guys aren't stupid. You think they can't figure out who the traitor is? I'm not a rat. Do what you got to do."

Frank closed the door and sat back down. His face softened. "I don't want you to turn rat. I hate rats ... have no respect for some scumbag who knowingly breaks the law and gets away with it by sending someone else to prison in his place."

"What're you trying to pull now? Reverse psychology? Going to be my buddy?"

"You notice anything familiar about me?"

"What? So you look a little like Clint Eastwood." Trick smirked and looked away. "Not as tall."

"I'm going to take a big chance with you, tell you

some things I hope I don't regret." Frank leaned forward, clenched his fingers tight, tapping his thumbs together. "I just found out, by accident. Swear to God. About two-and-a-half weeks ago, running a background check on you. One thing led to another. Seemed like a lot of coincidences, too many, so I dug further."

"What're you getting at?"

"What are the odds? Maybe if I had been around … you wouldn't, you know … turn out like you did, on the wrong side of the law."

Trick got an uneasy feeling in his stomach. "What in the hell …?"

"I'm your father."

Trick's head flinched back. "Bullshit."

"I realize this is a lot to take in." Frank tugged at the knot in his tie, pulling it down a couple inches, then unbuttoned the collar of his white dress shirt. "I was young, fifteen, so was she. Neither of us had any say in what happened to you."

"Wait a minute." Trick waved his hands away. "This is all too fucking weird. You got some proof of this?"

Frank lifted the edge of his desk mat and held up a large manila envelope. He leaned forward and handed it to Trick. "Here."

Trick opened the envelope and removed a birth certificate.

While Trick looked it over, Frank continued, "I pulled some strings. Being a cop has … let's say … privileges. I was able to track down and open sealed documents. There's no doubt in my mind. I'm surprised I didn't see it written on your face. You look a lot like her … my old girlfriend, the one who gave birth to you. Yeah, a little like me too."

"So you're trying to tell me this is real." Trick

scrutinized the yellowed sheet of paper. "It hasn't been doctored in some way?"

"Of course it's real. You think I'd go to the trouble of creating a false document. What for? To convince you I'm your father when I'm not? I spent years looking for you but always ran into a dead end. But after I looked into your background ..."

"OK, let's say I'm buying this act. Who is she ... my mother, this Priscilla Grannon?"

"She was a nice kid. Died in a car accident about eight years ago. Black ice on the road. Hit by a truck. No one's fault really. Neither of them should have been out that morning. She was heading to work at her real-estate office. Sorry."

"Just for the hell of it, let's say I believe you. Did you have much contact with her?"

"No. After our parents found out she was pregnant, they broke us up. Sent her to live with an aunt in Michigan and was forced to give you up. She stayed out there, graduated high school, all that. I went looking for her when I was about your age. Found her living in Saginaw, married with a couple kids. We spoke one time. It was hard, painful for both of us. She had a son and daughter that she loved very much but said you were never out of her thoughts. She kept saying, 'It wasn't fair, it wasn't fair.' Neither of us knew how to find you back then. That's the way it was set up."

"So you're saying I got a half-brother and sister?"

"Um hm. You got family out there you never knew about. The rate you're going, you'll never meet them either."

"I'm having a hard time swallowing all this. Some thief by the name Krupnik claimed he was my father too."

"Stanley Krupnik? About fifty years old, six-foot,

dark hair?"

"Yeah." Trick's eyes widened. "That's the guy."

"That's not his real name, by the way. We have him in custody. Picked him up trying to run a confidence scam on an undercover officer."

"He stole a gold watch from me and a lot of cash."

"We have his belongings in holding. We did retrieve a lot of cash from his car. And I remember a solid gold watch."

"That stuff's mine." Trick pointed a thumb at his chest.

"Any inscription on the watch?"

"Yeah, there's an inscription, *To Patrick, May you always obey the Golden Rule, Pop.* Got the watch from one of my foster fathers. What about the money?"

"If what you say is true, I'll get your watch back." Frank wagged a finger. "But, unless you can prove that cash is yours somehow, forget about it."

"What now? I got to go away? Be separated from my boy again?"

"I might be able to fix things. You know, you're really not a bad guy. Just in a bad business. You have a reputation … never used drugs. That true?"

"Yeah, never touched the stuff. I was in it for the money."

"All that's over now." Frank waved a hand. "For good this time, I hope."

"Definitely. I thought I was through when I got out of the joint. But I'm in a tight spot. Owe some rough sons-a-bitches a lot of dough. If I don't come up with it, something real bad could happen to my son."

"Let me see if I can take care of that." Frank folded his fingers together. "Who do you owe and how much?"

"You kidding me?"

"Does it look like I'm kidding? Give me the score."

"All right." Trick leaned forward and put his hands on the edge of the desk. "First, there's a guy by the name Edward Starnes. I owe him $40,000 for a kilo he fronted me and another $30,000 for bonding me out. He's charging me ten-percent interest."

"I know of him. We've been after this character for some time. So far, everyone's been afraid to testify against him. Where's he live?"

"The Ishnala section of Palos Heights. Usually drives an orange 53 Chevy pickup, real nice, all restored. Got a guy that works for him called Moogie. Don't know his real name. I think he might come from Decatur like Starnes. Carries a piece, collects for him ... screwy mother, nobody to fuck with."

"I'm nobody to fuck with. I belong to the toughest gang in the United States ... the police. We got guns and make the rules." Frank pushed a pen and pad of paper toward Trick. "Write down his address."

"You'd really do this for me?"

"That and a lot more. I'm the only thing standing between you and prison. The higher-ups want you back in now. You violated your parole when you got busted at the Hilton and again when you didn't show up at your parole officer's. I convinced everyone you're working with me to set up bigger people. I lied, told them I needed you on the streets for a little while."

"Well, I guess I should say thanks for that. It's allowed me time with my son and to bury Ginger. It was important that I was there for Pat during that.

Thank you."

"*Prego.*" Frank nodded. "Only problem with all this is, I put my reputation on the line for you. When they find out you're not cooperating, I'm through as a detective."

"Well I ... sorry if I fucked up your life. Don't know what to say."

"Doesn't really matter. Either way, I'm through. What I'm going to tell you now is of the strictest confidence. I need to know that I can trust you."

"I never had anyone go out on a limb for me. No one. If you're being straight with me, I'd never betray your trust. My word's my bond."

"Understand, this information could really get me in dutch, big time." Frank squinted. "I've been making some moves of my own. Skimming coke from the evidence room the last few years. Replacing it with cut after it's been tested. Got a guy who moves it for me. I protect him. Far as the force knows, he's just my snitch." Frank spread his hands out. "I bought a boat, a nice one, and a little seaside hotel with a bar and a ten-table restaurant on the southern coast of Italy. Got a local lady over there, Maria, runs things for me. I'm putting in my papers, retiring. Haven't talked about it with anyone but you so far."

"I'd never say anything to anyone. What good would it do me to betray you? You're offering to help." Trick shook his head. "You sell coke and get rewarded. I sell coke and go to prison. Well, no one ever promised me life was going to be fair. While you're out there enjoying the good life, I'll be rotting away in some cage."

"Not if I can help it. I know a guy ... can set you up with a new identity, passport, everything. I might be able to smuggle you out of the country and over to Italy." Frank put his right palm to his chest. "I'll personally watch out for your boy until you see him again. He's my flesh and blood too."

"Holy fuck. That would be unbelievable." Trick couldn't contain his excitement. "I better tell you everything. I found a bag that was thrown from a car on 55 about a month ago. It had drugs and a lot of money in it, two-hundred-and-eighty-five-thou. I paid off a debt to Starnes by giving him the three kilos that was in the bag. Remember those Latino guys, the ones hanging on my car at the funeral?"

"Yeah. I took notice. They looked out of place."

"I don't know who the hell they are or where they're from but they showed up saying the bag belonged to them. They took all the dough that was left, but they're leaning on me heavy to pay them back for the missing drugs. I don't know how they found me." Trick leaned back and rubbed his temples. "Unless maybe there was a second car following behind on 55 and they saw my car on the side of the road where the bag was thrown, or saw me with the bag getting in my car. Something like that. Only thing I can think of."

"If that's the way it went down and these guys are affiliated with one of the larger street gangs, all they'd need is a license plate to track you down. It's not like the old days; gangs have infiltrated the Chicago Police Department. Get the picture?"

"Yeah, sure." Trick raised his eyebrows and nodded. "Someone on the inside could have run my plate. Then they cased me."

"Tell me everything you can about these guys."

"I only saw them four times, including one time they chased me in traffic. They're always in the same car, that coffee-colored Olds you saw at the funeral. The guy that seems to be in charge is the short, stocky one. Black shiny hair slicked straight back like the old gangster movies. The big guy's face is pockmarked, always wears a leather Bulls jacket. The other two are obviously brothers, maybe twins, average height and build, rough looking. Oh yeah, the Olds, it's got fog lights and a Mexican flag sticker on the back bumper."

"Surprised you don't have a whole gang after you."

"Unless … unless these four are doing something on the side. Keeping it from the gang so they don't have to split it up or pay tribute to the leaders. That would explain why it's only those four."

"Could be." Frank nodded in approval. "Good thinking. I'll have the surrounding area police keep an eye out for these guys."

"It all makes sense now." Trick tapped a finger to his temple. "That's how they knew when I changed cars. When I got busted at the Hilton, I was driving the white Pontiac. It would have been in the police reports. Then at the funeral, they didn't see the Pontiac and figured I was in the rental. All adds up."

Frank looked up from jotting down details. "Hopefully, we'll find these guys. Maybe get some charges on them, lock them up for a while."

"I can't get over all this. It's ironic. You selling drugs." Trick tried to suppress a grin. "I guess crime does pay?"

"I've got my scruples. I never planted drugs on anyone. Never took a bribe. Never lied in court against a defendant. Believe me, that shit goes on all the time." Frank pointed to his shoulder. "I've been shot, stabbed, bitten and spit on. I even had a female perp falsely accuse me of sexual battery. Right or wrong, after putting my life on the line all these years, I'm walking away with something to show for it." Frank sat back and folded his hands behind his head. "I made my last skim two weeks ago. Just waiting for my guy on the street to finish turning it into cash. Then I'm through. Walking away from everything."

"The war on drugs is bullshit anyway." Trick didn't try to hide his scorn.

"I see this stuff up close every day." Frank tapped an index finger on his desk. "It's a sham. A war on people, not drugs. Locking up guys like you is a punishment but it does absolutely nothing to stop the flow of illegal drugs in this country. As soon as one dealer's taken off the street there's another ready to jump in and take over his customers. As long as there's a demand for drugs and the supply is already in the country, it's business as usual."

"The way I look at it," Trick replied, "drugs aren't a sin, like rape, murder or theft. Things like that have always been wrong and always will be. Drugs are more of a political crime. At one time they put cocaine in Coca-Cola. For all we know it might be legal again one of these days."

"Call me a hypocrite." Frank shrugged. "I know what I did was wrong. But in the scheme of things, what I put back on the street is like a grain of sand on Oak Street Beach."

"Agreed. When do we get the ball rolling?"

"I'll stall but it won't buy much time." Frank's voice had a slight growl. "The higher ups want results, reports, updates. You have to disappear. Now."

"What about my son? I'd rather die than leave him."

"You got to trust me here. I'll watch after him. Where's he staying?"

"I really don't see that I have much choice," Trick

said, picking up the birth certificate again. "But … I believe what you're telling me." Trick jotted down Karen's address and phone number. "Here," he said, handing Frank her information, "Pat's staying with this lady, Karen, temporarily."

"Good. I'll pick him up as soon as possible. Should be no more than a few days. You're making the right choice. I won't let you down. Call this Karen and tell her I'll be by to pick him up." Frank smiled and nodded. "You know … I respected the way you handled yourself the first time I put you away. No whining, bellyaching. You kept your mouth shut and did your bit like a man. If I'd have known you were my son, things would have been different. Something about you haunted me, couldn't put my finger on it. It was your mother's sad face looking back at me when you were taken out of the courtroom in cuffs back in 82."

"Things are moving so fast. One minute my life is over, the next … things are looking up. Wow." Trick rubbed his face. "Tell me more about Italy. I've never been there."

"Oh, it's beautiful where my place is. A lazy little paradise, not even a dot on the map. None of this ice and snow, below zero bullshit we got here. Fish and shrimp fresh out of the sea every day. I make a Lobster Fra Diavolo that'll straighten your pubes."

"Why would you do all this, stick your neck out, trust me?"

"You're my flesh and blood. There hasn't been a day I didn't think about you, wonder where you were, how you turned out, what you looked like." Frank's voice softened. "I've been alone. Couldn't trust anyone … considering what I've been doing. Couldn't allow anyone to get too close. Guys on the force think I'm antisocial."

"Yeah, see what you mean. Been the same for me."

"We need to trust each other. You're the only real family I have. You and Patrick. He looks like a great kid. Love to get to know him, be a real grandfather. After you disappear, I'm going to pull some strings, call in a couple favors and get myself appointed legal guardian of Pat. Then after I make my quick, surprise retirement, I'll bring him out to Italy. You'll be able to spend the rest of your life close to your son. But you won't be able to come back to the states for a long, long time. Not until everyone forgets about you or dies off. At least until the statutes run out."

"I don't mind leaving as long I'm going to be with Pat. Now that Ginger's gone," Trick shook his head, "there's nothing holding me here."

"One more thing. How 'bout I call you Pat? Can't get used to that name … Trick. Besides, you're starting a new life. You need a new name, a new last name too."

"No problem. That nickname came to me when I was a thirteen-year-old punk. Seemed cool at the time but that's not who I am now, not who I want to be." Trick leaned forward and smiled. "There's something I got to know. Are we Irish?"

"My father," Frank made the sign of the cross and continued, "was from Ireland, born in County Cork. My mother was full-blooded Italian, her maiden name was Siciliano. Your birth mother was Irish and Dutch, a little French too, I think."

"Damn. After all these years I'm starting to feel like I know who I am. Like I have roots."

"That's great, but now we have to uproot you, replant those roots across the Atlantic." Frank leaned forward and stretched his hands out across the desk. "You need to disappear until I'm ready to smuggle you out of the country."

"God, I dread being separated from Pat. I've been away from him so long as it is."

"This is the best possible outcome for your situation. If everything works out the way I planned, we'll meet you out there in about three or four weeks." Frank smiled and winked. "Let's tie up any loose ends right now. I want you to go straight to a safe house I got set up. Don't stop anywhere for anything. You can get new clothes in Italy."

"My Pontiac's parked at Midway, in the long-term lot. Here." Trick pulled the parking stub from his pocket and handed it to Frank. "I've been driving a rental from Hertz I picked up at Midway. It's back at Duke's Drive-In, where your guys picked me up."

"I'll take care of the vehicles. What else?"

"I got some money and a revolver stashed behind a mirror in the bedroom wall of a condo. Bottom left hand side. There's some things in the top right drawer of the dresser, title to the Pontiac, some pictures and stuff."

"Here." Frank pushed a pad of paper and pen toward Trick. "Write down the address."

"The key's on here," Trick said, handing over his key ring.

Frank jotted something down on a memo pad and slid it across the desk. He unlocked his drawer and retrieved a set of keys. "There's a dark blue Bonneville in the parking lot. When you walk out of here, avoid making eye contact with anyone. That bar on the southwest corner of 135th and Harlem, leave the Bonneville there with the keys locked in the car, under the mat. Call for a cab but don't use your real name. Have them drop you off at Paddy Bs on 143rd in Orland. Don't go in. Walk straight to that address. It's right down the street. You'll be safe there for a while. There's food, a new toothbrush and stuff, everything you'll need for a few days. Don't answer the door for anyone but me. Don't answer the phone. Don't even open the drapes," Frank said, handing Trick the keys.

"Gotcha." Trick stood and put his hand out. "Thanks. You're saving my life here."

"You're so much like me, a loner." Frank clenched Trick's hand. "Maybe it's not too late for guys like us to learn."

"I got a feeling we will."

Chapter 50

Driving to the safe house, Trick pulled his jacket open and looked at the title to Ginger's new LeBaron sticking out of his pocket. He thought about Pat cooped up in Karen's apartment and how it could be a month until he saw him again, providing he was able to get out of the country safely. He desperately wanted to say goodbye in person and reassure Pat that he could trust Frank and that it would be alright to leave with him. He thought about Frank's orders not to stop anywhere, then glanced at the title again.

Approaching 135th Street on Ridgeland Avenue, at the last second he turned left instead of right. Continuing east, Trick spotted Starnes and Moogie getting into the orange pickup in the parking lot of the White Hen Pantry. They recognized him, hopped in and squealed out after him. The pickup passed a school bus and sped up to catch him. Scrambling for ideas, Trick turned right onto Cicero Avenue and weighed his options.

Seeing Starnes fly around the corner in pursuit, Trick sped up, just making the yellow light at 137th Street, but then slowed down as he passed the Crestwood Police Station. Through his rearview mirror he saw Starnes hesitate at the light, then go through while it was still red.

Trick saw the sign for the El-Dorado, got an idea, and pulled into the parking lot. As he was getting out of his car near the front entrance, Starnes barreled in right after him, screeching to a stop, throwing gravel and dust in the air.

Hurrying into the restaurant, Trick was greeted by the hostess. "How many?" she asked with a toothy smile.

"Oh, just one," Trick answered in a controlled voice, trying to appear nonchalant as his heart raced. "But I have to use the bathroom first."

Trick headed to the rear of the restaurant but instead of turning right to the bathroom, he walked through the swinging half-doors leading into the kitchen. He heard a man with a Greek accent call after him, "Hey! Where you going?"

Trick nodded to a cook who was working over the flaming grill, dripping facial sweat onto the sizzling steaks and burgers. He bumped into another cook who was carrying a tray of chicken breasts. The tray, along with the cutlets, crashed to the grimy, grease-smudged floor with a loud bang. The cook at the grill, shrouded in steam and smoke, raised a cleaver and hollered, "What you doing in here, *vlacas?*" Trick pushed the cook in front of him to the side, stepped over the spoiled food and dashed out the back door, running fast as he could toward the apartment complex to the west. As soon as he reached the first tree, he hid behind it and surveyed the area behind him. A gray bunny scurried out from the bush next to him and across an area of dried mud. Trick gasped when a hawk swooped down, snatched the tiny animal and carried it off. He never heard a rabbit make a sound before but the future meal of the hawk emitted a high-pitched squeal that made Trick feel queasy.

With no sign of Starnes and Moogie, he continued running in the direction of Leonard Drive. He cut between the buildings, continued west three blocks, and went around to the front entrance of Karen's apartment.

"Please be home," Trick panted. He frantically pushed the intercom button watching for Starnes' pickup.

"Who is it?" The garbled voice came through the slotted metal plate next to the vertical row of buttons.

"It's me, Patrick Halloran," he answered, putting his mouth close to the intercom, then stepping back from under the awning so Karen could see him. Grabbing the handle and pulling the door open the second he heard the buzzer, Trick flew up the stairs two at a time.

Karen opened the door with a wild look in her eyes. "I hope this means you're here to take your son, for good. Ever since you told me not to let him out of my sight I've been freaking out."

"Uh ... no, I'm sorry. I can't take Pat right now. Where is he? I need to talk to him for a few minutes."

"He's taking his after-school nap." Karen motioned toward the bedroom. "Look, how long do you expect me to take of care him? I took my car in. It's got a cracked engine block. The money you gave me didn't last long; I was behind on my bills. I seriously need to find a job. If you don't take him with you now, I'm calling the police and have them come pick him up."

"No, no, please. A man by the name Frank Murray is going to contact you. He's a cop, a detective, you can trust him. I gave him your number. He's going to come by and take Pat off your hands. I promise. Just a few more days." Trick reached into his pocket and pulled out the title for the LeBaron. "Ginger signed and dated the title to her car in the hospital last time I saw her. I want you to have it. Go ahead and take it to the currency exchange and have it transferred into your name. I think Ginger would be happy it went to you for taking care of Pat."

Karen's hand moved slowly toward the title, then snatched it. "I can't believe it. I love that car."

"I want you to drive Pat to and from school. Don't let him take the bus. Now I need a little time alone with him." Trick glanced out the picture window, thankfully seeing no sign of Starnes and Moogie. "Call me a cab. Tell them it's for Patrick Murray."

Trick walked into the dimly lit bedroom, knelt next to the bed and gently shook his son. "Pat, I have to talk to you."

Pat sat up and scratched his ear. "What is it, Daddy?"

"I'm sorry, but I have to go away for a while."

"You promised you weren't going to leave me again." The disappointment on Pat's face pained him.

"It won't be as long as last time." Trick put his hands on his son's cheeks. "Maybe just a month, that's about thirty days."

"Mommy's gone," Pat's voice broke between sobs, "and now you're leaving me too."

"The last thing I want to do is leave you but I have to. I just have to." Pat's little body shook as he cried. Trick took him in his arms and patted his back. "I'm sorry it has to be like this. Please don't cry."

"I hate you. You're a liar." Pat pulled away and repeatedly punched Trick's chest.

"Please try and understand." Trick grabbed Pat's fists. "It won't be long. I'll see you before your birthday. I promise."

"You're a bad daddy," Pat whimpered.

"Please don't say that, pal. Please." Trick pulled Pat's hands close to him. "There is nothing in the world more important to me than you. I'd do anything to protect you."

Pat looked away with tears in his eyes.

"I have to go now, but before I do, there's something important I have to ask you."

"What?" Pat looked at him with watery, red eyes.

"If anyone asks about me, don't tell them what I said about seeing you in a month. Can you keep our secret? It's real important."

"Yeah." Pat nodded, his lower lip quivering. "I can keep a secret better than anyone. I know you weren't in college. You were really in jail and I never told anyone." Pat wiped his cheek with the back of his hand. "I didn't even tell Mommy I knew."

"Oh, Pat. I'm so sorry." Trick thought of the emotional hell he went through at Pat's age and wanted so much better for his son. He remembered being close to six-years-old and pulling a chair up to the refrigerator at one of his foster homes to get a popsicle without getting permission. His foster mother caught him and slapped him so hard that he fell from the chair to the floor, dislocating his shoulder. The foster father heard the commotion and stomped in. He pulled shirtless Trick to his feet and shoved the shoulder back in place. "Quit crying, ya baby," he yelled in Trick's face with beer and cigarette breath. "Next time ya ask first."

"I'll do my best to give you a good life when we're together again." Trick brushed back Pat's blond locks with his fingers. "A very nice man is going to come by in a few days and take you on a trip. His name is Frank. You can trust him."

Chapter 51

Under a starless sky, Frank and his younger partner Jimmy 'The Owl' Garcia sat in an unmarked car in front of the house next to the Starnes residence.

"Why we here, Frank?" Owl pushed up his round tortoise shell eyeglasses.

"Something I got to do for someone. I wouldn't ask you to be here if it wasn't important."

"I'm glad to help but just kinda surprised you asked me. The other guys call you 'Lone Wolf' behind your back. Say you never let anyone get close. Do as much as you can on your own."

Frank waved his hand away. "I really don't care very much what people say."

"Yeah, I can see that." Owl abruptly changed the subject. "Heard you took nationals."

"No, took state in high school. Third in nationals, my junior year at Michigan. I wrestled at 165. Can you believe it? That was twenty-five years ago. I've only put on about fifteen pounds since then, not bad for five-eleven," Frank said, patting his stomach.

Owl rapped his fingertips on the front dash. "So, we gonna shoot anybody tonight?"

"I hope not. Let's see how it goes. Hey … that looks like Starnes' pickup now." The 1953 Chevy pulled up next to the curb in front of the Palos Heights home. "Looks like he's got his muscle with him. Good. We'll kill two birds with one stone." Frank opened the driver's side door. "Just follow my lead."

"Starnes!" Frank called out with his gun drawn. "Hands in the air. Both of you."

"You guys cops?" Starnes turned to face Frank and Owl with his arms raised.

"Better hope we are." Owl pointed his pistol directly at Starnes' head.

"I only ask 'cause I already donated to the impotent policeman's fund," Starnes quipped.

Owl looked at Frank. "Funny guy, huh. Whadya think?"

"It's going to get a lot funnier." Frank turned back to Starnes and Moogie. "Empty your pockets. Put everything on the roof, then place your hands on the hood."

Frank held his gun on Starnes, who stood to Moogie's left. Owl patted them down as they bent over with their hands on the warm hood of Starnes' pickup.

"Hey, asshole. When we say empty your pockets, we mean everything." Owl pulled a pistol from Moogies' inside jacket pocket, then cracked him on the side of his head with it.

"Son of a fuckin' bitch," Moogie yelled, flinching.

"You callin' my mother a bitch? I'll shoot you in the head and swear you went for my gun," Owl said, moving closer to Moogie, who had blood trickling down the side of his face.

As Frank went through the contents on the roof of the pickup, Starnes asked, "What do you guys want? A monthly payoff? We can work somethin' out if you give us protection, inside info, lean on our competition."

Frank picked up a thick wad of bills held together with a rubber band and flicked through it. "How much you got here?"

"Forty Gs," Starnes answered. "You gonna take

my scratch?"

"No." Frank tossed the stack of money onto the damp grass between the curb and the sidewalk. "I'm not taking, I'm giving." Frank pulled an envelope out of his jacket and slipped it into the back pocket of Starnes' black jeans. "That's what you laid out for someone's bail a couple weeks ago. You're officially off his back as of right now. Don't ever contact this guy again, for any reason. If I hear different, I'm going to come back and cramp your style so bad you won't be able to jerk off without the law knowing about it."

"He owes me for more than the bail I laid out."

"Really? What else does he owe you money for? Drugs? Want to swear out a complaint?"

"OK, I get the point. But why you doin' this? What's you're angle? I gotta know." Starnes turned and looked Frank in the eye. "Someone we know turnin' snitch?"

"We're through here." Frank walked away and motioned for his partner to follow, but Owl stopped behind Starnes and raised the butt of his gun to hit him on the head. Frank looked at Owl and shook his head no.

"Think we won't find out?" Starnes called out in the cool night air. "That fuck goin' into witness protection? ... He a cheese eater now?"

Ignoring Starnes' barrage of questions, Frank and Owl got back into the patrol car and pulled away.

"This person you're stickin' your neck out for is a lucky so-and-so." Owl shook his head. "Lucky to have you in his corner."

Chapter 52

The hoarse bark of a dog filtered through the cracked plaster wall while Trick paced the worn area rug that set crookedly on the creaking hardwood floor of the living room. He turned the television on, only to see the same gray pattern of electronic snow as he did the last four times he tried it. Turning it off again, he walked the floor a few more minutes and then sat on the musty smelling sofa that was scarred with cigarette burn marks. The entire two-bedroom, one-story house seemed to have a slight odor of rancid potato chips. He picked up the *People* magazine featuring Cybill Shepherd that he already thumbed through several times. "TV's sexiest spitfire," Trick read from the cover. "Cute. But not as pretty as my Ginger." Dropping the magazine back onto the coffee table that had silvery duct tape wrapped around one leg, he turned on the cassette player as he had over and over his last three days of incarceration in the drafty safe house.

"Thank you," the pleasant sounding female voice emitted from the speaker, "*Grazie.*" "Pardon me ... *Mi scusi,*" Trick repeated along. "I don't speak Italian very well ... *Non parlo molto bene italiano.*"

Trick jumped when he heard a loud rap on the wooden door. He crept toward the peephole, then changed his mind and stood with his back to the wall. He flinched when he heard, "Let me in, it's me."

Realizing it was Frank, Trick breathed again. He

unlocked the deadbolt, unlatched the chain and opened the door of the weather-worn frame house.

"Thought you might like some real food." Frank stepped through the door. "I stopped at Mickey's. Got some beef sandwiches, ribs, fries ... none of that healthy bullshit."

"Great." Trick took the paper sack from Frank and set it on the coffee table. "I was getting tired of Campbell's soup and crackers."

"Didn't know how you took your coffee."

"Black is fine," Trick said as Frank handed him the hot paper cup from the cardboard tray. "You sure it's only going to be a month or so till I see my son again? I was away from him so long already."

"Three or four weeks, tops. I'll try to get out there before you." Frank pulled something from the pocket of his white dress shirt. "Here's your passport, Patrizio."

Trick sat on the couch and examined the document. "Patrizio Siciliano ... my gramma's maiden name. Nice. Hey, this is my last arrest photo. I'll be damned."

Frank set his coffee down, plopped on the couch next to Trick and opened the bag of warm food. "Thought you'd appreciate the irony."

"I'll appreciate it if we pull this off and I'm safe in Italy. I keep getting this bad feeling."

"Don't worry." Frank popped a French fry in his mouth. "It's not going to help anything."

Trick picked up the cassette recorder from the coffee table. "Thanks for leaving this book and these tapes about learning Italian. I've been studying night and day."

"I see. *Come va?*"

"*Bene.*"

"*Stupendo.*" Frank laughed and waved his fingers

like a fruit vendor on the streets of Rome.

"So, you don't think anyone will come looking for you out there?"

"Nobody knows nothing. Going to say I'm heading to Florida to bartend. If I cross paths with anyone I know in Italy, which isn't very likely, I'll just say I work there, not own the place."

"Makes sense." Trick brought his fingertips to his chest. "What if someone recognizes *me* there?"

"This isn't a destination spot. It's a tiny little town, a *cittadina*. You can only get to it by boat. *Non ti preoccupare.*"

"What? Speak English. I'm just learning."

"I said, quit fuckin' worrying." Frank leaned forward, closed his eyes and breathed in the aroma from the open bag of food. "Tomorrow's the big day. I'll be by to pick you up at 10:00 in the morning. There's a cabin cruiser, the *Topless Betty*, at Burnham Harbor that'll take you out to a cargo ship going straight to Italy. We need to be at the lake, no later than 11:00." Frank handed Trick an envelope with cash and directions. "Here. Everything you need to know is written down. You'll be working six days a week as a deck hand. Keep to yourself as much as possible, avoid answering personal questions."

Trick rubbed his forehead with his fingertips. "Can't shake this feeling. Like something's going to go wrong."

"I told you. Everything's set. Settle down. You worry about something too much, you make it a self-fulfilling prophecy." Frank pulled an Italian beef sandwich wrapped in foil out of the sack. "Come on, let's eat."

Chapter 53

"Had a bad dream last night. Hardly slept after that." Trick got in the passenger side of Frank's police car.

"In less than two hours, you're going to be on that ship." Frank patted Trick's shoulder. "It's all going to work out. Trust me."

Frank headed toward Lake Michigan, nodding and glancing over at Trick, who talked out of nervousness for several miles. He turned on his police radio and heard Owl's excited voice, "Frank, where you at?"

Frank picked up his hand-held speaker and pressed the button. "Yeah, I'm here. What's the problem?"

"What's the problem? You didn't hear? A perp grabbed a little boy, blond kid, as he was walkin' into Nathan Hale, the grade school on 135th Street."

"Nathan Hale?" Trick's face turned white. "Little Pat goes there!"

"Kid's name is Patrick Halloran," Owl continued, "same as the guy you busted that time."

"Oh, no." Trick covered his face with his hands. "Oh, fuck, no."

Frank switched on his overhead emergency lights and siren. "Where are they?"

"There's a high-speed pursuit goin' on," Owl's voice crackled over the speaker. "They're chasin' the perps on Southwest Highway right now. Headin' northeast."

Frank turned to Trick. "Don't say anything while

I got the transmission button down." He pressed the button and flew through a red light. "Owl, what's the make and model?"

"Late 70s Oldsmobile, dark brown," Owl answered. "Mexican flag sticker on the back bumper."

"That's them." Trick slammed his hand on the dashboard. "The guys I was telling you about. They got my boy!"

"Another report came in," Owl barked. "The vehicle was seen drivin' northeast on Columbus Avenue, over 90 miles an hour."

Frank pushed the transmission button down again. "I'm not that far away."

"Oh, no," Owl shouted, "they lost 'em. Went flyin' over the railroad crossin' at 82nd Place, just before a freight train came by. Chicago's involved now. High priority."

"Please, no, please," Trick repeated, his eyes glazing over.

"They lost 'em again," Owl reported, "somewhere on Kedzie, cut right through a funeral procession."

"Try to calm down," Frank told Trick, who was punching the roof of the car, every blow giving off a muffled, metallic thud. "Kedzie's right up ahead." Frank made a left and accelerated over the long Kedzie bridge with the clanging of train cars coupling below, past Nabisco bakery with its heavy aromas filling the neighborhood air, past the modest brick bungalows lining the street ahead.

"I'm only a couple miles behind these guys," Frank spoke into his speaker again. "I see the Chicago squads up ahead. I grew up around here, know a shortcut." Frank slammed on his brakes, skidding sideways as a little girl in a checkered coat ran out from between parked cars chasing a cat into the street. "Mother of God," Frank yelled, breathing heavily. The girl stood frozen in the middle of the avenue, staring at Frank. When he laid on his horn, she ran off and Frank continued pursuit.

After several minutes, Owl said, "They jumped on 55 headin' east, got a shitload of blue and whites on their tail."

Frank continued stopping traffic with his emergency flashers, siren and loudspeaker, going through red lights. "They won't get away," Frank reassured Trick, "not with all those squads right behind them."

"Son-of-a-bitch!" Owl yelled, "these fuckers sideswiped a Culligan truck, caused a big pileup on 55. Water bottles all over the road. Chicago Police cars stuck in the mess."

"Oh, God, no," Trick said, breathing heavily.

Owl continued, "They were last seen gettin' off at the Damen exit."

"I don't know where these guys are heading," Frank told Trick, "but they keep moving in the same direction, northeast." He made a right onto Archer Avenue. "We can't be that far from them." He raced through the red light at Archer and Ashland Avenue, causing cars around them to skid to a stop.

"There they are!" Trick screamed. The Olds made a left off Archer and into an obsolete industrial area. "They're heading toward the river."

Frank made a left one block before the street the Mexicans turned on and floored it. "We'll try to beat them to the bridge." He cut a quick right and squealed around the corner.

"There they are again! Cut 'em off!" Trick pleaded. "Cut 'em off!"

"You sure?" Frank barreled ahead.

"Cut 'em off!"

Frank pulled across the intersection, blocking the street. The brakes screeched and the nose dipped down sharply on the Olds as it fishtailed, then slammed into Frank's police car. Trick tumbled around as the cop car rolled over three times before resting against a telephone pole, passenger side up. Trick was piled on top of Frank, who seemed unconscious, but then he moaned. Trick climbed out the window using the steering wheel to boost him, his healing fingertip bleeding again.

The Mexicans' car was shrouded in a haze of steam from the busted radiator. Engulfed in the smell of skidding tires, coolant fluid, and gasoline, Trick staggered toward the Olds. The front end was smashed in, the bumper lying in the street. The brother in the driver's seat looked lifeless, his head resting on the steering wheel. His brother next to him sat back with his mouth open, face covered in blood.

The back door flew open and out staggered the big guy in the Bulls jacket with blood streaming into his eyes from a gash on his forehead. He waved a pistol and shouted, "I can't see!" Stumbling around, wiping blood away with the back of his hand, he fired three shots wildly, one coming dangerously close to Trick.

Trick picked up the front bumper of the Olds and swung it like a baseball bat, hitting the big guy on the side of his head, sending him to the street with a thud. The gun skidded across the old cobblestone bricks showing through the worn concrete.

Trick ran up to the rear passenger door to see Pat sitting in the middle of the back seat with a look of terror frozen on his face. The leader of the group, with his usually slicked back hair hanging in greasy locks on his forehead, had blood running from his nose. He sat on the other side of Pat holding a silver-handled razor against the boy's soft neck.

"Daddy," Pat cried. "Daddy."

"Are you hurt, son?"

"I'm scared, Daddy," Pat sobbed. A bump on his forehead seemed to grow before Trick's eyes.

Trick leaned in. "Let him go and I'll let you live."

The gang leader wrapped his arm around Pat and answered back, "*Chinga tu madre.*" He looked dazed and pulled Pat tighter with the blade against the horrified child's jugular vein.

While sirens blared in the distance, Trick hurried back to retrieve the big guy's revolver. He opened the chamber and counted. Two bullets remained.

A beat-up tow truck slowly pulled up, driven by a burly looking female with short cropped hair and a blue bandana tied around her forehead. She tilted her sunglasses down and questioned Trick with wide eyes. He glared at her and waved her away with the pistol. She shook her head and drove off muttering something Trick couldn't make out over the grinding of her gears.

Returning to the open door and pointing the gun at his nameless enemy, Trick said in a raspy voice, "I told you to let him go. Anything happens to him, I don't care if I live or die. I'm giving you till the count of three to let him go."

"I'll cut him, send him to Jesus," he growled, trying to duck his head down behind Pat's.

"One. Don't worry, Pat. Two. Close your eyes, Pat." Trick fired, hitting the gang leader in the elbow. His hand flew open from the shock, dropping the knife. He looked at Trick and said, "*Besa mi culo!*"

Trick fired again, putting one right between the young gangster's eyes. His head flew back against the window, mouth and eyes wide open as though he might say something, then slumped to the side leaving a smear of crimson on the window.

Trick reached in and pulled Pat close. His son, splattered in blood, was very still and quiet. Pat's eyes were glazed and appeared to be staring at nothing. Trick shook him, then lightly slapped his face. Pat started screaming and Trick held him tight.

The sirens of Chicago Police vehicles got louder by the second. Trick stood, pulled his jacket open and looked at the phony passport in his pocket. With pistol in hand he watched as three police cars sped toward the bridge. While Pat clung to his leg crying, Trick threw the pistol as hard as he could and watched it sail into the Chicago River. He got down on his knees and hugged Pat.

"I love you, Pat. I'll always love you no matter what happens, no matter where I am." He watched blue and white cars fly toward them across the bridge. "You're going to be OK now, Pat. The good guys are coming. Just wait here. They'll take care of you."

As Trick stood and pulled away, Pat cried, "Don't go, Daddy. Don't leave me."

"I'm sorry, son. But it has to be like this." Trick ran as fast as he could toward a warehouse. Just before disappearing behind the corner of the deserted building, he looked over his shoulder to see the first squad car pull up.

Epilogue

Trick jogged barefoot on the warm sand as soft waves lapped the beach and chattering seagulls swooped around, looking for morsels. He stopped and stretched, admiring the five ancient small hotels huddled close to one another and the smattering of tiny whitewashed houses behind them. The flat wall of rock, that rose a couple hundred feet behind the houses, reflected sun onto the quiet little fishing village. The sun-bleached pastel paint of the eighteenth-century hotels was faded but still colorful enough to attract the eyes from passing boaters. One building was yellow, one green, one orange and one pink. But the robin egg blue hotel in the middle was the one he really loved. He had been working at his father's stone and stucco *albergo* the last two days, doing everything from changing sheets to bartending.

Pat ran up, wet from playing in the water. "Dad, Dad, I love it here. And ... Maria's nice." Trick scooped his son in his arms, feeling the wetness from the sea on his bare chest. Trick kissed Pat's forehead, set him down and said, "Have fun playing."

Trick rolled his tan khakis up above his knees and waded into the shallow water. He grabbed the chrome ladder, climbed on board the *il Ladro* and eased into the deck chair next to Frank.

"Tell me something." Trick watched as the golden late afternoon sun approached its reflection in the ocean. "If I had turned rat for you, would we be here right now? Would you even have told me you were my father?"

Frank leaned back in his chair, crossed his bare feet on the polished brass rail of his vintage cabin cruiser and pulled a bottle of Moretti beer from the ice-filled cooler between them. Putting the bottle in his left hand, which was in a cast up to his elbow, he popped the cap, then flipped it off his thumb where it hung in the air, turning over and over before it made an almost imperceptible splash in the blue-green sea. He removed a Cuban cigar from the pocket of his white linen shirt, fished a cigar cutter from the pocket of his white jeans and snipped the tip. Lighting the cigar, he looked at Trick with a poker face and said, "What do *you* think?"

Trick grabbed a frosty bottle, looked over at the soft sands and turquoise water of the beach where little Pat splashed in the shallow water with Maria by his side laughing. He breathed in the fresh air laced with the aroma of cigar smoke and said, "I think sometimes you don't know if a situation is good or bad until some time has passed."

Frank blew a puff of smoke into the warm salty breeze. "True. And even though everything may seem to point the way, sometimes you have to take a different path to reach your goal."

Trick ran a thumb over the bump on his nose, then looked at his little finger with the missing tip and laughed. He leaned back in his chair and gazed up at the fluffy white clouds. They reminded him of giant cotton balls decorating the blue sky. He took a sip of cold beer then laughed some more.

Southside Hustle is also available on
kindle:

www.amazon.com/dp/B01DJHH030

33358024R00211

Made in the USA
Middletown, DE
10 July 2016